TO CHOOSE THE LONGSHOT

KENTUCKY DEBUTANTES OF THE GILDED AGE

BOOK TWO

LISA M. PRYSOCK

WILD HEART BOOKS

PRAISE FOR LISA M. PRYSOCK

"What a sweet, interesting, refreshing story of love and promise! Memorable characters and superb storytelling drive lingers in my memory. The sights, smells, sounds, fears and joys of the Lexington, Kentucky horse-racing lot make a marvelous setting and storyline. I was moved by Delia's struggles in facing the wealthy societal and family expectations and the decision to follow her heart."

— SUSAN G MATHIS, AWARD-WINNING
AUTHOR OF ELEVEN THOUSAND ISLANDS
GILDED AGE STORIES

The way of a fool is right in his own eyes, but a wise man listens to advice.

— PROVERBS 12:15

She said unto her husband, "Behold now, I perceive that this is a holy man of God, which passing by us continually..."

— 2 KINGS 4:9

CHAPTER ONE

A horse, a horse! My Kingdom for a horse!
—Shakespeare

Saturday, May 10, 1902
Lexington, Kentucky

"Are you ready, Delia, sweetheart? It's almost time." Pa patted her hand with his large rough one. "You look a little nervous."

"I *am* nervous." Today she, Delaney Lyndon, would marry Thaddeus Sullivan, son of the wealthiest horse breeder in Fayette County. And yet she clung to her father's elbow at the foot of the steps outside the First Christian Church. He looked nice in his best suit with a peach rose pinned to his lapel. "I feel as though I'm forgetting something, but other than that, I think I'm ready."

Delia had used lip balm to hide the fact she'd bitten her lower lip too much, a physical manifestation of the overwhelming stress and anxiety consuming her since before the Kentucky Derby. Time had flown by since last weekend's race in a frenzy of last-minute preparations for her wedding, with deliveries and fittings in rapid succession. And now, at long last, her big day had arrived. Despite her mother's meticulous planning and her family's support, a bad case of the wedding jitters and a sense of dread plagued her. Her stomach churned and flipped, unable to keep down a single bite of breakfast. The echoes of a disturbing dream haunted her, leaving her unsettled and on edge.

But thanks to the unwavering dedication of Mama and her trusted employees at their horse farm, Velvet Brooks, Delia had managed to make it through the morning without breaking down. Grace Mitchell and Frances Ellis, long-serving household staff, had kept everything running smoothly amid chaos. Grace filled the role of a lady's maid to the women at Velvet Brooks. Frances served mainly as a household maid, but she occasionally helped Grace or Willamena, their cook. Earlier today, Veronica and Gladdie, Delia's sisters, had tucked her shimmering white skirts, the long train of her gown, and her stunning veil into the carriage. Now she stood before the church steps, clinging for dear life to Pa's arm. She blinked several times as flashes of her dream echoed in her mind.

Pushing the dream away, she tried to focus on the day of sunshine the Lord had given. Her reception would take place at the Phoenix Hotel Ballroom. By now, Lexington's finest bakery would have delivered her three-tier wedding cake, placing it on a round marble-topped table in an elegant room to one side of the ballroom. She smiled to think of it. Their wedding cake would have a room unto itself. Such splendor awaited, if only she could make it through the ceremony without fainting.

Veronica, her oldest sister, acting as her matron of honor, stretched out her veil and the train of her wedding gown before dashing around her and Pa, lining up on the church steps with the other bridesmaids. The train of Delia's dress weighed more than expected, and she moved slowly in so much lace and satin. She could barely see through the filmy gauze of her veil, trimmed in elegant lace, shipped all the way from Paris.

Mama had slipped inside the church moments ago, taking her seat on the second pew on the left side, lovely in a sage-green concoction with a demi-train. Mama's seamstress in Lexington had designed it to complement Delia's peach wedding colors. The first few notes streamed through a few open windows as Aunt Celia Jane began playing Grandfather Spencer's favorite hymn on the piano, Charles Wesley's "Love Divine, All Loves Excelling." Her aunt had arrived the day before from Louisville with Uncle James to attend the rehearsal since no one else they knew played the instrument as well as Delia's father's sister-in-law.

The church doors swung open, and she caught a glimpse of Uncle James, filling the role of an usher, positioning the doors to keep them in place. She gulped again, hearing the music perfectly now. Her bridesmaids stood up straighter, fidgeting with their dresses before they began to proceed up the aisle to the magnificent hymn. Each carried a bouquet of peach roses tied with a sage-green silk ribbon. Glancing down at the slightly larger bouquet in her own hands, she managed a weak smile at seeing the delicate petals.

Veronica had disappeared inside the church, followed by their younger sister, Gladdie. Then Thaddeus's sisters, Tilly and Mary Louise Sullivan, proceeded inside. Their Sullivan cousins, Hazel and Flora, filed in next. Mama had said five bridesmaids and one matron of honor constituted a fine number. Delia could picture them taking their places to the left of the altar, all wearing flowing peach satin with demi-trains swirling at their feet. Their dresses featured white sashes at their waists, three rows of white lace ruffles at their hems, and sage-green piping on their bodices. Exquisitely fitted, they looked like the first breath of summer, perfect for a May wedding.

Thaddeus, dressed in a black suit, would also stand at the front of the little white church with his older brother—Henry, the best man—Tilly's twin, Percival, and three of Thaddeus's best friends. Edward, Veronica's husband, completed the groom's party. They would have lined up on the right side of the church before the bridesmaids entered, all wearing black suits with a peach rose pinned to their lapels.

Pa stepped forward, and Delia willed her feet to move, but they didn't budge. Joseph Lyndon stepped back as she clung to his elbow. "Time to go inside, princess."

A nervous laugh escaped her lips. "Oh, Pa, only you could make me laugh at a time like this. You haven't called me princess in a while."

"You do look like a princess today, and now you'll finally get to marry your prince."

"You don't look so bad yourself."

He grinned. "Your ma says I do clean up nice."

They climbed the steps. Aunt Celia Jane pounded out the traditional wedding march as if her very life depended on it. Delia kept her eyes forward, aware of the guests rising when they reached the doors. The pews creaked, and a sea of smiling faces turned toward them as she made her grand entrance on her father's arm. All of Lexington seemed crammed into the building.

A few feet down the aisle, she sought the face of her groom. Finding him, she relaxed a little when she met his blue eyes. Did he approve? His smile told her he did. Her heart pounded with an odd mixture of fear, apprehension, and excitement. Why did her lips quiver when she tried to return his smile?

They finally made it to the front of the church, and Pa let go, handing her over to Thaddeus. Just like that, as if she no longer belonged to him. Thaddeus tucked her hand into his elbow with another of his handsome smiles as he leaned toward her. She offered a weak smile in return.

Dizziness caused her to waver as the preacher, Reverend Burrows, said a short prayer and then began to address the congregation. Thaddeus steadied her. She couldn't hear many of the preacher's words, but she caught a few here and there. Something about dearly beloved gathering to witness. A moment later, she heard him asking if anyone knew of any reason these two should not be joined together in wedded matrimony. The dream flashed before her, and Delia stiffened.

Should *she* speak up? Had she arrived at the altar for the wrong reasons? Could marrying Thaddeus Sullivan finally put her fears to rest? No. She did not think it could, but she couldn't get any words out. Her mouth dry as the tail end of a summer drought, she swallowed.

She tugged her hand back, but Thaddeus wouldn't let go. She tugged again more firmly and managed to untuck her hand from the crook of his elbow. Twisting to her side, she picked up a handful of her white satin dress. A stirring of murmurs hummed from those in attendance, but she couldn't see many of their faces clearly through her veil. Her gaze locked on the doors as her means of escape. Her uncle had left them open. Like one of the horses from the Lyndon stables breaking into a gallop on Pa's racetrack, she broke into a run down the middle aisle, sucking in full breaths for perhaps the first time in the last thirty seconds. How could a girl breathe properly with a veil covering one's mouth, anyhow?

It didn't take long to reach the church doors. She burst through them and flew down the steps, shoes clacking and train rustling, as onlookers outside gasped. Behind her, commotion broke out. Someone sobbing—Mrs. Sullivan? Her father directing someone to go after Delia.

She ran toward the corner of the church, hoping to spot Pa's carriage, yet Mama would need it. But Charlie Ford, Velvet

Brooks's jockey, had ridden Midnight Sunburst—one of her father's most prized horses—to the wedding. She'd seen Charlie arrive while waiting with Pa before entering the church. Presently, she needed Midnight Sunburst more than Charlie did.

Rounding the side of the building, she hiked her skirts up a little farther in time to leap over several planters of more peach roses the florists had positioned along the perimeter. Delia landed safely, digging her heels into the ground as she teetered. Her train glided over the roses, and she kept going until something yanked her back. Drat! She stopped, twisting around to see what prevented her escape. Ah! The enormous holly shrub attempted to tangle with her dress.

She freed the train and turned back to the horses and carriages parked alongside the church her Spencer grandfather had helped to build. He'd preached there for most of his adult life until his retirement. Right now, he was likely fanning Grandmother Spencer to keep her calm. Both sets of grandparents, pillars in the Lexington community, would be mortified at her behavior.

She'd make them understand—once she did herself.

She hurried toward the beloved horse at the hitching post, tossing her bouquet of roses over one shoulder. Someone in the crowd caught it, and more gasps ensued.

Delia yanked at the lead until she managed to untie the horse. After a brief fight with her veil, she swiped it away, pushing the front layer up and over her coifed updo. She stuck one of her dainty heels into a stirrup and mounted. With a few quick sweeps of her hand, she arranged her skirts to hide the fact she would not flee sidesaddle. It could not be helped.

Feet clattered down the church steps, and voices she recognized called out. Some of her bridesmaids come to retrieve her? They would attempt to coerce her to exchange vows with her betrothed. No, she could not speak to them, nor allow anyone to convince her otherwise. She didn't know her own heart or what her dream meant, but she wrestled with an unshakeable sense of foreboding. Nonetheless, a few spectators pointed in her direction, apparently eager to help the bridesmaids catch up to her.

She tightened her hold on the reins as Veronica and Gladdie appeared at the corner of the church. Blocking her path to Church Avenue along with dozens of acquaintances who hadn't secured an invitation to the wedding stood a fancy Sullivan carriage with a team of striking white horses. Delia had no time to lament the fact someone had labored to decorate the carriage and the team with ribbons and flowers. It would have carried her and Thaddeus to their reception, but now she looked for a way around it.

"Delia, wait!" Gladdie lifted her skirts and waved her bouquet.

"Delia!" Veronica was right on Gladdie's heels.

More bridesmaids caught up to her sisters. A sea of peach dresses swarmed toward Delia.

To her right and left, a thick crowd of onlookers whispered at the spectacle as she urged Midnight Sunburst through them, steering the horse toward the road. Folks would have to step aside and let her horse pass. A couple of guests opened the church windows to observe her departure, but she paid them no mind.

"Let's go home, boy," she whispered in his ear. The towns-folk parted like the Red Sea.

When she cleared the thickest part of the crowd, she sat up straighter, digging her knees into her mount's haunches. She snapped the reins. "Yaw!"

Midnight Sunburst took off as her bridesmaids nearly caught up to her at the edge of Church Avenue. The horse broke into a powerful gallop, as if understanding the assignment. His strong muscles began to move in swift stride beneath the saddle, carrying her far from the scene.

As Midnight Sunburst's hooves thundered down Church Avenue, tears streamed down Delia's face—so many tears, not even the breeze could dry them as she sped along. Runaway bride or no, she refused to marry Thaddeus Sullivan today, or any other day—at least not until she sorted out the mess inside her head and heart.

Maybe Thaddeus would never forgive her for leaving him at the altar as Clay Grinstead had nearly done to Gladdie, but she would have to take her chances. At least Gladdie's episode had happened in private. Poor Thaddeus!

Riding hard toward Velvet Brooks, she told herself the town gossip did not matter. Well, it mattered a little, but they hadn't seen her dream. What did she care what they thought, anyhow? She'd rather face the wrath of her betrothed, her family, and her friends than contend with the consuming flames dancing in her dream. She'd witnessed a large building burning in the dream—one she didn't recognize—but why had it seemed like watching her future burn?

CHAPTER TWO

I am still under the impression that there is nothing alive quite
so beautiful as a horse.
—John Galsworthy

Ten months later, March, 1903
Lexington, Kentucky

"What's taken so long, Delia?" Thaddeus snapped his pocket watch shut, and his brows furrowed. "We'll be late to the auction."

Standing in the Velvet Brooks foyer before a mirror, Delia fussed with securing her latest hat creation with a few extra hatpins. "Thaddeus Sullivan, you know very well that I'm wearing a new outfit. I want everything to be just so."

He released a long sigh and held out his arm. "You look fine. Let's be on our way. You know how much I'd like to place a bid on a new horse. If we don't leave now, we may not have that chance."

She whirled around and placed her hand on his arm, offering her sweetest smile. "Ready." Did he have to be so impatient? Didn't he know how much effort she put into looking nice for him?

He helped her up into his fine carriage, and soon, they were on their way into Lexington, but his lips pressed into a thin, firm line. After about a quarter of a mile, she commented on how nice it was that the sunshine had appeared for the auction.

"Far better than rain." He nudged his hat farther back on his head.

"Indeed." Everyone had wearied of the spring rain turning everything to mud. But today, the rays of sunlight bathed them in glorious warmth. Except...her mood began to spiral since a slight scowl remained on his face despite her attempts at cheerfulness.

Turning toward him, she surveyed his appearance. "You are looking dapper, Thaddeus."

His shoulders relaxed, and she caught a sliver of a smile. When he began to whistle "Jeanie with the Light Brown Hair," something he did frequently in her presence because of her brown hair color, she peeked at him through her hat netting. Had his attitude softened? Dare she mention the other issue on her mind?

When his whistling ended, she sat up straighter. "I do have a matter of concern I'd like to discuss." She bit her lower lip and busied herself with arranging the length of ruffle from her pigeon-front blouse at the sleeve of her walking suit. Her heart beat a little faster. She dreaded bringing the matter up, but it needled her too much not to.

"What's that?" Thaddeus kept his eyes straight ahead, focused on Cornflower Road, their horses trotting along as he held the reins in his strong hands. Sullivan hands she had come to admire over the years, for the Sullivan brothers were all big, strapping Kentucky boys.

"It's about the way you allowed your horse to run Todd Breckenridge's horse off the course the other evening, and at the very first night race of the season, no less." She tilted her chin. There. She'd stated the case plainly enough.

The night races might not be formal races such as the Derby or the Phoenix Stakes, but nonetheless, what would their friends think? Why would he want to tarnish his good family name? And hadn't they discussed this very thing when she'd taken him back?

He bristled, his mouth agape. "I can't help it if he doesn't know how to steer his horse properly."

"Thaddeus, you know very well, it's considered cheating if you run someone's horse off the course." Delia turned toward him, her chin lifting again. "This is no time for poor excuses."

"I did no such thing." His expression indignant, he muttered under his breath, indistinguishable words.

"There are witnesses, Thaddeus, and there is talk." Didn't he care? Pa and Mama had raised her to guard her actions and her reputation. Shouldn't a person be above reproach?

"Let them talk. It's not my fault Todd's horse preferred to gallivant into the woods."

"Oh, so now it's the horse's fault." Delia shook her head.

They brooded in silence, him sulking and her gloved hands intertwined tightly. Peeking at him through the netting of her hat revealed another scowl upon his face.

Just great. They'd ruined their start to one of her favorite events of the year, but how she despised his standoffish behavior simply because she took extra time getting ready, and even more, his denial of how he'd unfairly claimed a win. Nobody wanted to refute the word or actions of a Sullivan, not even if flagrant cheating happened right before their eyes.

Though she hadn't witnessed the race with her own eyes, she'd heard about it from their jockey, Charlie Ford, when he'd discussed the incident with Chet Carmichael. No one knew the rules better than Charlie. Thaddeus didn't have to ask how she knew. He would know Charlie or any number of local friends might have informed her.

Thaddeus shrugged. "Look, Delia, sweetheart, it comes down to a difference of opinion. Let's not quarrel. I don't want anything to spoil our day." He scooted closer. Then he leaned over and kissed her cheek.

Touching her cheek, she blushed, unable to hide a shy smile. Maybe she worried too much about those night races. Perhaps she shouldn't judge the harmless fun he craved quite so strictly.

Biting her lower lip, she released a reluctant sigh. "You are right. Let's not ruin our day. I'll give you the benefit of the doubt, this time."

He gave her a cheeky grin. She'd always loved his full cheeks, an indication of how well Mrs. Sullivan fed and perhaps spoiled her middle son. She returned an affectionate smile.

Upon arriving at the fairgrounds, Delia accepted his hand as she stepped down from the carriage into the sea of folk from all over Kentucky gathered for Lexington's annual thorough-bred auction. After the long winter, it was a delight to get out and about. They'd barely found a parking space for Thaddeus's fine carriage with its black leather interior and the fancy Sullivan emblem.

She smoothed her burgundy walking suit and checked to make sure her hat remained pinned firmly in place over her fashionable updo. The jaunty bit of black netting over her eyes made her feel stylish and happy, as if nothing, not even her doubts about her relationship with Thaddeus or their rocky start in getting to the auction, could ruin her day. She'd sewn the netting and a half-dozen burgundy silk roses onto the hat herself. She'd leave her parasol in the carriage to have one less item to tend.

She didn't know why she liked this event so much, but ever since she had reached the age of about five, old enough to walk while holding onto the hand of a parent, she couldn't remember having missed one. The spring auction hosted by the Lexington Jockey Club provided an opportunity to enjoy seeing neighbors, friends, and family alike. She could connect with beautiful horses, glory in the signs of warmer weather ahead, and show off one of her prettiest new walking suits with another masterpiece perched upon her head.

Thaddeus, who'd tied the horses to a post, tugged the sleeves of his white shirt until his cuff links appeared at each wrist below his gray jacket. With his gambler-style hat and fitted boots, his broad chest filling out his suit jacket, he looked robust and handsome.

Once again, she was at his side where she belonged. Delia could hardly wait to show all of Lexington their happiness. And other than some trepidation when his old habits threatened to appear, she did feel sheer happiness at being back with the man she had once fled from. Of course, many locals knew they had reunited since he now sat beside her in church on Sundays again instead of beside Emma Pearson.

After she'd run away from him at the altar ten months ago, it had taken him a month to speak to her. She'd sent Carter Mitchell to return her engagement ring with a letter for Thaddeus saying, *I'm sorry. I had a horrendous dream the night before our wedding. It terrified me. Please forgive me.*

In truth, she hadn't expected Thaddeus to ever recover or forgive her, but he had surpassed her expectations. On Saturday, the seventh of June, a month after their wedding day, he had called upon her. They had discussed the dream and the fact she had taken it to be a warning. They also discussed their frequent arguments, his temper, his cheating at winning races, and how he made decisions for her. He had promised to work on those problems. He asked her to address some things, too, pointing out her flaws of complaining, dwelling on negatives, and pouting. She had agreed to curb those tendencies.

After the discussion, they had decided to give their courtship another go. He'd said he would give her the ring and propose again when he knew she wouldn't run away from him. They agreed perhaps a wedding with only immediate family would make it easier.

For a while, his mother didn't embrace their renewed courtship. She refused to permit Thaddeus to invite her to any family gatherings, but she eventually relented, and her frosty demeanor warmed again.

When Thaddeus hadn't given Delia's ring back by Christmas with another proposal, they'd broken things off again. He'd chased after Emma Pearson, whose father owned a warehouse near the stockyards, until one of Mama's brilliant plans—Delia attending the Valentine's Day Dance with Brent McIntosh—brought Thaddeus back to Delia's side.

Exasperating as Thaddeus could be, she still loved him, but she could only describe their courtship as bumpy at best. About as bumpy as a camel crossing the Sahara's sand dunes.

But hadn't she wanted to marry him for as long as she could remember? When they finally wed, all of her problems would vanish. She would take her place in the world as his wife. No one would consider her inadequate as Mrs. Thaddeus Sullivan. She would no longer live in the shadow of her two sisters as the invisible middle daughter. Perhaps she wasn't as vivacious as Veronica or as carefree as Gladdie, but whenever she was with her beau, his attention fed her sense of belonging, respect, and worth.

Not to mention, once she married, she would never need to worry about money again, and she would never need to wear a hand-me-down dress again. Of course, Mama saw to it that each of her daughters enjoyed a couple of new dresses each summer and fall, but the bulk of Delia's wardrobe came from her older sister's castoffs.

Even more importantly, with access to her own dowry and Thaddeus's resources as a Sullivan, she could find a worthy cause to support—such as her work at the library.

So why did she struggle with nagging doubts as they passed through the gates of the fence surrounding the long rows of stables and corrals? Had she done the right thing in pushing the fearful dream aside? Of course, she had. Most dreams were simply dreams, were they not?

Eagerness swelled inside at the prospect of assisting her beau in finding a champion horse to race. With Thaddeus at her side, they could forge a bright and happy future.

CHAPTER THREE

A horse doesn't care how much you know until he knows how much you care. Put your hand on your horse and your heart in your hand.
—Pat Parelli, Horse Trainer

The thick crowd milled about Delia and Thaddeus. It seemed everyone with even an ounce of affection for horseracing had turned out for the event, including many eager buyers and trainers from Tennessee, Indiana, and Ohio.

As some children ran past them, Thaddeus paused, smirking at the interruption. He waited for Delia to catch up and tucked her hand into the crook of his arm. "Remember when we were kids, running through these rows, getting into trouble when our parents weren't looking?"

"How can I forget? The auction is the best place. So much to explore...the smell of candied apples and fritters." She could already sniff out the treats from vendor carts, mingling with the scent of hay and saddle leather. Then she wrinkled her nose. "And horse manure."

"I'm looking forward to the fried chicken at the picnic lunch with our families. Mother said to meet them by the big oak tree near the pavilion at half past noon. Shall we stroll down this row? It looks promising." He gestured toward their right.

Promising...yes. The past winter had been one of the hardest in her twenty-three years. Adding difficulty to the unusually harsh weather, their broken courtship had left her sullen through most of the long winter months. Today, she saw signs of life everywhere, lifting her spirit. Spring had begun to blossom, and the morning sunshine had melted the frost on the bluegrass.

She lifted her chin and smiled. "Thank you, Thaddeus, yes. I want to see as many of the horses up for auction as possible before the bidding. Father is considering a purchase also."

"What do you think of this horse?" Thaddeus paused with her to admire a mare who returned their gaze, boredom evident in her eyes as she chewed on a tuft of grass.

"Hm. I like her chestnut coat, and..." She paused to scan the complementary auction guide, then pointed her gloved finger at the description of the horse matching the name on the corral plate. "It states right here, Belinda Blue has a champion bloodline, but I'm not impressed with her any more than she is with us. Shouldn't there be a bit more of a connection between a horse and her future master? There's a stallion up ahead who has caught my eye. Let's keep strolling."

"You've always had a nose for a champion, Delia. You chose my last winning horse. Thundering Wonder won nearly every race Father entered him in."

Delia flushed at his praise and looked down, a strange shyness coming over her. Thaddeus didn't compliment her often, but his blue eyes lit up with enthusiasm about her equine knowledge. Pa said his daughters knew winners when they saw them, and when it came to horses, her confidence seldom wavered. With Thaddeus behaving more attentively, she would do her best to give him her whole heart. After all, didn't most couples have their fair share of ups and downs?

Then Delia stiffened. Emma Pearson was passing by with her sister and parents. A glance at Thaddeus's expression told Delia he hadn't seen Emma or her family—or if he had, he didn't acknowledge them. He had his eye on a fetching horse on the other side of the row, farther up ahead. Tucking her hand more snugly into the crook of his arm, she kept her gaze fixed forward.

After admiring a mare and a gelding, they stood gazing at a feisty stallion in a separate corral. Thaddeus brightened and waved at Julius Anderson, Arthur Breckenridge, and Gebhart Pickett—sons of neighboring horse farm owners. Delia had known them for years, and Arthur was Todd's older brother. They'd attended Kentucky University together, formerly Transylvania College. And they'd stood at his side as groomsmen when she'd run away from Thaddeus. Would Arthur have something to say about the night race she'd mentioned earlier? Probably not. He wouldn't want to ruffle his friend's feathers.

Thaddeus turned to her, excitement in his eyes. "Should we say hello?"

"You go ahead. I'll catch up. I'm impressed with this frisky creature. He's such a beautiful bay. I'd like to observe him for a bit." Delia smiled, waving toward his friends. "Besides, Pa and Gladdie are headed this way. It will give me a chance to see if he found a new horse for Velvet Brooks."

Thaddeus released a thankful sigh. "All right, if you're sure you don't mind."

"I'm sure. Go on and say hello. I'll be right here."

He stepped toward his friends, and Delia returned her attention to the stallion, chuckling softly as the spirited horse stomped, performing a rebellious trot, apparently growing indignant about the crowd. Her father and younger sister joined her at the rails.

"What do you think about this gentle creature, Pa?" Delia glanced up at her father and smiled at Gladdie. "Have you seen any horses you like?"

"One or two, but I'm still looking. I have a few more rows to inspect before the bidding." Father tipped his hat farther back on his head to take in the view of the bay. He flicked his tail, continuing his flustered dance. "This one has a wild look. Is that why you refer to him as gentle, Delia?" He chuckled, amusement in his eyes.

"Yes. He's afraid of the crowd, but I think he has courage and spirit to match his agitation. Look at the way he prances. He is furious about being here, but inside, he's a baby waiting to be loved. I can tell by the sweetness under those fearful eyes, and I see intelligence there too. I'm not all that fond of strangers either." She kept her voice low. She shouldn't broadcast her opinion too loudly lest she attract others to bid on the same horse. "I think he'll perform for the right person."

Gladdie considered the bay, her head tilted to one side. "You've pegged him about right, in my opinion."

The horse neighed in further protest. His tail swished, and he turned left to trot in a skittish manner around the square pen. When he had nearly reached them again, he reared up, pawing the air with his front legs. Delia gasped and jumped back. His hooves came down a few feet from where she stood as he released another neigh.

"He doesn't look too happy." Gladdie also took a step back from the rail.

Delia made eye contact with the horse, and his nostrils flared. He sashayed off for another go-around inside the corral.

Movement in the crowd caught their attention. A burly man to their right turned from the railing and stepped in front of a finely dressed gentleman walking down the row with a horse on a lead, about to pass behind them.

"Ho, there! I say, how did you come into possession of my

saddle? Someone stole that saddle from me at the last spring meet!" The large man held up his hand to stop the gentleman, successfully blocking him.

"How dare you accuse me of stealing your saddle? I bought it fair and square with my hard-earned cash," the finely dressed gentleman snarled in reply, "two rows over at the saddle dealer, not ten minutes ago. He said it was brand new."

More people gathered at the bay's corral who intended to observe not only the horse, but now the growing argument between the two men. As the crowd thickened, the bay bristled inside the pen. Fearing a storm brewing, Delia drew in a deep breath. Pa would do something if it continued. Wouldn't he?

"If you check the reverse side of that saddle, you'll find my initials," the burly man insisted. "R-B-G. Carved 'em into it myself last spring before the meet. With this knife right here." He drew a knife from a leather holder strapped to his waist. As the bright morning sun reflected off it, gasps sounded from the ladies.

"You want to fight? Let's fight." The gentleman in the black suit dropped the reins to his horse, removed his suit jacket, and handed it to someone nearby. He began rolling up his sleeves as murmurs ran through the crowd. Ladies stepped aside, and all eyes turned on the two men ready to duke it out.

Delia bit her lower lip and glanced at Pa, who remained leaning at the rail, though he turned sideways to observe the argument. Gladdie huddled closer to her. They couldn't step away since the rail blocked them between the men and the horses.

"Gentlemen..." Despite his raised voice, Pa remained calm as he spoke. "Let's put the knife away and take your dispute elsewhere. This is a family event, and as a member of the Lexington Jockey Club, I must insist you abide by the rules of decency here. Besides, you are adding to the agitation of this horse."

Everyone knew her pa, and the men glanced toward him as they held their fists up. The muscular man had his knife in one hand, but now he returned it to its leather holder.

Adding fuel to the fire and punctuating her father's remarks, a loud backfiring sound released from one of the new automobile machines in the parking lot at the perimeter of the fairgrounds. It sounded as if a shotgun had fired. The bay inside the corral responded by rearing up again with another neigh. The horse's hooves landed on the top rail of the fence only a few feet from where Delia and her family stood. They whirled around.

Delia caught sight of three little girls huddled around the corner at the lower rails of the same corral, frozen, their eyes huge. Sisters, judging by their matching golden curls. She hadn't noticed them until now since they barely reached the top rail.

No one appeared to be looking out for them. Obviously, they wanted to see the feisty stallion, reminding her of days gone by when she had done the same, peering through the corral railings with her sisters. But the three-year-old colt couldn't jump since he didn't have enough room in the pen to make a go at the rail—meaning he would continue his campaign, bringing his hooves crashing down on the rails until he broke through to make an escape. Unless someone intervened.

Delia hurried past the arguing men who had now also turned their attention on the bay horse, along with everyone else. She slipped around the corner of the corral. Reaching the little girls—all under the age of nine or ten, she guessed—she scooped the youngest into her arms and took the other little one's hand to pull them away, assuming the eldest would follow her lead. "Hurry, girls, before the horse breaks through the rails."

The eldest also took the middle girl by the hand and

followed Delia. She guided them away from the fence, using her free arm like a wing to keep them moving away and together, seconds before the horse came crashing down on the rails again with the sound of wood cracking.

They reached a spot some yards away, closer to the neighboring pen and stable. Keeping the girls close to her and the youngest in her arms, Delia turned them toward the horse. He had broken through the top two rails, and most of the top rail and part of the second had crashed to the ground. Clearly, the heavy rails would have injured the girls if she hadn't acted swiftly.

The lip of the child in her arms quivered. The sweet angel could only be three or four. The one holding the oldest girl's hand might be a year or two older, perhaps five or six. Considering how well-tended they appeared—with their hair in tidy golden braids tied with white ribbons and wearing spotless matching white dresses, black stockings with no holes, and clean black shoes bearing few scuffs—their parents would surely appear at any moment.

"We're safer here, girls," she explained as the horse neighed again and backed up as if he might attempt to jump the fence, making the girls' eyes widen even more. Pa and some other men had leapt inside the pen. "Don't worry. The men will tend the horse, but let's stay here until then."

Who did the girls belong to, and why had she found them alone and unsupervised?

Just then, a man in a full-length leather coat, reminding Delia of buffalo skin or something Wild Bill Hickok would have worn in his Wild West days, leapt over the fence. His long, wavy golden hair and fluid movements made him seem as untamed as the horse—to which he was holding out a carrot. Delia couldn't take her eyes off him.

The oldest girl at her side stood up straight. "Uncle Jake!"

CHAPTER FOUR

The wagon rests in winter, the sleigh in summer, the horse
never.
—Yiddish Proverb

Uncle Jake?

Apparently, the men who'd argued over the saddle
had skittered away to resolve their dispute elsewhere. Thaddeus had disappeared somewhere farther down the row with
his friends. But all Delia could focus on was the man coaxing
the bay toward the stable.

The horse kept an eye on the offering as his nostrils began
to relax, flaring less than before. The man holding the carrot
spoke gently to the stallion, as did her Pa, working together to
urge him inside the stable as they walked backward, leading
the skittish horse to safe harbor. When their plan finally
succeeded, Delia sighed with relief.

She set the youngest girl on the ground and knelt to speak

to them at eye level with a friendly smile. "I'm Delaney Lyndon, but you can call me Delia."

The oldest one took the lead. "I'm Ruby. These are my little sisters, Ella and Mary."

"Nice to meet you, Ruby, Ella, and Mary. I have two sisters also. Are your parents here?"

"No, our parents are in heaven, but our Uncle Jake brought us. He's the one who gave the carrot to the horse." Ruby pointed, and Delia's gaze followed to where their uncle emerged from the stable with her pa. Well. He certainly had a way with horses. And he had charge of his nieces...who were *orphans*?

The men headed toward Delia and the girls, Gladdie meeting them at the rail, trailing behind.

"Uncle Jake" resembled the three girls with his blue eyes and blond hair. And Delia couldn't help but notice he possessed a strikingly handsome face with a strong jawline. Delia had never seen him around Lexington before, but with his tall height, dungarees, and leather boots, he fit into Kentucky as if he had always been here.

"Thank you, Miss..." their uncle began.

Delia rose to greet him.

He removed his hat, and after raking a hand through his shoulder-length hair, extended it to shake hers. He wore a friendly smile, his eyes bright. Seeing Pa caught up in a discussion with a friend, Delia shook his hand.

"Miss Delaney Lyndon, but everyone calls me Delia." He had a good, firm grip. She didn't like a weak handshake in a man. Pa said a weak handshake showed a lack of confidence, and one should never greet anyone in such a way. She gestured toward Gladdie. "My sister, Miss Gladys Lyndon, but we call her Gladdie."

"Delia—I mean, Miss Lyndon." He offered a respectful nod and another to Gladdie, then turned back to Delia. "Jake

Williams. Thank you for rescuing my nieces."

"You're most welcome, sir." Her brow arched. What reason might he offer for neglecting his precious nieces?

"I was asking the fellow across the row about a horse, but now I believe I'll place a bid on this frisky fellow. We've formed a connection. I like his spirit. In any case, I thought I'd only be gone a minute or two, and then all of this escalated." He waved toward the corral where several men had begun to repair the railing, bringing in new boards to replace the broken ones. "Anyhow, I saw you move the girls out of harm's way and decided to throw my efforts in with your father's."

"It's good that you did. That bay was determined to escape, but it appears he likes carrots." Delia's smirk drew a warm smile in response, and the girls giggled.

"I'm ashamed to admit, I'm better with horses than children. You must think I'm a terrible cad for leaving them alone for one second. Another valuable lesson learned in child-rearing. In my defense, we've only been together about a week. I put an advertisement in the Richmond papers for a nanny, but we've only just begun to have replies since my sister's home sold." He paused as Pa joined them, and they exchanged a handshake. "Jake Williams, sir."

"Joseph Lyndon. Nice to meet you."

The handsome stranger nodded at her pa and then turned toward Delia, a twinkle in his eyes. My, how blue they appeared in the sunlight.

"Where was I? Oh yes, Richmond—that's where they lived. I myself am from New York. But forgive me—I'm rambling. In any case, I am eternally grateful. How can I show my appreciation? I would have blamed my incompetence forever if any harm had come to them."

Delia cast a glance downward, smiling as heat warmed her cheeks. "I'm glad to be of help, and as you can see, they are perfectly fine. Perhaps briefly daunted, but a good lesson for them about horses. Ruby here, she knew what to do as soon as I came around the corner."

Ruby smiled at Delia's praise and looked at her feet.

"Thank you again, just the same. These are my nieces, Ruby, Ella, and Mary. We're keeping an eye out for a small farm to purchase. We're excited about finding a proper home and raising some fine horses, aren't we, girls?"

Ruby and Ella nodded, grinning at their uncle as he knelt, tousled Ella's hair, and tugged on one of Ruby's braids. The girls giggled in response. Mary climbed immediately into his arms, her chubby arms wrapping around his neck as he stood again, keeping hold of her.

"Yes, they introduced themselves to me. They are lovely girls." Delia smiled at their warm interactions, but Mister Handsome surely had his hands full.

"I must agree with my sister. They are very well behaved." Gladdie held onto her hat as she looked up at Jake, who towered over her and Delia with their petite frames.

"Thank you. I happen to think so, too, especially considering we're a bit cramped in our current living quarters." Jake's face twisted with a slight grimace.

"Where are you staying?" Pa crossed his arms over his chest.

"While we look for our farm, in two rooms at the Caldwell boardinghouse in town."

"Ah, yes. We know the Caldwell place. Listen...my wife is over at the shelter spreading out a picnic if you and the girls would like to join us. There'll be plenty of food." Pa waved toward the pavilions. "The bidding won't start until this afternoon."

"We'd like that, wouldn't we, girls?" Jake waited for the reactions of his nieces.

They nodded with enthusiasm, smiles lighting their faces.

"Mrs. Caldwell is an excellent cook and packed us a picnic lunch too." Jake shifted Mary to his other side, appreciation in his tone. "It'll do us some good to make friends in the community."

"Very good. Look for us by the great big oak tree, the biggest one by the picnic pavilions. I may know of some farms for sale, and one is not far from us."

Jake's brows shot up. "I'd like to hear about it."

Turning to Delia and Gladdie, Pa rested his hand on Delia's shoulder since she stood closest. "Jake mentioned he might be interested in racing horses one day." Looking over at Jake again, he added, "You've come to the right place for that. Kentucky has the finest equines in the country and some of the best race-courses around. If you do win the bid on the bay, as you mentioned, or any other horses, you are welcome to train them at Velvet Brooks. You can thank Delia for her quick thinking on behalf of the girls by bringing them to dinner sometime, once you're settled."

Delia flushed. She'd only done what any sensible bystander would have done. Although...she understood Pa was not only being neighborly and hospitable to a newcomer, but possibly gaining a new cash-paying customer who likely needed help acclimating to the world of horseracing.

"Thank you. Much obliged, Mr. Lyndon, Miss Delia, Miss Gladdie. We'll see you at the picnic." Jake lifted his hat. "I'd definitely like to hear more about training the bay at your farm, assuming we are blessed to win the bid."

"So then, you're making a bid on the bay?" When he nodded, Delia smiled her approval. "He has great spirit. Some-thing tells me he'll make a fine racehorse." And the two of them seemed a good match in temperament. Not to mention what the horse could mean to three little girls who had lost their parents and been uprooted. If Pa decided not to bid so Jake would have more of a chance, she could hardly blame him.

Jake grinned, a smile so wide, his blue eyes lit up. "I think so, too, if we can get him to run for the crowd instead of into it."

Delia and Gladdie chuckled as Thaddeus returned to Delia's side. What had become of him? He'd missed all the excitement.

"Sorry I've been gone for so long, but I think I've found a horse to bid on. I heard I missed quite a commotion. Someone said the bay broke through some of the rails and nearly escaped." Thaddeus slipped his hand around Delia's waist and then nodded at the stranger in their midst as he straightened his tie. "I'm sorry. I don't think we've met."

Pa introduced them. "Thaddeus, this is Jake Williams. While he helped me secure the bay, he mentioned he is from the Adirondacks. And while we dealt with the horse, Delia came to the aid of his nieces. Jake, this is Thaddeus Sullivan, the son of one of my good friends and owner of one of Lexington's finest horse farms. We happen to be neighbors too." Pa winked at Delia and Thaddeus. "But I think we'll be family one of these days—very soon, I suspect."

Delia couldn't help but glance at her beau, briefly meeting his smile, and then back down.

Did Pa's words infer an expectation of Thaddeus? If so, he didn't seem to mind. Or maybe her father implied he and Thaddeus knew something more specific than she did? Of course, Pa and Thaddeus had talked when they'd begun courting again last June, but they hadn't bothered to meet again in February after the dance. By then, Pa and everyone else had grown accustomed to the ups and downs of their testy relationship. Still, Pa's statement made her wonder if he and Thaddeus had spoken in recent days without her knowledge. She would press Thaddeus about it later, perhaps on the way home.

As for Jake Williams, she'd read of the beauty of Adirondack Park. While her curiosity stirred, she didn't dare draw further attention to herself by asking the stranger more about from where he hailed. Besides, the girls grew restless, as did Thaddeus.

Ruby spared them any further awkwardness by yanking on her uncle's sleeve. "You said we could look at more horses and buy candied apples, Uncle Jake."

"Yes, yes, I did. We had better be moving along, but it's been nice meeting all of you. Thank you again, Miss Lyndon, for looking after my nieces. You saved the day. We'll see you all by the oak tree at the pavilion."

Delia nodded and smiled as Thaddeus intertwined his hand in hers and Jake and the girls turned to go. Seconds later, Thaddeus whisked her away from Pa and Gladdie, explaining he wanted to show her the horse he had in mind.

"Tell me what Jake Williams and your Pa meant about you saving the day and rescuing his nieces. What did I miss?" Thaddeus's brow rose as he escorted her deeper into the long row of stables.

"Oh, it was nothing, really. The girls were standing too close to the rails where the bay was making a fuss. I just moved them to a safer spot and waited with them until their uncle could return." It wouldn't do to have Thaddeus notice her interest in the stranger. "Now, tell me about this horse you've found."

Still, she couldn't quell her curiosity about the bachelor uncle and his three young charges. Why had Jake decided to leave the Adirondacks and settle in Kentucky? A man who would walk around with carrots at the ready certainly had some instincts about horses, but how had he acquired such a love? And what, if anything, did he know about racing horses?

"Delia, you haven't heard a word I've said." Thaddeus jerked her from her musings, pulling her between two stables where no one could see them.

"I'm sorry. I'm just distracted trying to decide which horses are the best ones."

Unexpectedly, he drew her hand to his lips. "May I kiss you, Delia?"

"Oh goodness, Thaddeus." What if someone saw them? But

didn't she want him to kiss her? "I suppose, if you hurry." She giggled as he drew her into his arms, but then he pressed his mouth rather forcefully to hers, followed by a tender but serious look quite unlike him.

Did he mean to reclaim her notice after her encounter with Jake Williams? Before she could ponder that, he pulled her along to see the horse he wanted to purchase. And from there, she forgot about the stranger...for a while.

CHAPTER FIVE

Don't give your son money. As far as you can afford it, give him
horses. No one ever came to grief, except honorable grief,
through riding horses.
—Winston Churchill

Carrying Mary in one arm and lugging a picnic basket
with his other, Jake made his way toward the pavilions
on the eastern edge of the Lexington fairgrounds, Ruby and
Ella in tow. Would he find the attractive young lady who'd
rescued his three nieces among the Lyndon family members?
She intrigued him, even took his breath away for a moment
with her sweet, shy, demure smile.

But she had a beau. He didn't have time for such distrac-
tions, anyway. He had to focus on settling into the community,
making friends so his sister's children could thrive in a new
environment. He needed to find a small farm to purchase
where he could build a life for himself and his nieces. Some-

thing with a big farmhouse. Lots of bedrooms. Something not in a state of disrepair.

Yet of the two farms for sale he'd visited, neither enticed him. One out of his price range, the other with a small cabin. Joseph Lyndon had mentioned he knew of some properties for sale. And maybe he would be a helpful connection beyond providing training for his horse if he won the bid.

Mr. Lyndon spotted him right away as they drew near the picnic area, welcoming them with a hearty smile. "Good, you found us. Let me introduce you to everyone." He nodded toward an array of tables situated under a pavilion. "My wife saved some seats for you and the girls. Eleanor, here's our new acquaintance from the Adirondacks, Jake Williams, and his three nieces, Ruby, Ella, and Mary."

Eleanor Lyndon stepped forward with a warm smile, her pale blue gown fluttering in the breeze. "Nice to meet you, Mr. Williams. Please join us. May I help with your picnic basket? Let me have a look at these adorable girls."

She set his basket on a table while some of the other ladies finished spreading blue-and-white checked linen cloths on the tables. He inhaled the aroma of mouth-watering foods other women placed down the middle of the longest table—probably several drawn together. He didn't see Miss Delia Lyndon yet.

"Thank you, Mrs. Lyndon. Nice to meet you too." Jake clasped her outstretched hand. Then she knelt to exchange a few words with Ruby and Ella.

Another lady about the same age stepped forward with a look of delight fixed on his nieces. "Aren't they sweet darlings?" She shook hands with each of his nieces. The feathers on her expensive hat waved in the breeze as she spoke to the girls, asking their ages.

"This is Mrs. Caroline Sullivan." Mrs. Lyndon gestured toward her friend.

As Jake bowed over Mrs. Sullivan's hand, Mrs. Lyndon knelt to Ruby's eye level. "You must be a big help to your Uncle Jake."

Ruby's white bows at the end of her braids bobbed as she nodded with a shy smile.

Mrs. Lyndon helped Ruby and Ella find a seat as another gentleman stepped toward him. Maybe Mrs. Sullivan's husband? Mrs. Sullivan took Mary from his arms and carried her to a seat near her sisters.

"And this is Caroline's husband, a longtime friend, Harold Sullivan." Joseph drew in Mr. Sullivan with an outstretched arm. "A fellow board member of the Lexington Jockey Club. Harold, meet Jake Williams from upstate New York."

Jake squinted, extending his hand. "I believe I met your son, Thaddeus, earlier. Nice to meet you and Mrs. Sullivan. Mr. Lyndon mentioned you are neighbors."

"That's right. Glad to meet you. Welcome to Lexington and one of the best auctions in all of Kentucky." Mr. Sullivan gave him a hearty handshake. "I hope you like pie. The ladies have brought two apple pies, a peach pie, one pecan, and two cherry pies." Mr. Sullivan nodded toward the baked goods on another table, a twinkle in his eye.

Jake grinned. "Nothing better than pie."

Gratitude and relief filled his heart to see Mrs. Lyndon and Mrs. Sullivan fixing plates of food from his picnic basket for the girls. It was certainly nice of them to also add other foods like pickles, beets, and bits of cheese to their plates, rounding out what the boardinghouse owner had sent along from the provisions already on the table.

Movement to his right caught his attention before Mr. Lyndon could introduce him to more of the folks gathered around. Miss Lyndon, the pretty one named Delia, whose quick thinking had spared his nieces from harm, arrived with Thaddeus Sullivan at her side and greeted some of the others. When she smiled in his direction from the other side of the table, he nodded and returned a smile, causing her to look down. Sweet, shy young lady.

Too bad she had a beau. Though Mr. Lyndon had said he thought Thaddeus would become family soon, maybe the fella hadn't officially proposed yet. On second thought, who was he kidding? A humble former stable hand and a stranger, he didn't stand a chance with a lady so fine and fashionable as Miss Delia Lyndon. Probably not a good idea to show any romantic interest—not if he wanted to make friends with her kinfolk and the Sullivans he'd just met.

Mr. Lyndon waved him forward, leading him toward a couple seated at the far end of the long table. "Let me introduce you to our eldest daughter and her husband, Veronica and Edward Beckett. Edward is an artist. Veronica is holding our grandson, Eddie Junior." Turning to his son-in-law and daughter, Mr. Lyndon added, "Jake is from New York too."

Veronica Beckett smiled up at him from her seat with a contented countenance, her looks similar to Miss Delia Lyndon's and their younger sister's. Three brunette beauties with rosy cheeks, likely on account of the bounty of fresh air in the countryside.

"Nice to meet you." Edward rose from his seat, reaching out across the table, shaking hands with him.

"An artist? And from my home state too. Glad to meet you." Jake maintained an eye on his nieces, but he angled to face Mr. Lyndon's son-in-law. Edward Beckett had a commanding presence, maybe because of his height. Good, firm handshake too.

Edward's face brightened. "Yes, an artist. Stop in and visit my gallery sometime. A special exhibit begins this coming week."

"An art exhibit?" Jake cocked his head. Impressive.

Delia stepped near her older sister and took her infant nephew into her arms. She cradled the baby against her shoulder, resting her chin on the child's bit of hair, sniffing his baby scent. She certainly possessed a natural mothering instinct. No wonder she'd spared his nieces from harm's way. Did she realize she had such a gift?

Edward placed a hand on his wife's shoulder, smiling down at her as he spoke. "We just opened the gallery a short time ago. Took us some time to find the right location, but we finally did after a lot of prayer. In any case, the special exhibit begins Monday and lasts until eight o'clock each evening through Friday. We're on the corner of Mulberry and Main. Tickets are fifty cents each."

He shouldn't keep staring at Delia, so he nodded in Edward's direction. "Thank you. I'll try to stop by. I have no talent in artistic endeavors whatsoever, but I do appreciate artwork."

Veronica placed folded hands on the table. "We've shipped all of Edward's artwork by train from Manhattan to fill our gallery, and with both of you from New York, I'm sure the two of you will find plenty of things to chat about."

Mrs. Beckett had a southern drawl like Delia and the rest of her family had, one that made him smile, and somehow, relaxed him. These folks weren't uppity, but dare he say, kind of laid back?

Jake nodded. "I'm sure we will find plenty in common." But he had to stifle an inclination to ask Edward more since Mr. Lyndon urged him along toward some others he pegged to be in their twenties, all blond, possibly kinfolk to Thaddeus since he stood with them.

"Now that you've met my son-in-law and eldest daughter, most of the Sullivan clan are here. There are five siblings, but the eldest, Henry, and his wife Rose, are still viewing some of the horses. They'll be along later. You've met Thaddeus."

Thaddeus nodded curtly, his arms crossed over his chest.

"Oh, yes. Hello again." Jake returned a nod. Odd. Thaddeus didn't offer to shake hands or utter a greeting. He seemed...

prickly. Ack. Not his problem if the Sullivan fellow refused to return the courtesy of a polite greeting. Did he detect a territorial stance in the way Thaddeus glowered with a piercing stare, or did he imagine it?

"And the Sullivan twins are here, Percival and Matilda. And this is Mary Louise, the youngest. We know them fondly as Percy, Tilly, and Mary Lou." Joseph gestured toward each of the Sullivan siblings beside Thaddeus as he mentioned their informal names.

These three Sullivans heartily shook hands with him. Far more polite than their brother. How would he remember all of their names? Tilly and Mary Lou wore fashionable hats and gowns. Percy wore some fancy casual duds and one of those flat boater hats, a style he liked, but not for himself. Maybe he should cough up some funds to purchase a leisure suit or something nicer than his usual work attire. He had a suit for Sundays and special occasions, but he preferred his dungarees and work shirts.

Delia moved toward where his nieces sat, having returned Eddie Junior to his mother. Sweet of her to strike up a conversation with Ruby, Ella, and Mary. She deserved someone nicer than that stuffy, stewing Thaddeus fellow.

Joseph led him next to a table beside the long one where a foursome of elderly folks sat with two other ladies a bit older than Mrs. Lyndon. "Jake, I'd like you to meet my father, Colonel Lyndon, joining us with my mother. They have retired from horseracing and farming to live in town, but my father is the visionary behind Velvet Brooks Farm."

The colonel, an elderly man with white hair, reached for his cane and began to rise from his seat, his silver-haired wife nodding from beside him.

"No, no, please don't get up, sir. It's a pleasure to meet both of you. Thank you for serving our country." Jake reached out to him with a handshake. Had he said the right thing? Had the colonel fought in the Civil War, or was it a nickname indicative of something else? No one corrected him, and the sparkle that flickered in the colonel's eyes told him he'd gotten it right. So these were Delia's paternal grandparents.

The Lyndons and Sullivans made a grand bunch. They all dressed so fine, like the patrons of the Sagamore, the resort where he'd worked. Evidently, these folks were among some of the leading and most successful families in Lexington, given the fact Harold Sullivan and Joseph Lyndon were members of the Lexington Jockey Club. Apparently, their roots ran deep in Kentucky—at least three generations back for the Lyndons. His dearly departed Uncle Caleb, a former horse trainer in Baltimore circles, would appreciate them. He had a feeling his sister and her husband, a doctor, would have approved, too—if they hadn't passed away.

Mr. Lyndon held his hand out toward the other couple seated across from the colonel and his wife. "This gentleman is Reverend Spencer, my wife's father. He's retired from preaching, but he helped make our church what it is today. Perhaps you will join us for worship services with your nieces. The First Christian Church on Church Avenue. The sweet lady at his side is my lovely mother-in-law, and these two ladies are her other daughters, my wife's sisters, Aunt Eliza and Aunt Ida."

"Nice to meet all of you." Jake shook hands with the reverend and nodded toward each of the ladies as they waved and nodded in return, each wearing fine hats and spring gowns with elegant shawls or fine walking suits for the outing.

Had he finally met everyone? Could they sit down and eat? How had Mrs. Lyndon and Miss Delia managed with his nieces? He turned, searching for them.

"Well, I don't know about you, but I can't wait to feast on all of this food." Mr. Lyndon clapped him on the back. "Shall we take our seats?"

"Yes, I'm starved, and it all smells so good." Jake couldn't ignore the grumbling of his stomach. Had he been absent for too long from his nieces? A glance in their direction told him they were fine. Mrs. Lyndon still hovered over them, but where had the lovely Miss Delia gone? He spotted her seated near his nieces, with a seat reserved for him and Thaddeus on her other side.

This should prove interesting. What would he say to her? Bowls of food were being passed around, everyone helping themselves to potato salad, fried chicken, biscuits, three-bean salad, and slaw. Jake slid into the open seat between Delia and Ruby.

Mr. Lyndon raised his voice. "All right, everyone, let's quiet down so we can hear Grandfather Spencer lead us in prayer."

When the retired reverend's prayer ended and someone handed him a plate, Jake released a sigh, eager to eat his fill from the plethora of foods, happy at the prospect of having at last made some new friends. Of course, he'd met everyone at the boardinghouse, but they seemed as lost as he did. Visitors or newcomers, like himself. Here, except for Thaddeus Sullivan being standoffish, it almost felt...as if he'd come home.

Surrounded by good Christian folk who remembered to pray before a meal, and displaying fine hospitality, put him in mind of his family and friends back east. His parents would approve of these folks too.

Maybe he'd done well in choosing Lexington as a new home for himself and his three charges. A fresh start for them, away from the reminders of his sister's passing, and in a place he could grow his dream of racing horses and build a fine boardinghouse.

Now, if he could only think of something polite to say to Miss Delia Lyndon and others in her set seated across from her and Thaddeus. They all talked, still passing food around.

Someone passed him a basket of flaky biscuits thick enough to put those made by the chef at the Sagamore Resort to shame.

He plucked one from the offering in time to accept a jar of delectable cherry preserves. Then someone passed him a plate with butter molded into the shapes of leaves and flowers, maybe to celebrate the arrival of spring. The butter and preserves were probably made from livestock and fruit raised on their farms too. The ladies in Kentucky sure could cook. Of that much he was certain after he'd tasted a bite of the chicken.

Could he begin by remarking on the food as a means to strike up a conversation with Miss Lyndon? He'd have to wait. Someone chatted with Delia about various townsfolk they'd seen at the event. He shouldn't interrupt.

He'd at least like to get to know her a little better, on account of owing her a debt of gratitude. If only she didn't have a territorial beau seated on her other side. Judging by the cuff-links the fella wore and his finely dressed self and family, the Sullivans seemed mighty prosperous. Would he measure up to them? Maybe if he learned all he could from Mr. Lyndon about horseracing and farming.

He tasted more of the chicken. Could he also learn to make fried chicken that tasted this good?

Delia turned toward him with an arched brow. "And how is the fried chicken, Jake? May I call you Jake?"

"Yes, please. Call me Jake. The chicken is delicious. Thank you." Now what could he say to her? Tongue tied, he struggled to come up with something interesting.

"I'm happy you like it. And I hope you win the bid on the horse." She offered him another of those demure smiles that lit up her chocolate-colored eyes.

"I sure do, too, thank you." He yearned to ask for a tip about placing a bid, but then he might sound foolish. "I would sure appreciate prayers toward that end."

"Of course, I'll be happy to pray that you win the bid. You and your nieces deserve a chance at that horse. Perhaps few will bid on him since he behaved...so wildly." She buttered a biscuit as she spoke. "I haven't seen a horse pitch a fit like that in a long while, but I do believe it may work in your favor."

Jake smiled. "I sure do hope so." Could he ask more about her pa's farm?

Thaddeus leaned toward Delia. "Would you like to go riding next week when I'm home from my hunting trip?"

Delia turned toward her beau. "That sounds very nice, Thaddeus. Perhaps on Wednesday morning? We could take a picnic lunch along. I'm sure Gladdie would like to accompany us."

"Sure, I'll be your chaperone." Gladdie rolled her eyes and then chuckled.

Hmm. Jake should get to know Miss Delia Lyndon better, even if only to annoy Mr. Rudeness. Perhaps he could work up the nerve to ask her on a similar outing if he won that bid.

And maybe he should acquire something like what Mr. Lyndon wore for the occasion? A tweed jacket with a crisp white shirt, brown tie, and trousers. Jake had never allowed himself to dream of owning a piece of land before, but he soon would. Selling his late sister's home in Richmond would make it a reality, though bittersweet.

Mr. Lyndon probably earned a small fortune from fees for training horses, selling horses, and winning races. He should do all he could to emulate the man and acquire such knowledge to add to what he knew of horses. Running a stable for a resort had done little to boost his confidence, but he did remember a few things Uncle Caleb had mentioned over the years. First things first, he needed a champion steed. And a farm with a grand old Victorian house so he could transform it into a fine boardinghouse to rival others he'd seen over the years. Horses and offering hospitable accommodations were the only things he knew after working for a resort most of his life. If he couldn't offer upscale, he could at least aim for charming.

Thaddeus now dominated the conversation with a discussion about getting everyone together for a game of horseshoes later that evening at the Sullivan property, making it awkward to speak to Miss Delia.

Would he fit in with them? Not that he cared much for what other folks thought, but one day, maybe he'd feel he truly belonged. Certainly, if he won the bid on that horse at the auction, because then he would be working toward the same thing as these folks. He'd have a horse with as much chance as anyone's to prove himself on the track.

Ruby tugged on his sleeve. "Uncle Jake, Mary needs you to sit next to her. She's making a mess."

A few chuckles met his ears. Jake dutifully switched places with Ella, ending up too far from Miss Lyndon to easily converse. But did he notice a sympathetic glance and one of those shy smiles from her when he had settled into his new seat and swapped out their plates? Would some other opportunity to get to know her come along when he didn't have his nieces to tend?

Did he dare ruffle the feathers of Thaddeus by pursuing her? Jake didn't have to ponder the matter for long, for Thaddeus made no attempt to converse with him, didn't invite him to the horseshoe event, and did everything in his power to prevent Delia from speaking to Jake during the remainder of the meal. How had Mr. Lyndon been duped by this rude lad into thinking he'd make a good son-in-law?

'Twas doubtful Mr. Lyndon's daughter would seriously consider him, anyway. He was a few years older than most of them at twenty-eight, and why would she want to be saddled with three children who weren't her own? Furthermore, if her father hoped for a match for her with Thaddeus, best to stay out of the crosshairs. No, he'd find a way to thank her for her brave actions and keep his mind on being the best guardian he could be to Ruby, Ella, and Mary.

O n Sunday, before leaving the church service, Delia waited with Gladdie near the pew where she'd sat with her family and her beau. Why did she always have to wait for Thaddeus? She bit her lower lip. She shouldn't complain, even if only to herself. She'd promised him she'd work on that. Besides, he waited for her sometimes. And at least she still had a beau. Many ladies did not have the same blessing, but could she truly count it a blessing?

Presently, he absorbed himself in a hearty discussion with his friends to finalize some plans for a hunting expedition. He planned to come to Sunday dinner at the Lyndon household before leaving for two days of hunting, returning by Wednesday for their horseback ride. She would have to attend the special exhibit at Edward's new gallery without him on Monday.

Jake Williams moved toward her with his three nieces. They must have slipped into a pew somewhere behind her shortly after the service had begun. Jake certainly had cleaned up nice, looking quite dapper in a suit and tie.

"The girls and I couldn't leave without saying hello." Jake held Mary in one arm while Ruby and Ella smiled up at her.

Would Ruby like a hat in the style girls her age were wearing? Perhaps Delia could make her one. She resisted straightening Mary's hair bow. How on earth did Jake manage without any help?

"We picked these for you, Miss Lyndon." Ruby held up a bouquet of pansies.

Delia's brow arched. She couldn't hide her smile as she accepted the delightful offering. "What a lovely surprise. How very kind of you girls. Thank you."

Jake wore a shy grin that belied a little embarrassment about the girls giving her flowers.

"It's nice to see you again, Jake." Gladdie shook hands with him.

Mama turned around from where she stood nearby, speaking with Grandmother Spencer. "How nice to see you and the girls here today, Mr. Williams. I hope you enjoyed the service. Will you and the girls join us for lunch? There's plenty of food."

"As much as I wish we could, Mrs. Lyndon, Mrs. Caldwell went to extra trouble to make Ruby's favorite, roasted chicken." Jake tousled Ruby's hair. "Perhaps another time?"

"Of course. The invitation stands. Perhaps when you are settled. My husband said you'll be coming by on Monday about training your new horse, and he mentioned showing you a farm for sale near our home. Maybe I'll see you then." Mama smiled warmly at him before adding a special wink for the girls. "If you'll excuse me, I must help my parents into their buggy." She hurried away to lend her support to Grandmother.

Jake turned his attention back to Delia. "We should be going. I promised Mrs. Caldwell we wouldn't be tardy for the Sunday meal, but it sure is nice to see you again. We enjoyed the service."

"Very nice to see you again too. May I be among the first to congratulate you on winning the bid on the bay? I'm only sorry I wasn't there to see it, but Pa told me all about it."

"Thank you. The girls and I are filled with joy about acquiring the horse."

When his blue eyes lingered on her, heat rose to her cheeks. "Thank you again for the flowers."

"You're welcome. See you soon. Bye, Miss Gladdie." Jake smiled warmly at her and then offered a nod in Gladdie's direction before turning to leave, steering his girls toward the main doors.

"Bye, Miss Lyndon. Bye, Miss Gladdie." Ruby clutched a Bible, looking much too big to be hers, but she managed to wave. Ella followed suit, waving from her side. Mary leaned her head on her uncle's shoulder, but she gave Delia and Gladdie a shy smile.

"Goodbye, Ruby, Ella, Mary." Gladdie waved, too, grinning.

"Be good for your uncle, girls." Delia sighed as they shuffled through the crowd. Why did her heart skip a beat each time she saw this man and his charges?

Now that he had acquired such a fine horse, Jake stood a chance of becoming the proud owner of a champion on any of the thoroughbred racecourses of America. She had a good feeling about that horse, and Jake—truth be told—though she didn't know exactly why.

Gladdie snapped her fan open and began waving it rapidly. She whispered to Delia behind it. "He really likes you, and so do his nieces. And what a handsome gentleman."

Did Jake truly have some degree of attraction or a romantic interest in her? "I do like the way he wears his hair in a ponytail like Paul Revere." Delia released a tiny gasp at herself for speaking the compliment out loud, but then she and Gladdie turned and looked at each other, bursting into a quiet fit of giggles. They were still in church, after all. But the sanctuary had nearly emptied, so few would care if they shared a private laugh about how handsome the new stranger in their midst appeared—except her beau, of course, bidding farewell to his friends.

Still grinning far too much, Delia waved her fan. And Gladdie wore a terrible smirk. It did her heart good to see Gladdie laugh. Maybe she had finally begun to heal a little from Clay Grinstead jilting her. But Delia certainly couldn't let Thaddeus speculate on the reason for their humor as he turned toward them, raising his brow. She and her sister straightened.

Thankfully, Thaddeus slipped his arm around Delia's waist and gave her a peck on the cheek instead of questioning her. But his eyes followed Jake and his nieces as they exited.

"Are your plans settled?" She slipped her hand behind her back, hiding the bouquet of pansies. Would he cast blame on Jake for something the girls had done spontaneously—at least as far as she knew?

"All set, and now to enjoy lunch at your house before I depart. You and Gladdie are welcome to ride with me. I brought Father's buggy today."

Gladdie nodded to Delia, and her beau led them down the main aisle. Would he notice the bouquet? She positioned her hand with the delicate blooms under her Bible in such a way as not to smash them. Why did she feel the need to hide them? They weren't from Jake, but the very mention of the man or his nieces might bristle Thaddeus. *Please don't let him notice the flowers, Lord.* The very last thing she needed was another disagreement with her beau over something pure and innocent.

But as she settled into the buggy, her mind drifted far away from Thaddeus, a fact that needled her. Did Gladdie's words ring true? Why did the newcomer stir her with the way he stared into her eyes when he spoke to her?

She pushed away thoughts of Jake Williams. One day soon, Thaddeus would pop the question, and she would finally become Mrs. Thaddeus Sullivan. Jake was merely a distraction she didn't need to concern herself with except as a client for Pa and a new face in the community.

CHAPTER SIX

No philosophers so thoroughly comprehend us as dogs and horses.
—Herman Melville

On Monday, nearing the end of her shift at the library, Delia scooped a stack of books from the main counter. If she hurried, she could return the books to their proper place on the shelves before Gladdie and her parents arrived to pick her up for the special exhibit at Edward's gallery.

She'd nearly finished returning the books when Gladdie entered the library, trailed by Jake Williams, the very last person she expected to see. She'd prayed last night for him and the girls, asking the Lord to help them find the perfect place to build a happy life together. How good of Pa to think of the farm across from them. Would the Victorian farmhouse be too large for Jake's needs?

"Gladdie...and Jake? Hello there." She kept her voice low, but her brow arched. She turned her attention back to returning a book to its rightful place because presently, she stood on tiptoe and didn't relish the thought of it landing on her head. Unable to reach the top shelf, she had nearly resigned herself to retrieving the stepladder when Jake reached over Gladdie's head, giving the book a nudge.

"Thank you." She couldn't help but smile. It warmed her heart to have his assistance. He was tall, and helpful, two more things to like about him. Drat! Shouldn't she only have thoughts for her beau?

Curious as to why he had come inside the library with her sister, she crossed her arms over her chest, enfolding the last book in her hands against her bodice. "I think I can venture a guess. Are you accompanying us to the exhibit?"

He nodded. "I am." Then he held up five tickets. "I purchased tickets for your whole family. Part of my thank you for rescuing the girls at the auction."

Why did her heart leap a little at the prospect? She couldn't help but smile again. Placing a hand on her hip, she shook her head. "You shouldn't have, Jake. That was very kind of you."

"Our parents are waiting for us in the carriage. Is your shift finished?" Gladdie eyed the last book Delia clutched.

Delia walked around to the next aisle before responding, Jake and Gladdie following, and slid the book into its proper place on the shelf. "It is now." Delia held out empty hands. "I just need to get my cloak and hat."

And a stack of books to deliver, including some she'd set aside for Jake and his nieces, since they seemed too busy to worry about library visits until they were more established. She had selected four books for the girls, *Rebecca of Sunnybrook Farm, What Katy Did,* and *Black Beauty. The Jungle Book* for Mary.

She had set aside four for Jake, too, since she had no idea about his taste in books. *Moby Dick? The Pickwick Papers?* Maybe something more adventurous such as an Arthurian tale about the knights of the round table, *Le Morte d'Arthur*? Perhaps last year's trendy new release, *The Hound of the Baskervilles*.

Now she wouldn't have to deliver them. She could hand them to him at the end of the evening when their carriage dropped him at the boardinghouse. Would he like the books she'd chosen? Whatever he didn't want to read, she could deliver to others on her list.

How had he purchased tickets to the art show in advance? He must have stopped by the gallery earlier in the day if he'd spent most of his time with Pa at Velvet Brooks, or perhaps he'd purchased them directly from Edward or Veronica while at the farm. Had he decided to let Pa's expert staff train his amazing horse? Had he liked the farmhouse and land across from Velvet Brooks with the big barn, the trees, and its fishing pond? Would he make an offer, making them neighbors? She must refrain from asking lest she appear too interested, but some part of her could hardly hold back her curiosity.

Gladdie and Jake followed her to the main desk in the center of the library where the stack of books to deliver waited. She had to record her hours on the clipboard—if she could find it in the mess the head librarian had created.

"See you tomorrow, Miss Woodhouse," she said, keeping her voice low. Would the librarian stop typing to acknowledge her departure, or merely nod and wave them away? She could be somewhat mercurial, but then, so could Delia. Besides, she treated Delia and Miss Daphne Broadhurst, the other librarian and a local spinster, kindly, often giving them handmade book-marks and other treats. Delia's great love for books helped her overlook the spinster's moodiness.

"Do have fun at the exhibit." Miss Woodhouse turned her head to one side and peered at Delia over the top of her wire-framed eyeglasses which had slid farther down the bridge of her nose. The forty-something spinster then nodded toward Delia's sister. "Nice to see you, Gladdie."

Gladdie brightened, standing up a bit taller, leaning against the counter portion on the other side of the enormous desk. "Always nice to see you, too, Miss Woodhouse."

Miss Woodhouse inspected Jake, where her gaze lingered. Delia hid a smile. Of course, her gaze would linger. Jake was exceptionally handsome. Strong jaw. So tall. Broad shoulders. Kindness and warmth in his perceptive blue eyes.

"Have you met Mr. Jake Williams? He has recently moved here from Richmond." Delia continued sifting through the piles of papers on the desk in search of the clipboard.

The librarian offered a smile. "Ah. Welcome. Nice to meet you. Sorry. I'm drowning in overdue book notices to send out in the next post." She resumed typing a letter on the clunky new typewriter Delia longed to have for writing her stories, but Miss Woodhouse did steal a few more peeks at Jake between plunking out letters of the alphabet.

"Glad to meet you, Miss Woodhouse." Jake stepped back, undaunted by her choppy greeting. He craned his neck to take in all the books on the shelves around the large room, a pleasant expression on his face. Admiration for the sea of literary works surrounding them?

He and Gladdie didn't seem to mind the fact Delia kept them waiting. Gladdie reached for a book on the counter and began reading the back cover description.

Delia stood up straight, hands on her hips, brows furrowed. "Have you seen the clipboard? It's not hanging on the hook where we usually keep it."

"No idea." Miss Woodhouse shook her head, casting a sweeping glance around the desk. "I'm sure it's here somewhere."

Delia sighed. Tapping her foot, she bit her lip to refrain from asking how Miss Woodhouse had buried the all-important record of their work hours. Everyone used it, including the other librarian, Miss Daphne Broadhurst, who was not working today. Miss Woodhouse didn't usually spread out her work to this degree on the desk the three of them shared.

Finally finding the missing clipboard on the far side of the desk under a mountain of papers, Delia jotted down the time of her departure.

She hastened to the coat room near the main door, her arms laden, Jake and Gladdie on her heels. Snatching her cloak from a hook, she balanced the books precariously under her chin, unable to put the cloak on.

"I'll carry those for you." Jake plucked the stack from her hands as if it weighed a feather. Large hands and long arms made the books fit easily into his care.

"Thank you. A few of those are for you and your nieces, if you'll remind me to give them to you before the evening ends." She may as well let him carry them to the carriage. Why did he have to behave like such a perfect gentleman when she ought to be thinking of her own beau? She considered loyalty a high requisite in any relationship, requiring it from herself, first and foremost. But this man...how he distracted her.

Jake perked up, his eyes brightening. "That's very kind of you. The girls will be delighted."

She rattled off the names of the books she'd selected for them as she swung the cream cloak around her shoulders and hooked the top button into its loop. The cloak worked well with her peach day dress, more than suitable for viewing the exhibit with its cream lace embellishments and cream silk-covered buttons along the sleeves. She reached for one of her hat creations with its peach silk flowers and ribbon trimmings, securing it atop her head, tying the wide ribbon to one side of her jawline. "I guess I'm finally ready. Sorry it took me so long."

Eagerness appeared in Jake's blue eyes as he glanced up from the books he held. "I've been wanting to read *The Hound of the Baskervilles*. The title has me intrigued. Have you read it?"

"No. It's always making the rounds. You can tell me about it when you're done though."

"Are you reading all of these other books, Miss Delia?" His brows shot up.

She chuckled, shaking her head as they followed her outside to the carriage. "No, just delivering them to some elderly folks in our community who are shut in. Would you stow those under the seat?"

Would it be all right for Jake to accompany her family to the gallery? Mama must think so, or she wouldn't have agreed to any of this. Others might raise a curious brow, but what could Thaddeus or anyone else say since Jake would accompany the whole family? Still, why did she have an uneasy feeling?

~

Jake's brows furrowed. Delia's mother had said her daughter volunteered for a pittance. She hadn't mentioned Delia delivered books too. A highly commendable endeavor.

He climbed into the open family carriage last, sitting beside Mr. Lyndon, while the ladies settled on the seat facing them.

Jake offered a sheepish smile along with his greetings, then added, "I hope you won't mind me accompanying your family to the gallery. My intention is to thank Delia properly for rescuing my nieces at the auction." He searched Delia's face for a reaction, but she busied herself with tucking a few strands of her brunette locks into place under her lovely spring hat. When she did gaze in his direction, she smiled, her cheeks turning a deeper shade of pink before she turned away again.

"Not at all." Mrs. Lyndon smoothed her gray silk skirt. "It was very kind of you to purchase tickets for all of us."

Mr. Lyndon tapped his cane on the floor, and their driver navigated the conveyance into the busy city street. Such a change of pace from Green Island where isolation had greeted him day in and out.

And once again, Jake was underdressed in a mismatched coat and breeches, without a top hat or suit to rival the one Mr. Lyndon wore. He'd dressed for the tour of Velvet Brooks Farm and to meet Red Brickman, the trainer. Perhaps he should remedy his sparse wardrobe sooner rather than later.

"Edward will be thrilled to see all of us arrive in support of his work." Gladdie lifted her chin to have a look at the traffic ahead.

Delia's eyes sparkled. "I'm particularly excited to see Edward's painting of Diamond Comet with our groom. Poor Carter posed for hours while Edward worked on the portrait."

"Diamond Comet?" Jake turned toward Mr. Lyndon with a raised brow.

"One of Gladdie's favorite horses and a champion from our stables." Mr. Lyndon's deep voice and his smile told Jake of his pride in the horse.

"I must say, our groom was a good sport." Mrs. Lyndon released a ladylike chuckle to match the good-natured smirk upon her face. "I don't think he complained one time even though it took many days."

"You will buy the portrait, won't you, Pa?" Delia leaned forward slightly.

"Of course, but we won't take it home until after the exhibit ends on Friday. Edward may bring it to me, I suppose. I want to let all of Lexington view it so Diamond Comet will be etched in the minds of our community as the legacy he is." Mr. Lyndon relaxed in his seat.

Delia released a sigh of relief. "Good. Veronica said there will be a number of paintings on display on the main floor, but the special exhibit will be on the second floor. Each of the three paintings in it will feature a champion horse." She located a pair of gloves from a pocket hidden in her skirts and proceeded to don them.

"I tried to coerce Edward and Veronica to tell me who the other horses are, but their lips are sealed. They said we had to wait until the exhibit along with everyone else." Mr. Lyndon waved a hand, a brooding expression appearing on his face as he rested a hand on his gentleman's cane. If Jake didn't know better, he would say Mr. Lyndon was aggravated about not being "in the know."

"Edward and Veronica wouldn't give me so much as a hint." Mrs. Lyndon's shoulders drooped.

Jake had to stifle a chuckle.

Delia folded her hands in her lap and focused on him. "How are the girls today, Jake? Are they in school yet? Who is caring for little Mary?"

Leave it to Delia to express concern for his nieces. He kept discovering more reasons to like her, but her pretty smile drew him most. "I thought it wise to settle them into a routine as soon as possible, so yes, I've enrolled them in school. Mrs. Caldwell offered to watch Mary today, and she said she'd pick the girls up from school."

"Mrs. Caldwell is very kind and efficient. I'm sure she will look after them properly." Mrs. Lyndon tilted her head to the side of the carriage to see what caused a delay in traffic. "We're almost there, but poor Nathaniel. How will he ever find parking? Who would have thought there would be this much traffic on a Monday when simply driving a few blocks and around a corner?"

"Is everyone in Lexington going to the gallery for the opening day of the exhibit?" Gladdie craned her neck too.

Delia's mouth dropped open. "I think so. That long line of people from the gallery stretches all the way around the corner, and I can't see the end of it."

Jake twisted in his seat to peer over his shoulder. In addition to the line of patrons on the sidewalk, many drivers in all sorts of conveyances attempted to find parking. One of those new noisy machines tooted a horn. A sign reading *Beckett's Art Gallery* hung above their destination, its letters containing exactly the right amount of fancy swirls. Turning back to the Lyndons, he grinned. "Judging by the bottleneck of carriages and that long line, Edward's exhibit shall be a grand success."

Mr. Lyndon asked their driver to drop them near the end of the long line. After a twenty-minute wait, the Lyndons and Jake finally entered the gallery. Inside the main door of the long, narrow building, Edward and Veronica welcomed them with exuberant smiles, both flushed from the excitement. Veronica kissed and hugged her parents and sisters while Edward offered hearty handshakes to Jake and his father-in-law. Jake handed Mrs. Beckett the tickets.

"Follow me, everyone." Edward led them to the staircase, leaving Veronica to collect more tickets at the door as she allowed another group to enter behind them. "You may take all the time you like to view the portraits downstairs after you see the special exhibit upstairs."

At the top landing, Edward turned left and headed down a spacious corridor toward the front of the gallery facing the street below. He beckoned them under a wide square arch flanked with velvet burgundy drapes, tied back with gold braided cording.

The exquisite entrance led into a drawing room of sorts. The room, wide as the building, featured arched windows on three of the four walls and a white fireplace at one end. A few well-placed chairs and benches occupied the perimeter along with some potted ferns and palms. A pale shade of eggshell-brown paint on the walls with white wainscoting panels created a bright and airy space with a calming effect. The flames from a few sconces flickered against the walls, but the tall windows offered excellent lighting with their burgundy drapes drawn open. Sunshine illuminated three massive portraits on brass stands, situated on a room-sized black-and-gold Oriental rug with burgundy highlights. Suspended from the high ceiling, a chandelier housing dozens of candles also lit up the space.

Patrons meandered about the room, taking in every detail with approval in their eyes. A few other paintings of Edward's hung on the walls, all with country scenes one might encounter in Kentucky—farms, fences, barns, animals, country folk, and farmhouses.

Jake's breath caught in his throat, and Delia's eyes were wide.

"This is so lovely, Edward. You and Veronica have been keeping secrets from us, but very good ones, I see." Mrs. Lyndon smiled with approval at her son-in-law, her voice low so as not to disturb the other guests.

Remaining off to one side of the group, Edward clearly basked in her praise.

"I am overcome with the beauty of this space, Edward," Delia murmured. "You've done a magnificent job of creating the perfect gallery. I liked the warehouse style with the wood floors and the simpler lighting downstairs, but *this*...this is breathtaking."

Jake could not agree more.

"Thank you. I had a great deal of help from Veronica." Edward shifted his weight. "After you view the main portraits, I should return to help her with the guests downstairs. But don't forget to try some of the refreshments being served downstairs before you go."

"Thank you, Edward," Mr. Lyndon said. "You know I'm buying the painting of Diamond Comet, right?"

A wide smile spread across his son-in-law's face. "Veronica said you would."

As Delia approached the first portrait, Jake sidled up beside her, his arms clasped behind his back. He could hardly wait to hear her thoughts.

"Ohh," Delia breathed. "Look! It's Longfellow, from Nantura Farm in Midway, Kentucky." She pointed to the title of the painting.

Hadn't his Uncle Caleb mentioned the horse a time or two? "Wasn't he a champion from the 1870s?"

"Yes. John Harper owned him. Pa can tell you all about John Harper and how close he lived to Woodburn Stud Farm. How clever of Edward to choose to paint Longfellow."

"Do you think Harper named Longfellow after the poet?" Jake's brow arched.

"I don't think so. They say Longfellow was seventeen hands high. I think he was simply a tall horse with very long legs." Still smiling, Delia moved on to the next portrait as the other family members also circulated before the paintings, Mrs. Lyndon clinging to her husband's arm. Gladdie stood with an arm crossed in front of her waist and a finger planted on her chin.

"Just like our dear Edward to feature our Diamond Comet and Carter here in the middle." Delia gazed at the painting for a long while, leaning forward to inspect every detail, her eyes bright.

"The smile on your face tells me the painting does the horse and groom justice." Jake stuck close to her side, keeping his voice low. He'd purchased the tickets as a thank you to her, after all. Why did he discover as much joy in her eyes and just being there at her side as the artwork gave him?

She nodded, twisting to smile at Edward, standing a few feet away and behind them. "So nice to see Diamond Comet's name, our groom's name, and the name of our horse farm in the title. Everyone will applaud Edward for this."

Edward turned a little red at the compliment despite the weak smile on his face.

They moved toward the final portrait, and Delia read the title. "And here is Aristides, the first Kentucky Derby winner. My goodness, Edward has put quite a bit of thought and research into this. And so well done."

The way the lighting enhanced Delia's peach silk bow and the flowers of her hat, complimenting her dark hair, mesmerized Jake nearly as much as the gallery and its paintings.

Once Jake and Delia had sufficiently praised Edward and thanked him for sharing his art with the world, Jake turned toward Delia, his brow rising. "Shall we go downstairs and look at his other artwork?"

She nodded as her pa stepped up beside them.

Mr. Lyndon patted Edward on the back. "Well done. Well done, Edward."

Delia gestured toward the staircase. "Others want to see this space, and Edward doesn't want the room to be overcrowded. We should move along."

As Edward rejoined his wife downstairs, Jake followed the rest of the family toward the gallery on the first floor. Soon, Jake and Delia stood before a series of lighthouse portraits while her family and other patrons admired pictures farther down along the same wall. Waiters served appetizers and glasses of pear juice punch.

"I'd like to purchase something for our new home. Something the girls will like. Do you think they'd prefer something like this?" Jake motioned toward the lighthouse picture he liked best.

Delia tilted her head and paused, tapping her chin with a gloved finger. "I'm sure they would, but I think they might like this family picnic scene a little more." She led him to another set of oil paintings.

"I do like the way the dog is stretched out, and the colorful flowers in the meadow, and the happy expressions in this one." Jake smiled as he beheld the scene.

"Yes, it pulls me right in. I love scenes that capture the essence of country life." Delia accepted a glass of pear juice and a cracker with goat cheese from a waiter's tray. "Did you decide to train your horse at Velvet Brooks?"

He nodded. How pleasant it was to converse with her, inhaling the fragrant scent of green apple perfume each time she moved. "Yes, as a matter of fact, I did. And I plan to make an offer on the farm across the street. It's perfect for us."

Delia turned one of her pretty smiles and those big brown eyes framed by delicate eyelashes on him. "I'm glad things are coming together for you, Jake. You are handling your transition to Lexington so well. I'm sure you and your nieces will soon be settled and find great happiness here. Our community has much to offer and a rich heritage to share."

"Thank you, Miss Delia. I can see why my sister and her husband chose to settle in this state." Jake stood up taller. For some reason, her approval and genuinely warm encouragement made his heart expand. He couldn't tell her how much he had needed to hear words such as those she had expressed.

One day, perhaps he, too, would be able to say that heritage was a part of him, as it seemed to be for the Lyndons. Doubts plagued him about his decision to uproot his nieces from Richmond, but at least they didn't have reminders of what could never be again lurking around every corner. He and the girls had embarked upon an adventure together. He couldn't say for certain where it might lead, but nonetheless, a whole new life brimmed with possibilities.

Hmm. Could he work up the courage to ask Delia on a picnic with his nieces? Would that be considered inappropriate, given the fact that she had a serious beau? Would Mr. Lyndon be unhappy if Jake pursued his daughter? Would Mr. Sullivan turn him out of Sullivan's Savings & Loan, the bank where he'd opened a new account? Would Delia spurn him, scoff at him, find such an invitation audacious? She might consider him below her station in life or feel greater loyalty to Thaddeaus Sullivan than Jake imagined. Perhaps if he invited her whole family...

"Delia, dear, look who's here. Thaddeus has just arrived." Was that Veronica's voice?

Jake turned as Mrs. Beckett joined them, resting a hand on Delia's forearm. Thaddeus Sullivan trailed her sister by a few feet, another glowering expression under his lowered brows.

Delia spun around, her eyes wide. "Thaddeus, you're back early from your hunting expedition. Is...is everything all right?"

Jake didn't trust the fellow—why, he couldn't say exactly. Delia's beau reached her and twined his arm around hers, pulling her a few steps away from Jake. She nearly lost her footing before recovering her balance, but Jake had to stop himself from reaching out to steady her.

Thaddeus raked a hand through his hair. "Arthur and Gebhart are fine, but Julius had an appendicitis attack. We decided to cut our trip short and get him to the doctor. The physician is going to observe him for twenty-four hours and admitted him to the hospital. The rest of us went home and cleaned up. Then I decided to come into town to see if everyone was here at Edward's exhibit. And right I was. Here you are with..." His brow arched, and he grimaced, turning a sour face on Jake. His chest puffed out and he squared his shoulders.

"You remember our new friend, Jake Williams, Thaddeus." Sweetness on her face, Delia gestured toward Jake.

Meanwhile, someone had drawn Veronica aside to inquire about a portrait.

Jake took a step forward with an outstretched hand. "Good to see you again, Thaddeus." Maybe an offer of a handshake would simmer this fellow down. But the glare emanating from him! Should he put both fists up and prepare to defend himself in the middle of Edward's fine gallery?

Thaddeus sneered at him and took one more step back, pulling Delia with him.

Delia's smile disappeared, replaced with a crushed expression, disappointment in her eyes.

Jake could only shrug and withdraw, letting his hand drop to his side. Terribly rude fellow.

"Thaddeus…" Mrs. Lyndon stepped toward the three of them, her arm still wrapped around one of her husband's, pulling him gently along, her voice soft, like a polished southern belle's. "How nice of you to support our Edward's artistic endeavors. Back so soon from your hunting excursion?"

Mr. Lyndon stared at a painting nearby, hands in his pockets, his wife's arm still clinging. Reluctantly, he turned toward them and raised his brows. "Oh, hello there, Thaddeus. Everything all right?"

While Thaddeus repeated the situation that had brought him home early, Veronica drew near and leaned toward Jake. "What a lovely picture." She spoke in a low tone. "Have you decided on it? Shall I wrap it in brown paper and ring it up for you at the register?"

"Thank you, yes." Jake carefully removed the painting from the wall and handed it to her. After rummaging for his wallet inside his frock coat pocket, he withdrew a bill large enough to cover the purchase.

"I hope you enjoy the special exhibit." Mrs. Lyndon patted Thaddeus on the arm as if soothing his obvious ire. "We showed Jake around at Velvet Brooks earlier today. He will be training his horse with us. Then we all decided to come out and show our support to Edward. We picked Delia up at the library on the way."

How wise of Mrs. Lyndon to articulate the situation. She had made every effort to clarify things for Thaddeus—so he wouldn't do anything stupid.

Delia bit her lower lip, her brows scrunched together, concern evident in the lines creasing her forehead.

Thaddeus's stern expression did not soften much. He offered Mrs. Lyndon a half smile but otherwise kept a suspicious glare trained on Jake.

Gladdie caught up with the party and inquired about going home.

As she spoke with her parents, Thaddeus turned toward Delia. "Since you must be going, I'll see you on Wednesday for that horseback ride, darling." He wasn't even looking at Delia when he spoke the endearment. On that word, he aimed his cold stare at Jake. Delia flinched as he tightened his hold on her arm.

Jake's fist clenched. Why didn't anyone else see the problem? Mrs. Lyndon and Gladdie were still absorbed in an exchange about leaving. Mr. Lyndon had turned back for a glimpse at a painting. Jake wanted to ask Delia if she was all right, but why make a scene and ruin Edward's special exhibit?

Probably best to step away and take some of the heat with him in case Thaddeus continued to direct his displeasure at Delia for being there with him. Jake sauntered toward the register to claim his purchase, kicking himself for not intervening by calling Thaddeus out. The man was a cad. Plain and simple.

Thaddeus struck him as the sort who would wrestle Delia with verbal wars, arguments about anything and everything until he had his own way. Jake had known temperamental folks like him before. He'd seen plenty of them come through the Sagamore Resort over the years.

Veronica handed Jake the wrapped painting, and he thanked her absentmindedly, keeping an eye on Delia as she said good night to Thaddeus. Mr. Lyndon stepped up to the register to pay for the painting of Diamond Comet, and Jake moved aside.

"Edward will deliver it to you on Saturday," Veronica assured her pa.

"That will be fine. Splendid event. A wonderful turnout." Mr. Lyndon turned to his wife and the rest of their party. "Everyone ready to head to the carriage?"

"Good night, Thaddeus. See you later." Delia waved to her beau.

Was Jake wrong, or was that uneasiness in her eyes?

Thaddeus nodded. "See you Wednesday."

Ignoring the last chilling stare Thaddeus turned on him, Jake followed the Lyndons as they filed out of the gallery, the portrait tucked under his arm. He did his best to keep a space between him and Delia as they returned to the carriage, though he would rather put a protective arm around her and ask if she was all right.

Why had Delia fallen for the Sullivan fellow in the first place, a man whose temper simmered for no good reason? Jake had only tried to thank her for her courageous act by purchasing tickets for her and her family to support Edward Beckett. She deserved far better than a volatile husband in her future.

And why didn't her family seem to notice the way Thaddeus behaved? If they did see it, did they overlook it because they considered him a fine catch for Delia?

Would she consider Jake in Thaddeus's stead? And how might he win her affection when he had nothing to offer but a life of hard work and three children to raise?

CHAPTER SEVEN

A mother's love for her child is like nothing else in the world. It
knows no law, no pity. It dares all things and crushes down
remorselessly all that stands in its path.
—Agatha Christie

Two weeks later, Delia returned to Velvet Brooks on
Glorious Day Dreamer. Her ride constituted one of the
last she would enjoy with the colt before his intense training
under Red Brickman—their trusted horse trainer who worked
exclusively for Velvet Brooks—began. Pa planned to enter
Glory—his stable name—in several races for two-year-olds.

The birth of Glorious Day Dreamer, preceding Veronica's
marriage to Edward, had sparked renewed hope to the whole
family and cheered up Gladdie, easing her broken heart.

The colt had a bright future as one of Velvet Brook's star
horses. Once horses passed the age of four, their racing career
generally concluded since fewer races existed for four-year-
olds. The rigor of four years of intense training and racing

usually relegated a stallion to become a leisure-riding horse, unless a stallion had a good pedigree and race record, in which case he could go on to become a breeding stock stallion. Healthy mares at Velvet Brooks could become broodmares from the ages of two to fifteen, ideally, according to Pa.

Delia had raced Glory hard, galloping across the entire width of the farm from the barn to the creek's edge on the western side of the property. The horse's breathing had already returned to normal, and he'd hardly broken a sweat. From what she could tell, he had the strength and stamina of a horse at the end of a racing season instead of one coming out of a long winter pent up in the barns. If Glory did as well as everyone hoped on the track, he might become the sire of an incredible legacy, like a handful of other horses who'd lived at one time or another on their farm.

After dismounting in front of the veranda of the main house, she handed the reins to Carter Mitchell. The farm's loyal groom wore a wide smile as he stroked Glory's long nose. "Atta way, boy."

"How did he do?"

"Miss Delaney, I keep blinking, thinking I've read his time wrong." Carter held up his stopwatch. "One minute and fifty-seven seconds. He be fast. It's not even April yet."

Delia let out a whistle under her breath. "I can hardly wait to tell Pa."

"He'll be right proud." The groom tipped his hat toward her. "I'll walk him for a well-deserved cool down."

"Thank you, Carter. Nice job, Glory." She patted the horse, and the groom led him toward the big horse barn. She watched them walk away, brushing some dust from the sleeve of her green velvet riding habit, and hurried inside, anxious to find Pa.

She paused in the main hall to remove her hat before the mirror. The ride had cleared her mind, too, about matters concerning her beau. Thaddeus had come calling for several horseback rides since the special exhibit at the gallery, including the one on the Wednesday following as he'd promised. He hadn't brought up anything about the gallery visit or mentioned Jake on their ride or since that evening in Edward's gallery. Perhaps he'd considered Mama's explanation and calmed himself down.

The newcomer had certainly troubled him, so she avoided any mention of Jake Williams around Thaddeus. He'd never gripped her arm so tightly before, and the infuriating moment had taken her by surprise. His manners had been less than commendable as well. Had she made a terrible mistake by giving him a second chance?

Otherwise, it seemed their relationship had resumed with ease since his hunting trip, settling into a semblance of routine. He came calling for horseback rides or tea in the sitting room once or twice each week. They spoke about the weather, the latest news in the papers, and outings they looked forward to in the summertime.

Low voices sounded from the library, reminding her she wanted to speak with Pa about Glory. She recognized her parents speaking but tilted her head toward the open doors at hearing her name mentioned while she plucked the hairpins from the matching velvet hat with its long scarf trailing down her back.

Setting the hat aside on the narrow table beneath the mirror, Delia stepped closer to the double doors.

"I don't know, but some competition can't hurt," her mother said. "Then our Delia will have options. Isn't that what we want for our remaining single daughters? Options, secure marriages, and bright, happy futures?"

"You have a point there, Eleanor," Pa conceded. "Options are better than no options. And I like him. I agree, we should add him to the guest list."

Who did they speak of, and why did their conversation

involve her marital future—or rather, the lack thereof? This reminded her of Mama's matchmaking efforts regarding Veronica, and an uneasy feeling settled in her stomach. She pulled the jacket of her riding habit down and rounded the corner into the library. Didn't she have enough disaster in her love life without their help? "Add who to the guest list?"

Mama looked up from where she perched on the edge of Pa's desk with the trusty household notebook and ledger in her hands, about to jot something down.

Pa leaned back in his leather chair, his brows furrowing with a contemplative look. "There you are, Delia. We were just speaking about you."

"I thought I heard my name." Dismissing the matter for the moment, she dove into her news. "I've just returned from a ride on Glory. I wanted to tell you how fast he broke into a gallop and how well he did. He circled from the barn all the way across the lawn to the creek and back again in under one minute and fifty-seven seconds. He barely broke a sweat, and if his breathing is any indication, he has more endurance than most of our other horses this early in the spring. He's incredibly strong and fast."

Pa grinned. "As I said before, he's a champion. Excellent news."

"It's not the same as running on the dirt track, of course, but I thought you'd like that number." Delia took a seat in the chair across from her father's desk and arranged her velvet skirts, looking between her parents before fixing her gaze on Mama. "Now, what's this business about a guest list?"

"As you may recall, your father and I are finalizing the details for our dinner party this coming Friday evening." Mama glanced at a guest list scrawled into the ledger. "We've invited Thaddeus and his parents, Mr. and Mrs. Breckinridge, Mr. and Mrs. Pickett, and your father and I were discussing the idea of inviting our new neighbor, Mr. Jake Williams. Of course,

Edward and Veronica will be coming, too, and Gladdie. It will make an even fourteen guests, seven pairs."

"I see." Delia's eyes widened. She'd seen Jake discussing something with Pa and Red, probably training methods, but, in the saddle on her way to deliver some library books to some elderly folks in the area, she hadn't stopped to chat. She had waved and smiled from astride her horse instead. "Yes, it would keep the number of guests even for pairing at dinner."

"Mrs. Sullivan and I think his three nieces are adorable." Some days Mama liked Mrs. Sullivan, and some days she didn't. Delia could understand. Caroline Sullivan had a great deal of influence in the area. Best to keep on her good side, but she could put on infuriating airs at times.

"We'd like to make him feel welcome to the neighborhood since he purchased the farm across the road, and also because your pa has taken him under his wing by inviting him to train his new horse here. Everyone knows Red Brickman is one of the best, and it so happens, he works for us." Mama brightened, sitting up straighter where she perched. "I'm not sure if Jake realizes yet what a wonderful opportunity this will be for him and his horse, but in any case, he has turned out to be a good paying customer for Velvet Brooks. Your pa gave him a small discount since he's just getting established, but it's always nice to have new clients."

Delia's brow rose. Why did Mama have a special gleam in her eyes? "I can tell you're up to something. What is it?" They'd spoken of her marital future and having options only moments ago, but now her mother wandered about the rosebush with talk of Jake's nieces and inviting him to a dinner party.

"As I said, his three wards are adorable." Mama leaned forward with her smile wide as the creek at Velvet Brooks. "Don't you agree?"

"Yes, I do." What did that have to do with her, though? Ever since the picnic lunch at the auction, Mrs. Sullivan and her mother had taken Jake and his nieces to heart. Her mother had sent an apple pie across Cornflower Road to welcome them. Thaddeus's mother had sent a crate of fresh oranges. She'd heard about it from their servant Frances Ellis, who'd heard about it from Jake when she delivered the pie. "And...?" Delia drummed her fingers softly on the arm of the chair.

Mama set her ledger aside and, rising from her perch, paced between the fireplace and Pa's desk. "Yes, well, we were thinking the dinner party might encourage Thaddeus to officially propose again sooner if we include him as a guest, with his parents and none of his siblings. My guess is, Jake Williams will have much to share with you about his new horse and racing plans."

"Of course, you'll conveniently seat me near Jake. And you think Thaddeus will protect his territory and speed up another offer of matrimony before Jake can steal me away." Delia drummed her fingers on her skirt. "But maybe I don't want Thaddeus to speed things up. Maybe I'm still figuring out if we are suitable."

Her mother's eyes widened, and her mouth dropped open. "What's to figure out? I'll never understand why you left him at the altar in the first place. He's a Sullivan, a graduate of Kentucky University, among the best the state has to offer. You should be thankful he's forgiven you and keeps coming around. He's a nice young man, and except for the Emma incident, I find no fault with him. To be fair, you were apart at the time."

"You don't see his flaws like I do." Delia did her best to keep her tone level and calm, but her temper simmered. Was the jealousy Thaddeus had displayed concerning Jake escorting her family to the gallery justified? She wasn't so sure, and she had a feeling her parents had dismissed it or were blind to it. She had not fully dismissed it. No, it whirled about in the back of her mind, right along with the rude behavior he had shown.

"I suppose he has a healthy dose of the Sullivan temperament, but what man is perfect? I daresay I haven't met a perfect man yet."

Pa cleared his throat.

"Present company excepted," Mama added. Her parents smiled without looking at each other. "In any case, you and Thaddeus are dragging your feet. You've known him your whole life, and you are twenty-three now. About the same age as when Veronica married. It gets harder to attract a husband after your early twenties. Ask my sisters."

Delia sighed. "I know. You've told me many times."

"What else is there to know about Thaddeus? He's a fine gentleman, ready to settle down, but he's waiting on a signal from you. You should do your best to encourage him. Show him you are finally ready."

Absorbing Mama's words, Delia looked down at her hands. "Sometimes I think I'm ready, and other times, not so much. I'm not sure he is ready either."

Her mother sniffed. "All this business about being ready could cause you to lose him. Time is not an unlimited commodity, my dearest daughter. Slowing your courtship down again could end tragically. Pa and I don't want you to miss your chance for security. We'd like you to experience the joy of sharing your heart and life with a husband. I'm sure you'd like to have children and a family of your own. Of course, we won't be able to afford another extravagant wedding like the one you ran away from, but something elegant and small...a parlor wedding, perhaps."

"Of course, I want a husband, children, and a family of my own, but I'm not in any hurry." Delia fixed her eyes on the view through the front window behind Pa's desk of the horse barn. In truth, she had always had doubts about Thaddeus. They clashed and adored each other all at once.

Then she'd met Jake. In the weeks since meeting the newcomer, she'd grown more confused and reluctant than ever.

One day, she wanted to marry Thaddeus, and the next, doubts swallowed her whole. Her mind drifted more often than usual to when he'd broken things off with her to cavort about town with Emma Pearson. Had he intended to pursue Emma when he first mentioned them splitting apart after last Christmas?

"Don't you remember when I said you should accept Brent McIntosh's offer as your escort to the Valentine's Dance? Did it not bring Thaddeus running back to your arms, begging for a second chance?" Mama slid the ledger onto the desk and paced in the little area between Pa's desk and the fireplace, then turned and faced Delia, hands on her hips.

"It did bring him back, but it doesn't mean it will work again if Jake speaks to me at the dinner party." Delia's chin tilted. And if Jake did so, would Thaddeus make a scene? "I don't want to rush into a marriage. My doubts continue, just as they did when I ran away on what should have been our wedding day."

"And my pocketbook knows it right well." Pa scoffed. "Don't marry anyone if you're not sure. He'll never forgive you if you leave him a second time, and I'm not sure anyone else will either."

"Trust me, my darling daughter..." Mama slid into the chair beside her and twisted slightly to look at her face to face, softening her voice. "Few men ever feel truly ready to tie the knot. One minute, they are convinced it's the right thing to do. The next, they run into the arms of some other woman they have no feelings for whatsoever, like Thaddeus and that Pearson girl. Is that what's bothering you? You must let it go. Your part is to know your own heart and make up your own mind."

"It's not Emma. Maybe a little. It's mainly my inhibitions, Mama."

And Aunt Eliza's words which swam about in the darkest corners of her mind. *My dear niece, I don't care how many ponies your pa buys you or how many pretty dresses you wear. You don't hold a candle to the Sullivan girls, and you never will.*

Her meddling parents didn't mean to ruffle her feathers and turn her thoughts to darker days. Mama, the main source of interference with the futures of her daughters, meant well. And she had triumphed with her matchmaking efforts in the outcome of a happy union for Veronica. Mother liked to say Pa had found Edward Beckett through his mutual friendship with Leviticus Beckett, but Delia suspected otherwise. Her mother had a few high society friends from New York. She took occasional trips by train to visit them, and she maintained a healthy correspondence with each.

When Veronica had locked herself away in her room after her parents had said she should marry Edward, it hadn't gone well for anyone in the house. Veronica had argued, cried, pouted, stewed, and simmered. It was a wonder her temper hadn't burnt the house to the ground. If only she had an ounce of Veronica's courage.

Instead of resorting to a match of wit or anger, she intended to talk her parents into a display of patience. She didn't want to create unbearable tension in the household. She had to live with them, after all.

She took a deep breath. "I know you have my best interests at heart, but the right husband is worth waiting for. Jake Williams may have some merits worthy of my consideration. But I don't need my parents plotting out my romantic life as you did for Veronica. Your meddling may have worked out for her, but it may not yield positive results for me."

Immediately, she wished she hadn't used the word *meddling*. Mama pressed her lips together in a firm, thin line. Pa's brows furrowed. Delia squirmed in her seat.

"We aren't plotting out your life. We are merely guiding our daughters into safe harbor. All we're saying is to keep your options open, Delia. And do stop doubting yourself." Mama reached out and patted her hand.

Pa leaned forward and folded his large hands together, resting them on his mahogany desk. "Thaddeus and Jake both seem like suitable husbands, each worthy of your consideration. I realize we haven't known Jake for long, but I've spent a good deal of time getting to know him these past few weeks. I suspect he has an interest in you, and I believe in time, it could develop into something more if encouraged—that is, if you are unhappy with Thaddeus. Although, the man surprised us all with his forgiving heart, and he must love you since he keeps coming back. On the other hand, Jake is a hard worker who knows horses. I believe he could have a promising future here." Pa rose from behind the desk to toss another log on the fire. Spring mornings and rain in Kentucky meant drafty rooms, and today seemed especially chilly. "If it were me, I would make them earn my favor." He used the metal poker to move the logs around until oxygen circulated to fan the flames. "You bring much to the table, Delia, especially with your sizeable dowry from your Grandfather Lyndon. There is an old saying in the stock industry I learned from my old friend, Edward's father, Leviticus Beckett, not to sell yourself short."

"Maybe, but Thaddeus doesn't need my dowry." The Sullivans owned a bank, a hotel in Richmond, and their sizeable horse farm with plenty of crops each year—not to mention their income from horseracing and training and investments in railroads and coal.

Her mother cleared her throat. "The fact remains, all men of great wealth appreciate additional wealth, and not every gentleman is suitable. We've worked hard to build the Spencer-Lyndon name. We cannot simply marry you off to anyone. Besides financial security, a good husband should have certain merits—like faith, for instance. He should make a good father."

"Yes, I realize all of those things." Delia refrained from

rolling her eyes. If only she hadn't sought out Pa to tell him about Glory, maybe she wouldn't be up to her ears in their meddling. But then she wouldn't know Mama intended to push her toward making a decision to either marry Thaddeus or consider Jake Williams.

Mama continued, undeterred. "Not everyone is honest and good. Some men can bring a woman great harm and even bring a good family name to ruin."

"I think you should trust the fact you've given me a sensible head." Delia rose from the chair, anxious to shed her velvet riding habit for something cooler. She circled around to stand behind the chair, resting her hands on the leather. "I'll think about all you've said, but I would prefer things to unfold naturally. I'll attend the dinner, but I won't be rushed into any marriage until I'm certain of love *and* security. I am praying about it. Isn't that what you've always taught me to do?"

"We can't argue with prayer and maturity," Pa agreed.

Mama acquiesced with a nod. "I'm sure everything will work out satisfactorily in the end. In the meantime, Jake will receive an invitation to the dinner."

She nodded and hurried upstairs to the solace of her bedroom, her thoughts a jumble as her parents' words echoed through her mind. Could she really lose the chance to marry Thaddeus or anyone at all if she didn't manage her steps and decisions carefully?

She reached for her Bible on her nightstand and flipped through it until she located the book of Jeremiah. She found the seventeenth chapter and read the verse she had underlined once again. *The heart is deceitful above all things, and desperately wicked: who can know it?*

Silently, she bowed her head and prayed. *Dear Lord, You see the dilemma before me. Please show me what is in my heart and what I should do.*

Did she trust Thaddeus to look after her for the rest of her life? Did the Lord want her to marry him? It would make everything in her world just right. In spite of a few doubts, she would cling to becoming Mrs. Thaddeus Sullivan until the Lord showed her otherwise.

But why couldn't she hear the Lord's voice about the matter? Why did she have this verse on her mind? Was something wrong in her own heart? And why couldn't she stop herself from thinking about Jake and his nieces? Indeed, she'd found herself praying for his little family almost every night. Had the Lord put them on her heart and mind for a reason?

CHAPTER EIGHT

A man that advances in spiritual and in temporal matters at the same time, minding to keep the spiritual first, will not let the temporal lead him; he will not place his heart upon his farm, his horses, or any possession that he has. He will place his desires in Heaven, and will anchor his hope in that eternal soil; and his temporal affairs will come up as he advances in the knowledge of God.
—Jedediah M. Grant

The evening of the dinner party arrived, and all of Velvet Brooks hummed with activity. Carter Mitchell lit the lanterns along the lane leading to the house, at the sign to the farm, on the veranda, in Mama's rose garden, and on the back porch. His wife, Grace, styled hair for Eleanor and Delia while Frances Ellis styled Gladdie's hair. They helped them into their evening gowns, and Delia swirled around in front of the full-length oval mirror in her bedroom, enjoying the floral creation and the feel of the shimmery fabric.

Mama had splurged on the gown after their talk in the library. The seamstress had worked day and night to have it ready on time. Delia could only sigh with relief because Mama had finally stopped insisting she wear Veronica's hand-me-downs. Brand new, the gown made her feel like a queen.

The spring taffeta displayed large pink and peach roses on a cream background, each rose surrounded by sprigs of green leaves and stems. The skirt flowed down to three ruffled tiers. The bodice featured a pigeon-front cream lace panel insert leading to a high-neck lace collar and three-quarter-length sleeves of lace puffing out beneath the elbow before a wide ruffle dangled above her wrists. The seamstress had designed a floral cape, the ends of it gathered, meeting at a pink rosette sewn into the center above the wide band around her waist. A demi-train swept over the floor with her every move.

Grace stood back and admired her completed look, nodding with approval in her eyes. "You look gloriously beautiful, Miss Delia," she said breathlessly. "You'll be the crown of Velvet Brooks this evening."

"Thank you for helping me get ready, Grace."

"You need a necklace. Let's put your heart-shaped locket on, the one your parents gave you for Christmas." Grace fished in the trinket box on the vanity until she found it.

Delia sat down at the vanity again, allowing her to fasten the clasp.

"There you are. You look radiant. Now don't be shy and remember to smile. Hurry downstairs and help your mother greet the guests. Some are already arriving. You don't want to be the last one to arrive at our own dinner party." She opened the bedroom door wide and held it for Delia, shooing her out into the hall. "Ah, here is Gladdie, ready and waiting."

"Frances just helped me with a few finishing touches. Martin just brought little Eddie upstairs and said Veronica and

Edward arrived." Gladdie patted her hair, tucking one of an array of silk flowers in place.

If Martin, their family butler, had just brought their nephew upstairs, then guests certainly had begun to arrive. Delia turned back to her servant while her sister waited at her bedroom door. "Grace, do you know who is looking after little Edward Junior this evening? Is someone coming from Rose Glen?" Veronica's cottage on ten acres of Velvet Brooks land had been a wedding present from their father.

Grace shook her head. "No worries, dearie. Frances and I are taking turns watching him upstairs in Veronica's old bedroom whenever we aren't needed downstairs."

"All right, then. I guess I'm ready." Delia stepped out into the hall, joining her sister, and they proceeded to the staircase landing. "You look lovely, Gladdie. I'm surprised you didn't try to escape at the last minute." Gladdie had skipped the Valentine's Dance for two years in a row, ever since Clay jilted her. She had thrown herself into tending matters at Velvet Brooks, becoming reclusive in her behavior.

"I'm only attending because Mama will throw a fit if I don't, and she assures me Percival Sullivan isn't invited. You know how he annoys me." Percy had dropped off numerous calling cards and bouquets of flowers, but only after Veronica had finally married, shutting the door to his chances with their older sister. Gladdie had never shown any interest in Percival, considering him the "equivalent of pestilence." Rarely did she "appear" at home to any of her other callers. Pa had said to pray for her and be patient. He'd said time and Jesus would heal her wounded heart, and thankfully, Mama agreed. "Should he find some way to attend, I will make a grand escape, and you'll have to tell Mama I've succumbed to indigestion."

Delia rolled her eyes. "At least your sense of humor is intact."

As they descended the steps, they lifted their gowns. Her

sister's simple cream lace dress with its tiers of ruffles and puffed sleeves was a hand-me-down from Delia. Gladdie had added a periwinkle satin sash, matching the ribbon and flowers woven through her braided chignon.

In the wide hall below, Thaddeus and Jake Williams joined the elder Mr. Sullivan, Delia's pa, their brother-in-law Edward, Mr. Breckenridge, and Mr. Pickett as they chatted near the door to the library. Thaddeus kept an approving eye on her entrance, but Jake's mouth dropped open as he beheld her.

For a brief moment, Delia had no idea where to focus her gaze. She kept one hand on the banister and another lifting her skirts, doing her best to descend gracefully. Finally, she centered her attention with a warm, shy smile on Thaddeus.

Her beau drew her to his side, stepping forward to greet her when she and Gladdie reached the hall. "You look lovely this evening, Delia. Like a spring flower."

"Thank you. You're looking handsome yourself, Thaddeus." How nicely he filled in his dinner jacket and white shirt, his white bow tie telling her he had dressed with care for the occasion.

Jake wore a dignified gray suit and burgundy tie. He had cleaned up nicely also, having pulled his long blond hair into a ponytail. Why did his wild looks attract her when she tried to keep her mind on her beau? Confusion swelled in her mind and heart, adding to her generally shy nature.

"Welcome to Velvet Brooks, everyone." Delia greeted the guests with a simple nod, afraid to shake hands with anyone lest she find herself doing the same with the attractive newcomer, now on Thaddeus's other side. An inner nudge warned her that touching Jake Williams might ignite a spark between them.

Her instincts cautioned her to avoid Jake at all costs, but the expectation of her parents weighed heavily on her. Didn't they want her to speak with him and get to know him? And the small guest list meant she would likely encounter numerous opportunities for discussion with him. Earlier today, she'd observed his stallion running training circles in one of their corrals under Red Brickman's watchful eyes. Circles gave the horse a feeling of routine, safety, and calm. The training would work wonders on Jake's spirited stallion. Perhaps the bay would be a safe introductory topic.

While the men began a robust discussion about the status of their spring plantings, Gladdie nudged her. "We should greet the women guests."

Delia turned to Thaddeus and spoke in a low voice. "If you'll excuse us, gentlemen."

Thaddeus and Jake nodded. The older gentlemen looked too absorbed in their dialogue to notice.

Delia followed Gladdie down the hall toward the music room beside the entrance to the rear garden where their mother, Veronica, Mrs. Sullivan, Mrs. Breckenridge, and Mrs. Pickett gathered. The spacious area, perfect for dancing, held only the piano and a few benches along the walls. A door to their left led to the kitchen, and a set of double doors on their right led into the sitting room. The ladies gathered around one side of the piano, where Delia and her sisters would no doubt end up taking turns entertaining their guests before the evening ended. Perhaps there would be dancing too. A shiver of anticipation tingled her spine. Why did she detect a yearning to dance with Jake?

"Here are my other two daughters. Everyone, you know Delaney and Gladys." Mama raised her cheek as first Gladdie and then Delia planted a kiss on it. They turned to do the same for Veronica, and then offer a warm handshake or embrace for each of the others present.

"It's nice to see you girls again," Mrs. Sullivan, dressed in a satin gown in an orchid shade, said before resuming her conversation with Veronica about a home remedy should little

Edward's croupy cough reappear. Edward had suffered with a severe cold shortly after his birth. Veronica had nursed him to good health again, but they'd endured a scare and numerous doctor visits.

"My father-in-law appreciates the books you bring him each month from the Lexington library, Delia," Mrs. Breckenridge said. About the same age as Mama, the lady possessed a kind demeanor.

"I'm glad he enjoys them." Sometimes Delia couldn't tell if the elder Mr. Breckenridge liked her coming around. A peculiar, reclusive fellow rumored to have amassed a tidy sum from racing horses, he seldom left his cabin. His face did sometimes brighten when Delia appeared, and he always returned the books on time. Occasionally, he asked her to bring him a specific type of book on a variety of topics ranging from history to literary classics to horse farming techniques.

"And my daughter enjoys the hat-trimming tea parties you host each month." Mrs. Pickett made her selection as Martin held out a tray of stuffed mushroom caps, apple and cheese tarts, and asparagus toast. "Abigail puts a great deal of thought into which hat she will transform before each tea. She is looking forward to the next one and has found an amazing bunch of plumes to work with for April's event."

"Ah, I'm glad to hear it. Perhaps we can wear our next creations to the Phoenix Stakes or the Kentucky Derby." Delia smiled to think anyone enjoyed her meager efforts.

"Speaking of the Derby, did you hear what they plan to roll out this year at Churchill Downs?" Mrs. Breckenridge's voice swelled with excitement. Everyone turned their attention toward her.

Mama leaned forward. "Joseph said the new managers and stockholders have built a brand-new clubhouse just beyond the finish line and added a grandstand alongside it with broad verandas for a promenade and display of gowns. We've heard the promenade has beautiful green chairs and sofas and a new ladies' reception room adjoining the new dining room, all of it finished in green and yellow club colors."

Mrs. Breckenridge nodded, her eyes lighting up. "That's not all. They've hung lovely green drapes with lace panels in the windows, added potted plants and trees, and someone told my husband they'll serve meals on fine china marked with a horseshoe and the club monogram. The men will have their own area for entertaining small parties too."

"Did you hear about the pennants? Apparently, horse owners can now fly their colors over the Derby stables during the day of the races," Veronica added as she selected an appetizer. "We'll be able to look out across the centerfield of the track now and see a colorful scene with all of those pennants flying in the distance."

"They're hoping to attract bigger racing names and famous horses from the East. This will eventually take Churchill Downs to a whole new level of popularity." Mrs. Sullivan turned to look pointedly at Delia. "The women will want to wear their best hats and gowns for the promenade. Keep helping the younger women, Delia. I'm convinced they'll have photographers and journalists on hand to capture photos of the best-dressed ladies. They'll publish them in a great many papers to attract the wealthy from the Pimlico racecourse and the like. So, you see, your work helping to keep the ladies in fashion is needed. It will not only give them confidence, but it will attract visitors to Kentucky races. This will help our economy."

"I will do my best to continue the tradition we've started here at Velvet Brooks, Mrs. Sullivan." Delia enjoyed hosting the monthly tea and hat-trimming socials, and she flushed with pleasure that her future mother-in-law's statements indicated she saw some value in her efforts.

"How are you keeping busy these days, Gladdie?" Mrs.

Breckenridge peered through a lorgnette at Delia's younger sister.

"I've been gardening and helping Pa's trainer with exercising the horses. During this past winter, I collected certain pine needles and medicinal leaves for tea, turkey tail and oyster mushrooms, and black walnuts too." Gladdie declined Martin's offer of appetizers, and he moved along to the next woman.

"That's quite a bit of foraging, young lady. I imagine your mother appreciates your contribution to maintaining a well-stocked pantry." Mrs. Sullivan's brow rose— as did nearly all of the other brows of the women at the mention of foraging— before she bit into some of the asparagus toast.

Mama intervened before they could draw conclusions about Gladdie's unique hobby, which Delia knew to be prayerful, soul-searching expeditions. "Gladdie has also been cross-stitching and embroidering Scriptures like the one on the piano." She reached for the framed Scripture. "This one is my favorite. 'Make a joyful noise unto the Lord.' I can hardly wait for the next one she creates. I'm doing my best to keep her in supply with plenty of colorful threads."

"It's beautiful, Gladdie," Mrs. Pickett commented as she inspected the framed verse.

Mrs. Breckenridge leaned forward to peer through her lorgnettes, mumbling her approval of Gladdie's work.

A commotion in the hall attracted attention before her sister could offer a polite reply, and Mama rose to the occasion. "I'll see what's happened, if you'll excuse me, ladies."

Thaddeus's angry voice drifting through the open door made Delia stiffen. What had happened? And how could she commit herself to a man who still couldn't contain his temper?

CHAPTER NINE

But the Lord said to Samuel, "Do not look at his appearance, or
at the height of his stature, because I have rejected him. For the
Lord sees not as man sees; for man looks at the outward
appearance, but the Lord looks at the heart."
—I Samuel 16:7, AMP

Jake resisted the urge to fiddle with his tie and raked a
hand through his hair as he stood in the hall, cloistered
around the door to Mr. Lyndon's library. The other
gentlemen wore black dinner suits with white vests, white
shirts, and white bowties. Why hadn't he thought to purchase
something more appropriate than his Sunday suit? He sucked
in a breath, but he made a mental note to remedy the matter.
Come next week, he'd pay a visit to the Kingsley Custom Tailor
Shop in Lexington.

Would he have a chance to speak with Miss Delia Lyndon?
My, she looked pretty as a picture. His eyes couldn't help but
follow her when she left to greet other guests.

"We harvested the spring hay, and we've planted fifty acres each of corn, oats, and wheat." Harold Sullivan sipped some of his punch.

Thaddeus nodded, standing up taller. "We should have a good harvest on the winter wheat, come the end of May."

"I've had some trouble keeping the deer out of our winter wheat fields this year," Mr. Pickett grumbled.

"We have too. They've been nosing around everywhere, hungry after the long winter. Our cook even found them nibbling at our kitchen garden one morning." Mr. Lyndon turned toward Mr. Pickett. "Hank Parker, our farm's manager, had an idea to deter them by setting up dried corn feeders some distance away from our fields. Seems to have worked."

Pickett tilted his head. "I'll have to give that a try."

Jake couldn't contribute much as the men conversed since he'd only just moved into the farmhouse across the way, but he listened, trying not to let his mind wander to Miss Delia Lyndon. Would she be willing to dance with a guest dressed so inappropriately for the gathering?

Then, Mr. Breckenridge turned, bumping him. The punch in Jake's glass splashed all over Thaddeus, standing on his other side.

"What'd you go and do a fool thing like that for?" Thaddeus stepped back, his voice a bellow that echoed down the hall.

Jake held up his free hand. "What a blunder! I'm terribly sorry." Now Delia's beau would have good reason to despise him.

Where could he set down his cordial to help the fellow out? Not seeing a table close enough to set his punch glass aside, he thought the better of it. Unfortunately, there wasn't anything he could do except offer his handkerchief.

Thaddeus swiped the offering from his hand with a grimace. He attempted to soak up the spill, but his shirt now boasted a bright pink splotch. A rather large one.

The butler hurried forward to assist. "If you'll follow me to the kitchen, we'll get you all cleaned up, Mr. Sullivan."

Mrs. Lyndon's soothing voice brought calm to the incident. "Thank you, Martin. I'm so sorry, Thaddeus, about whatever happened."

A groan and some indistinguishable grumbling emitted from Thaddeus as he turned and followed the servant. Helpless, Jake sighed as Miss Delia's beau traipsed away.

Jake hung his head. "The accident was my fault, Mrs. Lyndon." It wouldn't do to blame Mr. Breckenridge for bumping into him, who now spoke with Edward Beckett about something to do with art. Breckenridge held himself in a confident sort of way. Was he someone important in the community?

"Don't you worry, Mr. Williams." Mrs. Lyndon placed a comforting hand on Jake's arm. "Martin can offer him a fresh shirt. My husband has dozens upstairs."

Jake released a sigh. "Thank you for being such a lovely hostess. It was terribly clumsy of me."

She patted his arm and offered an understanding glance. "It can happen to anyone." Then she returned to the ladies. Would she tell Miss Delia what a mess he'd made of her beau?

~

"What happened, Eleanor?" Mrs. Sullivan inquired when Mama returned from the front hall a few moments later.

"It seems Jake accidentally bumped into Thaddeus, spilling his punch on Thaddeus. Martin took Thaddeus into the kitchen to clean him up. I hope he isn't too upset about it. Punch stains aren't easy to remove."

"These things happen." Mrs. Sullivan shrugged.

Mama nodded.

If only Mrs. Sullivan's son would prove so understanding. Thaddeus would be irritated. Delia would give him some time and space to recover.

When he appeared at her side to escort her to dinner, slightly agitated but otherwise calm, a large red punch stain remained across his crisp white shirt. She bit her lip and pretended she hadn't noticed. The stain took up so much of his shirt, surely Martin had offered to let him borrow one of Pa's white cotton shirts. If so, Thaddeus had declined.

In the dining room, her mother had used place cards, assigning Delia to sit beside Jake and directly across from Thaddeus—where he could observe her interactions with the newcomer for an entire meal.

Thaddeus was seated between Gladdie and Mrs. Breckenridge. Throughout the four-course meal where the guests spoke to each other over the tops of low vases filled with hyacinth flowers and white candles, Mrs. Breckenridge monopolized Thaddeus with every detail of splendor concerning the renovation of Churchill Downs. Poor Thaddeus! He did his best to appear interested, but Delia could tell he was bored out of his mind. Gladdie quietly partook of her split pea soup, spring greens, and roast beef, only able to rescue Delia's beau with a word here and there.

Meanwhile, Delia enjoyed an engrossing conversation about everything happening in Jake's world, including the work he was doing on his home and the various names his nieces proposed for his new horse. "Mary suggested Thumper, but Ella told her it wasn't a rabbit. I suppose somewhere in the mind of three-year-old Mary, the horse appeared to thump those railings down at the auction with his hooves—hence, the name she suggested." Jake sliced some of the roasted vegetables on his plate while Delia chuckled.

"And what does Ruby say?" Looking toward Jake, Delia suspended her fork in midair, a slice of carrot on the tines.

"As of yesterday evening, Ruby suggested the leading name of Horizon. We all like it." He tasted some roast beef. "Your cook is very good. This is so much better than my cooking."

Delia nearly choked on her carrot and held a linen napkin toward her mouth as she coughed. Recovering, she smiled, but curiosity could not prevent her from inquiring, "Am I to understand you are doing most of the cooking?"

He nodded and sampled a bite of the roasted potatoes. "I've purchased some applesauce and some canned vegetables to heat, but my cooking skills are limited to flapjacks, cornbread, bacon, fried fish, eggs, and potatoes."

"I see." Too bad the nanny he'd hired must not possess skills in the kitchen, but how wonderful of him to try. "I hope you'll find someone to help soon. Yes, Willamena is an excellent cook. She's been with us for as long as I can remember. And I must say, I like the name Horizon. An excellent name suggestion for a racehorse."

"I'm glad you agree. Maybe we'll try it out and see if the horse likes it."

A man who considered the horse's preference in a name? She couldn't help but smile. "Did Pa or Red think your horse can be ready in time for the Phoenix Stakes?"

"We're all hoping he will. He's breaking records on your pa's racetrack for Charlie Ford, but I'm well aware he's your pa's jockey. I'll need to find a jockey first." Jake's brows furrowed and he shifted in his seat.

Easier said than done for a newcomer with a new horse. "I'll pray you find just the right one."

"Once again, I find myself in gratitude for your kind prayers, Miss Delia."

Jake's response melted her heart. She bit her lower lip. How else might she encourage him? "Has anyone mentioned reading the advertisements in the *Lexington Gazette*? They occasionally list an advertisement for a jockey looking for work."

"I hadn't thought of that." Jake leaned forward, curiosity in his eyes.

She nodded. "Oh yes, and there is something else you could try."

"Do tell." Both of his brows rose as he sliced some of the roast beef on his plate.

"If you stop by the Lexington track at five or six o'clock in the morning, you'll be able to ask the jockeys when they come back from their morning rides. Even if most say no, word will spread among them." Delia sipped some of her tea.

Jake's mouth dropped open. "I had no idea. Thank you for the excellent tip. Has anyone told you how thoughtful you are?"

Delia lowered her gaze, hiding a smile. "You are most welcome."

Jake then told her about his plan to transform the Victorian farmhouse into a country inn. "Do you think the idea would be successful, once we find a cook and complete some minor renovations?"

"I think it's a solid idea. There are only a few boarding-houses in Lexington. With limited hotels, considering the rapid growth in our vicinity, there are seldom enough rooms available for visitors. Many folks travel here to purchase a horse, take in a race, or handle business matters. Others are looking for a way to escape the city and explore the countryside. Your farm is in an ideal location. It's not too far from the city, and yet the fresh air and clean water are restorative for good health." Delia took another sip of tea.

Thaddeus was staring at them. At least he didn't glower at Jake as he had at the gallery. With his parents and other guests in attendance, he seemed to be doing a better job of keeping his temper in check, except for that moment with the spilled punch.

Jake leaned closer, his enthusiasm palpable. "So there aren't other inns nearby, then?"

"There are a few rental cabins to the west, farther out in the countryside. A popular inn exists near a hot spring, a few hours' drive from Lexington. But no, not close to here. A place to ride horses on trails is exactly the sort of thing city folks want."

"I'm glad you mention these points. I thought if we could offer good food, comfortable and pleasant rooms, and two or three riding trails...maybe provide some fishing at the pond and other activities, we might have a unique country destination." Jake paused to look at her, his blue eyes alight.

Delia returned a warm smile, enthused about his plan. "I think it's an excellent idea. I can see the girls helping too. If you advertise properly, it could be successful year round."

Jake exhaled and sat up straighter. "Your opinion matters a great deal to me, especially since you've grown up here."

Unaccustomed to anyone asking for her opinion about a business matter, Delia could only smile and try to hide her wonder. As accurate as her input might be, some men wouldn't value a woman's opinion. Most gentleman would find any reason to disagree with a woman about business matters. Not Pa, though. "Have you mentioned your ideas to my father?"

He added some sugar to his tea and stirred. "I have. You echoed his sentiments."

"If my father didn't think you had a good idea, he would certainly say so. You could also mention it to Mr. Breckenridge and ask for his input. He is part of our city council." Mr. Breckenridge usually had good ideas on how to attract visitors to Lexington. He had staunchly supported their racecourse for years, not only for his love of the sport, but for economic reasons, opposing all who murmured about the ills of gambling and the like.

Jake's gaze traveled to where Mr. Breckenridge sat at the

other end of the table near her parents. "Thank you. Perhaps I'll speak to him before the evening is out."

"Tell me more about the Adirondacks. I've read about them, but I'm sure the area is more beautiful than words." She angled toward him.

"It's stunning. The trees are tall and thick. It's a luscious wilderness. Breathtaking. The waters at Lake George where I am from are among the most pristine one could ever lay eyes upon. Much of the area is rugged and unsettled. Undisturbed by progress."

"It sounds so beautiful." She tasted some of the asparagus toast. "Did I hear Pa correctly when he said you were employed by a resort in the area? The Sagamore?"

He sat up taller. "Yes, I worked alongside my father as a groom there. It's where I grew up and all I know. It's part of why I decided to give Kentucky a chance and strike out on my own. The experience should help me with running a small inn of my own."

"And that explains your skill with horses." Delia leaned back in her seat. His plans sounded admirable, and she could envision all of it. Oh dear, more things to like about their new neighbor.

After the dessert course, Thaddeus leapt from his seat the moment her father dismissed them from dinner, obviously eager to flee the matronly guest chatting endlessly beside him. He rounded the far end of the table and hastened to Delia's side, offering to pull the chair out for her. "Would you care for a stroll through the garden, Delia?"

After he pulled out her chair, she smiled with an arched brow, rising to meet him. Perhaps Mama's plan had played a part in this attentiveness, after all. Had his view of Jake speaking with her through the entire meal revived his desire to romance her properly, or did he merely flee the matron?

"Thank you, yes. I would love a stroll."

She accepted his hand, and he whisked her away from the dining room instead of following the other men into the library. She had to admit, Mama's plan seemed to be working again. Pausing in the entry, he waited patiently while she retrieved a shawl.

Outside, he steered her along the brick paths, guiding her with his hand on her back, bright lanterns lighting their way. Carter had done his job well, ensuring Velvet Brooks put forth a grand welcome. The scent of bright red and yellow tulips, purple crocus, yellow daffodils, purple and white hyacinth blooms, and clumps of dainty white flowers Mama called snowdrops mingled with the crisp night air to tingle and delight their senses. A swath of bright moonlight bathed everything with a golden hue. A few stars dotted the sky, peeking through milky clouds floating effortlessly above.

"Have you thought of a name for your new horse?" She paused to admire a patch of invasive phlox, returning from previous years to fill in a corner of one of the flower beds. She adored the way the pink and periwinkle blossoms took on the shape of little mounds, but her favorite daisies had yet to bloom.

"Not yet. Any ideas?" Thaddeus halted beside her, following her gaze, but flowers held little interest for him. Judging by the way his brows furrowed, his cheeks puffing out with a sigh, he pondered the name dilemma.

"Tell me more about the horse." Tucking an arm into his elbow, she turned him around and pulled him along. "Let's enjoy the swing. It's so romantic." Maybe she could stop thinking about Jake if they sat close together.

He allowed her to lead him toward the rear porch and up the steps. Seated on the swing, she scooted near.

"He's ready to race, an all-black beauty, and he rides like a streak of lightning," Thaddeus told her. "I have a good feeling about him. He doesn't hold back when he's running."

"I don't like the name Lightning for a horse. It's overused and associated with the enemy of our souls. I read it in a verse about the way you-know-who fell from heaven." She shuddered to think of it. "We should think of something else. Something to do with a reflection of his speed, agility, courage, and maybe his coloring." Delia spoke softly, clasping the shawl at her throat to ward off the cool breeze created by their swinging motion in the night air.

"Good points." The furrow in his brow disappeared as he relaxed.

"What are they calling him for his stable name?" She leaned her head on his shoulder.

"Black Thunder, but it's another overused name, though not at Sullivan Hill." He covered her hand with his larger one, his warmth reviving her fingers from the chill.

"You said his sire's name is Boomer, as I recall." Delia put her feet on the porch floorboards to stop them from swinging, grinning as she sat up with an idea. "How about Bluegrass Blaze?"

Thaddeus raked a hand through his sandy-blond hair, the same color all of the Sullivan siblings had in one form or another. His smile broadened into a wide grin, lighting up his blue eyes. He nodded. "Yes, I like it. Bluegrass Blaze is perfect. I knew you'd have an idea. I was going to ask before you mentioned it."

Moments like this made her happy—when Thaddeus shared his confidence in her or gave any sign of his approval. "I like it too. Bluegrass Blaze..."

He rose from the swing, pulling her up with him into his arms. "You're shivering. Let's get you back inside. They'll be looking for us soon. A kiss before we go?"

"Just one."

He brushed her cheek with a sweet kiss, causing her to flush. He took her by the hand, opened the French doors leading inside, and waited until she preceded him and the train of her gown passed before following.

The men had rejoined the women in the music room. When Delia sat down at the piano bench after Gladdie and Veronica had each played a song, she flipped through a few books of sheet music until she settled on a new tune by Hans Engelmann titled, "Melody of Love." Jake stepped up to her side and asked if she needed his assistance turning the pages.

"Thank you, yes, I'd very much like your help, if you don't mind." She wouldn't turn down an offer of assistance while playing in front of so many people. Her hands glided over the keys, a testament to the many hours she put into practicing.

When she finished singing along with her instrumental performance, everyone clapped.

Jake bowed over her. "You play and sing so beautifully, like an angel. I can think of few performances I have enjoyed so much and have seldom encountered such a lovely voice. Thank you for sharing it with us."

Delia flushed, unable to respond. She lowered her gaze to her hands in her lap.

Thaddeus leapt forward. "I've been trying to tell her much the same, though I think you have expressed it better than I ever could. Beautiful playing, Delia."

Somehow, before the watchful eyes of the other guests, Thaddeus's praise came across as less than genuine in comparison to Jake's heartfelt reaction. Did she detect a tone of contempt toward Jake in his words? Hopefully, no one else did, but as Mama said, maybe it would continue to spur Thaddeus toward honorable actions.

And yet...it was Jake she lost her composure around.

Delia rose as she addressed her beau. "Thank you, gentlemen. How about a song on the Victrola? We could play 'In the Good Old Summertime,' Thaddeus. I know it's one of your favorite tunes." She hastened toward the record player in the corner.

After the tune played, Thaddeus sauntered toward the library, scorning Jake's presence for the remainder of the evening. Though Thaddeus reappeared occasionally, he barely acknowledged the newcomer, stepping away whenever Jake attempted to join him in conversation. It would seem her beau had come down with a case of envy.

Delia and her sisters continued playing songs on the Victrola for their guests. A few married couples danced, but most mingled and chatted. Would Thaddeus ask her to dance?

When Gladdie played one of their newest records, "Tessie," he finally emerged and made the inquiry of Delia.

She leaned her head toward the Victrola, biting her lower lip. It could be her only chance to dance with him, but the lyrics of the song did little to invigorate her. One of the lines, "but one day we had a quarrel, we too," exemplified their relationship almost too perfectly. Why did Thaddeus choose this song to ask her to dance? Everyone in Mama's music room would take notice of it, surely.

"Oh, Thaddeus. I don't know about this song..."

He turned puppy dog eyes on her. "Let's dance, Delia. You know how much 'I love you madly.'"

She couldn't very well argue when he professed his love to her in that light, reciting lyrics from the one part of the song she couldn't deny appreciating. "All right. Yes, let's dance." She could enjoy the melody, for once in her life not caring what anyone else thought, couldn't she?

Thaddeus heaved a sigh of relief and Delia placed her hand in his and smiled, allowing him to lead her toward the middle of the room where even her parents and another of the older couples joined to dance alongside Veronica and Edward. Yes, tonight, she would dance.

For a little while, everything seemed fine as they moved

together, their hands intertwined as he placed an arm around her waist. The musky scent of his cologne made her heady, especially when he spun her around under the dim lights.

But then Delia caught a glimpse of Gladdie and Jake. Her younger sister crossed her arms over her chest and sat in the chair beside the Victrola, one foot swaying to the song, closing herself off to the world. Jake hovered nearby, standing where he could see everyone dancing, but he didn't ask her sister to dance.

The song came to an end, and Thaddeus returned Delia to her seat. "Do you need a glass of punch or anything?"

"No, I'm fine. Thank you for the dance."

"All right, then. I'll return in a little while. I want to talk to Mr. Breckenridge and see if he's heard anything about how Julius Anderson is doing since his operation." Thaddeus hurried down the hall to the library again. Couldn't he stay beside her and simply be her companion and escort for the evening? Didn't Thaddeus realize Jake would sooner or later have the advantage in his absence?

The way Jake stared at her with his warm smiles and those eyes that seemed to see her whole soul...and if only she could deny that the man from the Adirondacks stirred a longing in her. Was it his confidence and humility? His height? That ponytail? The mystery behind him? His gentlemanlike behavior? And something else...perhaps the faith and conviction she sensed in the way he conducted and carried himself.

Gladdie put another record on the Victrola, and "Pretty Molly Shannon" began to play.

Jake ambled to her side and cleared his throat. "M-may I have this dance, Miss Delia?"

Delia gulped. Was he finally asking her to dance? *Say something!* Why couldn't she find her tongue? "Y-yes, thank you, Jake. I'd love to dance."

She managed to place her hand in his, and he pulled her to

her feet. She tried not to leap out of her chair. Jake led her to the dance floor and pulled her into his arms.

Something about being held by him rendered her speechless as he steered them in a waltz, an arm wrapped around her waist in a reassuring and commanding fashion. They blended into the other two couples dancing alongside them, but she kept peeking up to gaze at his unreadable face.

They both relaxed a little, and his gaze settled on hers, his blue eyes sparkling in the glimmers of light. Perhaps he struggled as much as she did in finding anything to say, but his eyes told her more than words ever could have. During the line, "I'm always ready to sacrifice anything for her," he seemed to pull her closer. And again when the singer crooned, "I tell you, boy, there's none like her, she is the only one in her class."

When the dance ended, he returned her to her seat. Delia sighed, almost as if lost in a dream, snapping her fan open to calm her rapidly beating heart.

Veronica sat beside her, taking a rest from dancing. "What a wonderful evening, don't you think?" She sank farther into her seat, a radiant smile on her face.

"Indeed." Delia hid a smile behind her fan.

Did she detect Jake stealing glances in her direction? A marvelous evening, indeed.

As guests began their departure, Delia lined up with the rest of her family to say goodnight to their friends at the door. Jake lifted her hand, boldly brushing the back of it with a kiss. Heat rose to her cheeks. He said good evening, staring into her eyes as if Thaddeus didn't exist. Maybe he'd heard she'd run away from Thaddeus at the altar.

Jake's boldness made her want to laugh. No one else would dare interfere with a Sullivan but a newcomer. Instead, she stifled the giggle threatening to bubble up from her throat. She could hardly blame Jake for his forward behavior considering the cold shoulder Thaddeus had shown him throughout the evening.

"Thank you for a splendid meal and a lovely evening, Miss Lyndon," Jake murmured, still holding her hand.

Delia dipped her head. "Please bring the girls over to visit us soon."

"I look forward to doing so, and to seeing you again." He smiled, seeking her gaze.

She returned a warm smile, melting on the inside, but looked down again, hiding beneath her eyelashes. An undeniable magnetic attraction between them seemed to swell. Did everyone in the room feel it, or did she only imagine they did?

He moved along the line, shaking hands with Gladdie, Veronica, Edward, Mama, and last, Pa. The fact that he'd not only lingered beside her for far longer than his parting words to the rest of her family combined, but that he had kissed her hand, increased the heat in her cheeks. Gladdie exchanged looks with her while Thaddeus stewed nearby, a grimace on his face.

Thaddeus and his parents departed last. Mama would have said in so doing, they had made a visible and marked effort to protect their son's territory. When Thaddeus said good night, he took both of Delia's hands in his and held them, avoiding eye contact. "I'll come by in a few days, and we'll go for a morning ride if you like."

"I look forward to it, Thaddeus." When he finally looked up, she searched his eyes, but she couldn't read anything but derision in them. Most likely, his consternation pertained to Jake, not her, starting with the red punch stain, now faded to a pink splash across his shirt.

For now, it seemed Mama had achieved her goals. Thaddeus might come to heel as Mama expected, but was that what Delia really wanted? And Jake...had his apparent interest in her tonight been genuine, or merely intended to goad his rival? Would he, too, seek her out as promised?

CHAPTER TEN

For jealousy makes a man furious, and he will not spare when
he takes revenge.
—Proverbs 6:34, ESV

A few days later, a knock on the front door disturbed a
spring afternoon at Velvet Brooks. Martin rounded the
corner into the dining room where Delia sat at the table with
Grace, helping her polish the silver. Mama sat at the other end
of the linen-covered table, her ledger book open as she worked
on the menu. Gladdie practiced at the piano, pleasant notes
filling the hall and drifting through the rest of the colonial
farmhouse.

"Jake Williams, requesting to speak with Miss Delia,"
Martin announced from where he stood near the door.

Delia straightened. Had Jake brought the girls? Her heart
leapt a little at the prospect.

Thaddeus had not called on her since the dinner, but

perhaps he'd been busy preparing Bluegrass Blaze for the Phoenix Stakes.

Mama looked up, smiled briefly, and resumed writing. Her brows furrowed as she bent her head over her work. Her lack of comment told Delia she could respond as she wished.

"I'll speak to him in the sitting room if you'll show him inside and offer tea, Martin." Delia finished polishing a few more spoons before rising. She checked her hair in the mirror in the hall and, satisfied with her appearance, hurried into the sitting room so as not to keep him waiting too long. Gladdie had finished her piano practice, and Delia didn't see her anywhere. Jake stood near the unlit fireplace. Did he appear a bit tense—nervous, perhaps?

"Hello, Jake. What brings you to Velvet Brooks today?" Brisk and casual with her greeting to set him at ease, Delia positioned herself on one of the two sofas.

Jake stepped forward but maintained a proper distance. "I beg your pardon for the interruption, Miss Lyndon, but your father suggested I speak with you." Jake drew himself up taller, rotating the brim of his hat in his hands. "It seems I am in a peculiar dilemma, but perhaps you may be of some assistance."

"I see." She clasped her hands together in her lap. "How can I help?"

"Our Nanny Philips—Leonora—must take the next train to Richmond to help her mother through an unexpected illness for a few days, possibly as long as several weeks."

"Oh dear. What sort of illness?"

"Her mother has contracted a severe case of bronchitis and is on strict bedrest after suffering a collapse, as I understand it. She is in danger of developing pneumonia." He grimaced. "As a widow, she needs help, and Leonora is her only family."

Delia's eyes widened. "That is dreadful. Pneumonia can be dangerous for the elderly."

Jake nodded. "Yes, and I'm afraid it leaves me without

someone to look after the children while I try to establish our plans for the farm and assist with training Horizon for the Phoenix Stakes. We haven't found a jockey yet, so I'm the one riding her most mornings at dawn. I can train Horizon a little later each day after Ruby and Ella are in school, but I would still need someone to look after Mary during the day and her sisters after school. Between settling into the house, unpacking, making all sorts of repairs, training Horizon, and purchasing everything we need, I have my hands too full in Leonora's absence."

"Plus, you mentioned the cooking has fallen on your shoulders." She furrowed her brows as she considered the matter.

"Yes, that too. I was hoping perhaps you could step in temporarily to fill the nanny's shoes. I haven't found a house-keeper or a cook yet, so it's all somewhat chaotic, but I've been managing with the nanny's help, until this." He paused. "The girls know and like you, and I'm afraid we have few options since we haven't met many other folks in the area yet."

"I'm honored you thought of me." Delia smiled, her thoughts racing.

Her part-time work at the library could be rearranged with a note to the head librarian in Lexington, and she could ask Carter to take over exercising the horses she rode in the mornings, or take her rides earlier. Everything else she normally did at Velvet Brooks generally had some degree of flexibility. Under the circumstances, she couldn't possibly say no, but Thaddeus certainly wouldn't like the idea of her assisting the handsome newcomer.

Yet reading to Jake's girls went right along with her literacy work with other children in the community. She spent an hour each week tutoring several local children in reading who strug-gled with their school lessons. How could Thaddeus deny something so beneficial?

Seconds later, she made up her mind. "I would be happy to

fill in until Leonora returns. A few days or a couple of weeks shouldn't be too much of a hardship. It would give me a chance to get to know Ruby, Ella, and Mary. I didn't realize you were looking for a cook and a housekeeper too."

"Well, yes, ideally..." He flushed and crushed the brim of his hat in his hands.

Delia gave a brief nod. "I may be able to offer some minimal assistance in those areas until you find someone. I assume you'll be all right with Mary and the girls spending some of their time at either of our houses, since we're situated so close. I have some other obligations to squeeze in as well, and it would make things easier since there are plenty of us here at Velvet Brooks who may be useful. My mother, Gladdie, Veronica, Grace, and Frances may all be counted upon to pitch in if something in my schedule cannot be remedied."

"Of course, and I hope it's not too much trouble. I'm sure we could work those things out. Would you be able to start tomorrow?" He raked a hand through his long blond hair, his blue eyes full of hope. Looking utterly helpless and at her mercy—not to mention the fact his hair appeared more disheveled than usual—he began turning the hat in his hands again.

"Tomorrow is fine. Would seven o'clock be early enough to help the girls get ready for school?" She bit her lower lip. If Thaddeus appeared for the morning horseback ride he'd mentioned, she would need to decline in favor of something in the evenings. If he arrived after she'd gone to help Jake with his nieces, Martin could inform him of her unavailability.

Jake's eyes lit up with visible relief. "Thank you. Seven is good. We can iron out the rest of the details after Ruby and Ella have gone to school."

Delia rose from the sofa. Should she shake hands with him? Instead, she extended her hand toward the door, and they began walking that direction. "Then I'll see you and the girls tomorrow at seven."

Though she did her best to remain calm, why did she so look forward to the prospect of getting to know him better?

~

The next morning, Tuesday, Delia stepped onto the veranda at a quarter to seven with a sense of anticipation. Her family and the staff had taken to the idea of her filling in as a nanny during Leonora Philip's absence quite well. But she stopped short as Thaddeus pulled up on his horse in the driveway.

"Ready for our horseback ride?" He dismounted, looking happy to see her, except for the unexpected drizzle of rain matting his blond hair into a mass of curls, reminding her of the earliest of his school days.

He looked handsome as ever in his riding attire, but she didn't have more than a minute or two to explain about the latest developments. "I'm sorry, darling. I'm filling in for Nanny Philips for Jake Williams." She went on to bring him up to speed about Leonora's mother's condition.

"You're filling in for Jake's nanny?" He repeated it as if he hadn't heard half of what she'd explained, his brows rising.

"Yes, but can we go riding some other time." She tucked a stray lock of hair, loosened from her chignon, behind her ear. "I see you've brought Bluegrass Blaze. He is a beauty. I'm sorry I can't go riding, but later this evening, perhaps?"

Thaddeus heaved a sigh. "Drat. I promised Father I'd go with him to the Lexington Jockey Club meeting tonight. How long is this nanny business going to last?"

Delia descended the porch steps. "I guess it depends on how quickly Leonora's mother recovers. You may walk with me part of the way, but I must be going so the children aren't late for school." She hurried across the drive lined with sugar maples, curving around the front of the house toward the long lane leading to Cornflower Road.

Following her, Thaddeus led Bluegrass Blaze, the horse's hooves clomping. "I really must object, Delia." How indignant he sounded. A glance at him revealed the stern look she'd anticipated. "I don't think it's right for a girl I'm courting to take on employment for some other single fella. An eligible bachelor. In fact, we happen to be about the same age."

Delia jerked her chin up at Thaddeus's proprietary attitude. In fact, she'd heard Pa say Jake was twenty-eight...not that it mattered.

Thad hurried to catch up to her. "We have plenty of servants if Velvet Brooks can't spare someone. I can have one sent over to perform this nanny job."

Delia stopped in her tracks and swung around to face Thaddeus. She positioned her hands on her hips and glared at him. "Thaddeus Sullivan, his nieces know me, and they cannot simply be handed over to just anyone. Secondly, I don't see a ring on this finger for you to tell me who I'll help and who I won't." She held up her hand to remind him he had yet to officially propose. Where had her confidence come from to stand up to him? "Third, Pa recommended Mr. Williams ask for my help in this particular situation. And you're behaving like a jealous schoolboy ever since he accidentally spilled punch on your shirt."

"Maybe I am protecting what is mine. Are you saying you don't plan to listen to my opinion?" His brows slashed down.

She must not let him discourage her from helping Jake's nieces. "Thaddeus, you know you have nothing to worry about. We've been courting for over a year."

Pivoting, she continued toward the Victorian house. In truth, Jake had turned her head and her heart, and she kept her chin down as a twinge of remorse for her dishonesty nagged at her. However, she couldn't tell Thaddeus the truth. If she admitted to having some attraction to Jake, he would want to know more. She didn't know the answers to any questions he might pose. Plus, it might enrage him. And didn't she need to listen to the advice her parents had given since he dragged his feet about making an official proposal?

Thaddeus did not follow her. He stared after her for a while before finally mounting Bluegrass Blaze and turning around, riding off at a gallop toward Sullivan Hill. Obviously, she had made him angry. How angry, she didn't know.

She didn't have time to contend with him presently. Flustered, she marched on toward Jake's farm. What could she expect from *him* today? What did she know about Jake Williams? Nothing, absolutely nothing.

While she had to admit she found their new neighbor intriguing, she told herself she did not have any romantic notions toward him. Jake hadn't indicated in any exact words whether he harbored any romantic inclinations toward her, but some part of her wanted to discover where the road would lead, especially since Thaddeus continued to delay a commitment.

CHAPTER ELEVEN

I've read hundreds of cookbooks. Most of those cookbooks
don't even tell you how to get a steak ready, how to bake
biscuits or an apple pie.
—Colonel Sanders

Jake opened the door with Mary on one arm. Her golden curls tousled, she leaned a sleepy head on his shoulder. He grinned sheepishly and stepped back to welcome Delia inside, opening the door wider. "I'm so glad you're here." He couldn't begin to tell her how glad. "Please come in. We've been making breakfast. They've managed to dress, but I confess, I can't do hair. I can barely manage my own."

She smiled. "I'm glad to help." She looked around, unpinning her hat as she followed Jake. He led the way to the kitchen, straight down the center hall. They passed their sparsely furnished sitting room on the left, and then the library and music room on the right with a smattering of books, toys strewn about, and an upright piano against one wall. Farther down the hall, they passed the formal dining room on the right before he turned left into the kitchen.

What did she think of the house? She would barely have had time to take in her surroundings as he led her to Ruby and Ella. Jake tried to see the kitchen with its large stone fireplace and thick wooden mantel through Delia's eyes. The windows with the sink and cupboards below them ran the length of the rear of the house. Even for an overcast day with light rain, the panes let in plenty of light.

The girls looked up at Delia with wide smiles, their eyes bright. He'd managed to get each of them into their white dresses and black stockings with their black shoes that morning.

"Hello, Miss Delia. We've brought our comb and brush set downstairs." Ruby led her over to a counter to show her a mirror, an array of white hair ribbons and bows, and everything she might need to arrange their hair. "Could you put one of these bows in our hair?"

Delia hung her shawl and hat on a hook near the back door. "Certainly. Who's first?" She took the brush in her hands, and Ella stepped forward. Ruby handed Ella the mirror to hold and gave Delia a hair ribbon at the right moment.

Jake sat Mary down at the table and went to the stove. He hummed a tune as he flipped little cakes in a cast-iron skillet. This he could do. Another skillet sizzled with bacon, the smell tantalizing.

Soon, Delia finished styling Ella's and Ruby's hair and did the same for Mary while the other girls set the table. Mary had shorter hair, but Delia found a way to part it and add a little bow to one side. Mary smiled and kept patting it, clearly happy to have something in her hair too.

Jake placed a stack of fried cakes and a plate of bacon on the kitchen table as they gathered around. "Have you had breakfast yet, Miss Delia?" If he put a plate on the table, maybe she'd join them, even if only for a few bites. "I'm going to assume you'll join us for meals this week whenever you can—if you can put up with my cooking, that is."

"Thank you. I have eaten breakfast with my family, but I might manage a bite or two." Delia cast him a wide smile.

Good, she seemed to notice his attempt at humor. Brave girls, all of them, to endure his lack of cooking skills.

Delia poured the girls each a glass of orange juice. Then she took a seat, folded the linen napkin in her lap, and began slicing a flapjack into small bites for Mary. Ruby and Ella, following her movements, placed napkins in their laps too. At last, they had a lady's example they could emulate.

When Jake lifted his fork, about to take a bite, Ruby reminded him, "We forgot to pray." The girls stared at him.

"Oh, yes. You're quite right, Ruby." Jake shook his head at his own mistake. "We mustn't forget our prayers, or we might have a dreadfully terrible day."

His words drew a smile from Ruby and Ella. He bowed his head for the prayer, and they followed his lead, including Delia. He blessed the meal, asked the Lord to watch over them, and prayed for Leonora's mother to heal. He also thanked the Lord for providing Delia's help. Then he prayed for the girls to have a good day at school. Finished, he glanced up at the kitchen clock. "Ten minutes to eat and then be on your way to school, girls."

"It's a long walk." Ruby wore a pitiful expression as she explained to Delia. "Nanny Philips walks us to school."

"A very long walk from here." Ella's lower lip protruded.

"I'm assuming they attend the elementary school on the west side of Lexington."

"That's right." Jake took a bite of bacon.

"I remember when they finished the new two-story building last summer." Delia shared her smile between the girls. "Shall I walk with you? Is there a pram for Mary? I could borrow the buggy from our farm, and we could be there in no time at all."

"Your pa let me borrow a team and wagon from Velvet Brooks until we acquire our own and more horses." He poured some of the maple syrup onto his cakes and bacon. "Tell you what. I can hitch it up, and we'll all drive this week."

It would provide more time each day to get to know Miss Delia Lyndon.

～

Half an hour after breakfast, they had dropped the girls off in the schoolyard and turned the wagon toward home. Mary sat on Delia's lap, clutching her hand as the wagon rumbled over the country roads. Jake chatted about how he intended to buy a couple of cows, some work horses, more riding horses, and mentioned he had acquired some chickens.

"Chickens," Mary echoed with great enthusiasm, causing Delia to laugh.

"She really likes chasing the chickens." Jake tipped his hat back farther on his head and glanced at them. "I'll give you a tour of the farm and the rest of the house when we return. Then we can talk about their schedule and how Leonora has arranged a few things for us. I'm also hoping you can tell me what you think we need to do to transform the place into a country inn."

"I'll be glad to offer my humble opinions, although with your background, I'm sure you know more than I do."

He shrugged, holding the reins steady. "Suppose I do have a unique perspective, as my whole family worked for the Sagamore in one capacity or another. Me in the stable with my father from age thirteen on. My mother as part of the kitchen staff. My sister, Charlotte, labored in the laundry house until she married Calvin. My parents met working at some other hotel in the same area. They went to work for the Sagamore when I was about eight. Of course, my inn won't be nearly as grand as a resort or a fancy hotel, but it would provide for us, and it's what I know."

"Still, our countryside setting and those horse trails should be a steady draw. And now that I understand where your love for horses has grown from, I am wondering what gave you the desire to get into racing." Mary inspected the shiny buttons at Delia's wrists, her pudgy fingers and soft touch warm and tender against her skin.

"Well, I learned most of what I know about horses from my father and the racing part from my uncle. Uncle Caleb, my father's brother, was a trainer like Red Brickman. He was and remains quite well known and respected at Pimlico for his methods and successes in horseracing. We would go and see the races and spend time with him in the summers each year until he passed away suddenly from a heart attack. We were devastated, and even more so when Charlotte and her husband passed not long after my uncle."

"I'm so sorry to hear about these losses." Delia didn't know what else she could say to comfort him, but clearly, Jake had contended with great suffering in recent years.

A solemn look appeared on his face. He craned his neck to look down at Mary. Likely, to confirm the toddler had stopped fussing with Delia's hands and buttons and had begun to drift into a morning slumber. Then he added in a softer voice, "Losing Uncle Caleb and Charlotte has broken our hearts. Diphtheria stole Charlotte and Calvin from us. Not even Calvin being a doctor could save them. They contracted the disease within days of each other, according to the medical records I read through. They suffered with a severe case, but thankfully, their suffering didn't last long. Two weeks and then they..." His voice trailed away. "Anyhow, I went to visit them as soon as I could, but I was too late. I never thought something like this could happen to people in the prime of their lives. As for our uncle, over the years, I kept up a healthy correspondence with him. He used to visit us at the Sagamore every other year or so during the winter. I guess you could say he's the one who inspired me to get into horseracing and training. It's strange how it's come about through the passing of Charlotte, but here we are."

"I'm sure you will have many successes, just like your uncle. Red knows what he's doing. He'll be a big help to you. He has an excellent track record, no pun intended." When Jake chuckled, Delia flashed him a smile. Funny, how natural it felt, riding along with him with his niece asleep in her arms. For a short time, they drove on in silence.

"Have you thought of a name for the farm?" she asked when he turned the wagon onto his drive.

"No, but I'd like it to reflect something about the girls' mother since we sold their home in Richmond to have a fresh start here in Lexington."

A bold move, to be sure. Yet another reason to admire Jake Williams. She turned her face toward him with an approving smile. "I like the fact you aren't afraid of taking a chance on something some might consider a risk."

Jake shrugged. "I could see the memories of their mother associated with Richmond didn't help much, though we'd have had more support from locals who knew them there. In the end, after Charlotte and Calvin were laid to rest, I knew we needed this chance to begin anew somewhere. Thankfully, when Leonora answered my ad for a nanny after the auction, the newspaper forwarded her reply to the boardinghouse, and she decided to move here for the job. So far, she's been all her references indicated we should expect—kind, dedicated, and reliable."

"I'm so glad. I wondered how you found a nanny so quickly." Delia had only seen a few glimpses of Leonora. She seemed very professional in her black uniform with a white apron.

Nearing the farm, she took Mary's hand in hers to begin waking her, earning a sleepy smile from the toddler, who closed her eyes and began to drift off again. "Time to wake up, little one. We're home. Ready to see the chickens?"

Mary rubbed her eyes with her chubby fists. Her eyes widened at recognizing the barn where Jake parked the wagon. "Chickens!"

Jake jumped down from the seat. "Ready for the tour of the house? We'll see the chickens after that. At least the rain has stopped."

When he came around to her side, she handed Mary to him. Lifting her skirts a few inches, she held onto his free hand to jump down, careful to avoid the wagon spokes. She took Mary in her arms for Jake to unhitch the team.

Once inside the house, Jake showed her around. With three floors of rooms, including five bedrooms on the second floor and four more on the third floor, plus another sitting room besides, he had plenty of space to accommodate travelers.

Outside, Mary held onto Delia's hand while they toured two barns, the corral, met the chickens and their coop—giving the toddler extra time to run amongst the fowls—and inspected the icehouse and smokehouse. They circled around part of the fishing pond, strolled alongside the tree line beyond it, and returned to the house to admire the tidy rows in the kitchen garden. Jake ended the tour at the back porch. Sunshine peered through the clouds, warming everything, but the air still felt cool and brisk on their hands and cheeks.

"How about a cup of tea?" he suggested.

"Sounds good. What do you think, Mary?" Delia looked down at the sweet little girl clinging to her hand.

"Blocks and train," Mary said with a wide grin.

"Those are her favorite toys," Jake explained.

"Ah, I see."

Jake opened the back door and held out his hand, inviting them into the spacious kitchen.

Delia helped Mary inside with an expressive shiver. "I'll put the kettle on and make us all something light for lunch if you'll fetch the toys she likes."

"Deal." After situating Mary at the table, Jake disappeared to find her toys.

Delia set about making tea and hard-boiled eggs. She found some cheese and apples in the icebox and sliced those and the eggs. Meanwhile, she listened to Jake teaching Mary to identify alphabet letters on the blocks.

After walking around the farm and filling her tummy from the light meal, Little Mary's eyelids drooped again. Jake cleared their plates and began washing the dishes while Delia carried the toddler to her trundle bed for an afternoon nap in the room she shared with her sisters.

She returned to the kitchen in short order and refilled their cups of tea, joining Jake at the table. He brought a notebook and pencil, then opened the notebook to several lists of his ideas for the farm, divided by indoor and outdoor needs.

Setting his pencil aside, he raked a hand through his hair. "So now that you've seen the place, what do you think about transforming it? Can it be done? I'd love to hear your honest opinion."

"Yes, I think it can be done, but there's still a lot to do. You'll need an advertising budget, a household budget, and an outdoor budget for livestock, seed, and the like. I assume you'll grow your own oats and hay in some of those dormant fields, and I highly recommend acquiring a few bulls and cows for producing your own beef. It's expensive to feed folks. They'll expect good, hearty meals. You'll need more chickens, but I'm sure your flock will grow. A good team of work horses for plowing and the wagon, of course. You'll need a carriage to pick up folks at the train station. I'm guessing you already have plans for these things."

He showed her he had included many of those items and more to his lists. "I hadn't thought about having a nice carriage. You may be right about that. What else would you recommend?" He scribbled the word *carriage* in his notes.

"You'll need more riding horses and ponies, as you mentioned, and they will require more hay, oats, corn, and straw for bedding. You'll also need more saddles and tack for the guests to enjoy the riding trails." She paused, tapping a finger lightly on her chin. "Fishing poles and gear for the pond. City folk may not have any."

"Anything else?" Jake's brow arched.

Delia leaned forward with a nod. "Sleighs, cutters, and sleds for winter. Eventually, a selection of skates for when the pond freezes over, although most winters in Kentucky aren't cold enough for ice skating or sledding except for when we have a good snow. More lanterns. A proper flower and shrub garden. Plenty of roses and bulbs. Furniture for the front and rear porches. Hanging baskets of flowers, potted plants, and window boxes. Maybe a trellis arch."

Jake scrawled down her ideas as fast as she could rattle them off.

"I see you have a nice start on the vegetable garden, but I recommend doubling it to accommodate having more mouths to feed. I hope you have plans to hunt and build up the smokehouse with plenty of meat. The more self-sufficient you are, the less there will be to purchase."

"I do hunt and yes, I plan on stocking the smokehouse." He gulped and then drank some of his tea. "I'm afraid to ask, but what do you think about the indoors?"

She tilted her head to one side, afraid to tell him how much he still needed in that department. "I did notice the bedrooms have double beds, nightstands, dressers, and most have writing desks, but you'll need nice airy curtains in all of the bedroom windows, shades to keep them dark when guests want to sleep, more linens for all of the beds, and quilts too."

"Good ideas." He jotted down *curtains*, *bed linens*, and *quilts*.

"Not just any quilts. They should match the curtains. I personally think each room should have its own color scheme so you can place guests in either the yellow room, the pink room, or the blue room, for example."

"An excellent idea." Jake scribbled down more notes, and Delia sipped some of her tea.

When he looked caught up, she added, "More rocking chairs and settees inside the house. A tea table and maybe some lounge chaises for outside. Did I mention a porch swing? You'll need a well-stocked library. Guests will want a selection of books to read without having to go into town. Tablecloths for the dining room, and plenty of cookware, bakeware, china, and silver. I haven't taken an inventory of what you have, but you'll need a good tea service and dishes enough to accommodate maximum capacity. A fresh coat of paint on the porches, a bit of white picket fencing, and flowers by the road. Vases for fresh flower arrangements in every room. New drapes for downstairs with lace panels, and kitchen curtains for these windows. Towels and washcloths for bathing. New wallpaper and fresh paint in several rooms, though it looks as if the previous owner painted some of the rooms and updated the plumbing."

Jake continued writing fast, his head bent over his notes. "China, silver, tea service, fresh paint, wallpaper, white picket fence, more flowers, vases, towels, and washcloths. Got it. Anything else?" He sounded more than a little breathless.

She looked around, twisting in her seat to see if she had missed anything. "I'm hoping you have one of those new washing machines."

He nodded toward a corner of the kitchen. "We do. It's in

the pantry with the other cleaning items. The former owner left it."

"Oh good. You're going to need it. Washing clothing and linens for all of your guests would be a chore otherwise."

"This helps a great deal." Jake closed the notebook, then slid it aside. "A woman's influence is of great value to me in these matters. I'll need more of your expertise going forward so the place can have a feminine touch and feel like a home to our guests. If you're willing, that is..."

"Of course." She offered a shy smile. It was thrilling to be part of Jake's plans, and even more so that he valued her opinions. The man took every suggestion she offered as important enough to write down. And how refreshing that he didn't argue with her about them. "Now, we should probably discuss the schedule before Mary wakes."

After they picked up the girls from school in the wagon later that day, Jake remained outside to tend the horses, feed the chickens, and make a small fence repair to a section of the corral. Delia gathered the girls around the kitchen table and instructed them in making an apple pie using supplies from Jake's pantry. Ruby and Ella helped her peel the apples. Mary appeared content to pick up any peelings they dropped, and after a while, she wanted to stand on a chair to observe the goings on. Delia measured out the ingredients for the crust, but she let Ruby and Ella take turns mixing and rolling out the dough. Judging by their laughter and flour-covered smiling faces, the girls enjoyed baking.

After they placed the pie in the oven, she suggested the children clean up the mess and set the table for dinner. Having found some canned beans and cornmeal in the pantry, she began making corn muffins, allowing the girls to help her stir the batter. When Jake returned to find their supper almost ready, he looked relieved.

"Everything smells good in here. Wow! Is that an apple pie

too?" Jake's eyes danced, the golden-brown flaky crust drawing his attention. The whole kitchen smelled of cinnamon and nutmeg. She smiled and nodded since she couldn't get an explanation in. The girls swarmed around him, Ruby and Ella talking at the same time about how Delia had let them help with the baking.

"Just like our ma used to do with us, Uncle Jake," Ruby remarked, a smile reaching her eyes. "If you make more bacon, dinner will be all ready."

"Is that your way of requesting bacon for dinner?" Jake grinned, teasing Ruby. "I suppose I could sizzle up some more bacon strips. I do know how to cook bacon."

Ruby smiled in reply.

"Bacon!" Mary clapped her hands, making them laugh.

All in all, Delia's first day had gone well. She had learned more about the handsome newcomer, and now she had an idea about the schedule the girls followed. Jake needed a lot of help —more than she should allow herself to provide lest Thaddeus object. And Jake would someday marry a woman who would want to implement her own ideas.

Yes, she could only contribute in a few small ways and pray for Leonora to return soon—as she reminded herself on her walk home. Why did some part of her wish the nanny would take her sweet time? And why did spending time with Jake and the girls feel like having a happy family of her own?

Because the girls so quickly accepted her and Jake clearly valued her opinions and made her feel so useful and needed, sending her confidence soaring.

CHAPTER TWELVE

Jump, and you will find out how to unfold your wings as you
fall.
—Ray Bradbury

Throughout the remainder of the week, Delia returned to
Jake's home each morning, repeating a similar routine.
For the most part, each day progressed smoothly, except for
Wednesday's late-morning crisis after a long session of scraping
wallpaper upstairs.

Downstairs in the kitchen, while Mary contented herself
with the wooden mixing spoons, Delia used a chair from the
table to climb onto the counters and hang curtains on the long
row of windows. Walking on the counters felt strange. Mama
had given her a set of red plaid curtains from the linen
cupboard at Velvet Brooks. Jake had approved of the gesture at
breakfast. Then he'd gone to work outside somewhere.

When she finished, she put her hands on her hips,

surveying the new look from above. "What do you think of these, Mary?"

No answer caused Delia to glance down at the braided rug where the toddler sat only moments ago. Instead, the wooden spoons lay scattered about. No Mary. Surveying the rest of the spacious kitchen, she didn't see her charge anywhere.

"Mary?" she called out from atop the counter. Perhaps she'd gone looking for her blocks and the train.

Delia scrambled down and began searching through every room in the house, inspecting behind furniture, opening closets, and peeking under the beds. She didn't find Mary anywhere. Panic set in during the futile search of the first floor. Fear struck her heart with every passing minute of her search through the second floor. Having returned to the kitchen to search the pantry and cupboards, she bit her lower lip. Where could the child have gone?

The chickens! Dashing out into the hall and bursting onto the front porch, she stopped in her tracks, colliding with Jake.

"Whoa, there! What's wrong? You look white as a ghost." Jake steadied her, holding her arms in his strong hands.

"I can't find Mary anywhere. I've looked everywhere in the house. She must be outside. Maybe with the chickens," Delia blurted out.

"Okay, okay. Slow down. We'll find her. Let's go have a look at the chicken coop."

She nodded, then followed on his heels as they headed around the corner of the house. They crossed the lawn, then the drive, and finally, the henhouse came into view. With it, Mary came into their view, too, and Delia breathed a sigh of relief.

The child had found a way to lift the latch to open the gate and let herself inside the pen. Now, she ran exuberantly about, chasing after the chickens. She held a clump of feathers in both hands and occasionally stopped to shake the feathers away.

Then she caught one of the chickens, and clutching it to her chest, she squeezed it with all her might to give it as much love as she possibly could, laughing with glee.

"Oh, Mary, we have found you at last!" Delia followed Jake into the hens' abode. Once inside, she dropped to her knees and wrapped her arms around the child and the chicken she held fast to. "You scared Miss Delia."

Jake knelt beside them on one knee. "Mary, we've talked about this before. You can't go outside without your sisters, or me, or Nanny Philips, or Miss Lyndon."

Mary looked up at him with bright eyes, cradling the struggling fowl. "Chickens...hold..."

Delia set the child down and brushed the dust and feathers from her pinafore. "It appears there is more harm done to our feathered friends than to her. I don't think she understands yet."

"I think you're right. She's done this a few times before. If it happens again, I'll have to recommend we take the train away." Turning to Mary, Jake reiterated the consequences.

"No train?" Her bottom lip quivered.

"Not if you come out here again by yourself." Clearly, he was trying to sound stern, though a chuckle vibrated just below his words.

Delia couldn't bear to see her lips quiver and scooped Mary into her arms. "Into the house we go. I've hung the curtains if you'd like to see them, Jake."

"I'd love to see them." He followed them inside and stood back in the kitchen, a look of marvel written in his expression at how a bit of fabric had instantly transformed the kitchen into a vibrant, cozier, more attractive environment. "Now it's beginning to feel like home. How can I thank you?"

"I'm glad you like them. You thanked me enough by helping me find Mary. I'm sorry she escaped." Delia's eyes misted. What if something had happened on her watch?

"It's all right. Things like this are bound to happen with children around. Or so I am learning." Jake offered a tender and somehow reassuring smile.

"I should have been more careful, and it's entirely my fault. I should have checked on her more often while hanging these, but I discovered walking on the counters necessitates a bit of a balancing act." Delia nodded toward the windows.

He chuckled, crossing his arms over his chest. "I can imagine."

"The good news is, earlier this morning, I finished removing the faded wallpaper from the bedroom requiring the most attention. I'll begin hanging the new wallpaper you purchased after lunch. Are you hungry? Is that why you returned when you did?"

"Yes, I'm famished, and I need some coffee or tea." Jake poured himself a cup of tea at the stove.

Delia kept a closer eye on Mary after Wednesday's experience. On Thursday at noon, Jake came home for lunch once he'd completed his list of morning chores and outside work. They sat together with Mary at the table for some chicken salad sandwiches Delia had brought from the kitchen at Velvet Brooks. She and Mary had enjoyed walking there and back to retrieve them.

"Those were delicious," Jake remarked when she returned from tucking Mary into her trundle bed for her afternoon nap.

"I'm glad you liked the sandwiches, though I can't take credit for them. Willamena is a wonderful cook." Delia carried their plates from the table to the sink basin and then poured herself some tea.

"I forgot to mention how nice this tablecloth is. Please send my regards to your mother." Jake ran his hands over the red plaid linen cloth.

"I will." Delia had found the tablecloth in Mama's linen closet, and it matched the kitchen curtains, one of the reasons she'd selected them. She handed him a list of items she'd noted the kitchen lacked after taking an inventory of Jake's dishes and a few other household items. She focused her attention on the handsome man who no longer felt like a stranger.

"Thank you. This is most helpful." He patted the list, then his blue eyes lit up. "Horizon beat Red's best time for any horse on the Velvet Brooks track today."

"Wow! I'm thrilled to hear Horizon is doing so well, and I'm sure you're going to at least place in one of these upcoming races. Have you found a jockey yet?" She leaned forward, tilting her head to one side.

"Not yet." Jake reached for his teacup, casting her special notebook on the table a curious glance. "So...tell me, what do you like to do in your spare time, Miss Delia?"

"Oh, a variety of things. I usually work a few days a week at the library as an assistant, as you know. I advocate for children's literacy by tutoring one day each week and reading to more children at the library on other occasions. Once a month, I deliver books on horseback to some of our elderly. I also host a monthly tea and hat-trimming party for a few of the local young ladies. When I'm not involved in other ladylike pursuits, I occasionally find myself writing a short story." She placed a hand over her notebook. "That's what's inside the notebook. Between working on the wallpaper upstairs and looking after the girls, I plan to finish my latest short story."

"May I read one of your stories?" His brows arched.

Delia looked away, flushing, hiding her eyes from Jake. "I suppose I could let you read one. They aren't anything spectacular, but each one has a happy ending."

"All right, you choose one, and I'll read it."

She flipped through the pages in her notebook until she found one she could share. Sliding the notebook toward him, open to a short story about a horse and a young girl's spying adventures during the Civil War, she sat back in her chair. She sipped her tea, waiting patiently for him to read it. Occasionally, he'd glance up at her, smile, or laugh out loud.

When he finished reading it, he closed the book but kept it in front of him. "I liked the story a lot. You have a talent with words."

"Thank you. I'm glad you liked it."

"But why are you hiding all of these stories in this notebook? Why not submit them to the *Lexington Gazette* for publication?" He thumbed through the book, peeking at some of her other work.

She rose from the chair and attempted to snatch the notebook from him. "I have only given you permission to read one of them, Jake Williams."

He chuckled, dangling it away from her as he tried to peek at more of the contents.

She finally succeeded in retrieving her treasure from him. "They are not ready for the world yet. Besides, Thaddeus would detest it if I became a public writer. And I don't think they're good enough to inflict upon society." Delia began clearing their cups and saucers, stealing a glance in his direction. The mention of her beau's name had cast a solemn look upon Jake's face.

"You shouldn't let Thaddeus squash your talents and dreams. You must have ten good stories there if the one I read is any indication. I do hope you'll choose some of these and polish them. You could earn funds if a newspaper editor chooses to print them. Plus, you might help someone with your gift instead of hiding it."

"Maybe so, but Thaddeus would never allow it."

He dropped the discussion with a furrowed brow, but maybe she'd better not bring her notebook to his house anymore. He might ask to read more of her stories, and she certainly wasn't ready to share them. Still, Jake's modern view of women impressed her. Perhaps New Yorkers kept up better with new ways of doing things than Kentuckians. She had to admit, his thoughts gave her much to consider.

Later the same afternoon, as she tried to press two long pieces of wallpaper onto the wall and smooth out any wrinkles, one after the other fell onto her in quick succession.

"Oh dear!" She toppled about trying to free herself from the glue-covered wall-hangings. One of her feet stumbled onto something that rolled—maybe the little wooden car belonging to Mary's train set. She couldn't look down, and she couldn't see anything but paper as her foot glided forward.

A pair of strong arms caught her.

"The two of you really don't have to wear the wallpaper," Jake's voice said over Mary's giggles.

Delia clung to his arms while he held her steady and flung the two large sheets of paper aside. She sputtered in his embrace, finally free of the sticky paper. "I wasn't expecting you so soon. Is it time to collect Ruby and Ella from school?"

"Yes, but first, you required rescuing from a most dire predicament." A smirk turned up his lips, and his eyes danced with amusement.

"A predicament, indeed." Blinking, she looked down to discover Mary had attracted dozens of tiny scraps of wallpaper strips in her hair and clothing from being underfoot, crawling about in the bits of old wallpaper on the floor. Some of the pieces stuck to her face and arms too. "Oh, Mary! Look at you." She couldn't help but laugh at the mess they'd made.

"Is that a bit of glue on your nose?" Jake chuckled softly.

As he held her steady, she glanced up, and their eyes locked onto each other's as she quietly slid the train car away with her foot before she could step on it again.

"Uh, I think I should clean the...wallpaper off of Mary." The statement came out in a whisper. Melting in his embrace, she went hot. How nice his strong arms felt. So much better than the sticky wallpaper wrapped around her. He kept one arm around her waist, the other supporting her back. Her balance had returned, but why did she want him to kiss her?

Along with his smile, desire flared in his eyes. Did he see it in her eyes too? His tone soft and tender, he managed a reply. "I've finished repairing the ladder to the barn loft and hitched up the team." His voice sounded hoarse.

She didn't move.

He leaned closer and ever so softly brushed his lips across hers. It happened so fast, she forgot to breathe. Delia's eyes closed for a moment at the touch of his warm lips on hers, the smell of his musky cologne making her dizzy. Goodness...she'd wanted him to kiss her all week, perhaps since the first time she'd laid eyes on him.

Releasing her, he stepped back, his arms dropping to his sides. "I'm sorry. I shouldn't have taken such a liberty..."

He dodged out of the room, and as his boots clambered down the steps, she wanted to stop him. Had he not enjoyed the kiss as she had? Or had he apologized because he respected her courtship with Thaddeus? She didn't know what she wanted anymore. Keeping one's heart open to the possibility of a romance with either gentleman had fully rendered its share of confusion. Only one thing she knew for sure—she didn't regret the kiss.

Delia picked Mary up, hurrying across the hall to the powder room. Thankfully, the farmhouse had updated plumbing. Soon, she had the toddler cleaned up, having plucked away the wallpaper. She washed both of their hands and faces to remove any sticky glue residue.

Downstairs, she tied on both of their bonnets, put on her shawl, and helped Mary into her spring coat. Outside, Jake put Mary onto the front wagon seat first. Then he swung Delia up into the seat, his lips pressed into a firm line, his jaws clenched.

All week so far, he'd driven her to and from the school. How she'd looked forward to those drives. Sitting close to him made her heart beat faster, the attraction between them strong and flourishing, hanging in the air over them like a tree branch, beckoning her to pluck the fruit thereof.

And now, she didn't know what to say in the awkward silence. If she told him she had liked the kiss, she betrayed her feelings for Thaddeus. If she expressed regret, he might never kiss her again. Unable to deny her attraction to both Jake and Thaddeus, she decided not to say anything at all, unless he brought the kiss up. They spoke no more about the matter.

But his kiss left her wanting another.

After picking the girls up from the school, he came inside to see them settled into their routine, helping the girls out of their coats, reminding them to listen to her. A knock on the door interrupted them, and Jake answered it, the door creaking as it opened. "Telegram for Jake Williams," the voice at the door said, drifting to where Delia sat in the rocking chair in the front sitting room with Mary climbing onto her lap.

Jake thanked the person who had delivered the message. A few minutes later, he appeared in the parlor doorway, an opened envelope and notecard in his hand. "Leonora writes that her mother has improved and is out of danger. She'll be returning on the two o'clock train this Saturday afternoon and asks us to pick her up at the depot at four-thirty."

"Oh." Delia looked down over Mary's curls at the children's book in her hands. Ruby and Ella played with their dollhouse on the floor, a few feet away. She instinctively hid her eyes from Jake, wrestling with disappointment and relief. Did he feel the same mixture of feelings? "I'm glad her mother has improved. I'm sure you'll be happy to have her home so things can return to normal."

He looked at her as he tucked the telegram inside his shirt pocket. "It's for the best." Clearing his throat, he added, "I mean, it will be good for the girls to have Leonora return, and I can't expect you to put your life on hold for much longer. You've done a wonderful thing for us, and we will be sad not to have you here."

His response spoke volumes. Her heart sank. *It's for the best* echoed in her mind, but she could now be free from her dilemma, able to return to horseback rides and her courtship with Thaddeus. Her beau had sent a bouquet of daffodils to Velvet Brooks, telling her he would call upon her on Saturday evening. And yet, she would miss Ruby, Ella, Mary, and Jake. Why did her heart hurt so much?

"I don't want you to go." Ruby's voice quaked.

"Can't you stay?" Ella's eyes looked hopeful.

Mustering her strength, she looked up at Jake where he stood in the hall, staring at her and his nieces. "We should all have a picnic supper tomorrow at Velvet Brooks after school so I can say goodbye. Not a permanent goodbye, but a sort of last hurrah before Nanny Philips returns," she suggested. "Pa said he thinks the weather will be sunny and warm. No more spring rain."

Jake's brows rose. "A picnic?"

She nodded. Had she detected hope in his voice? "I'll have Willamena make something special for us."

The girls murmured their agreement, but their response lacked the expected enthusiasm.

"I'll only be right across the road, girls. You can visit anytime." Despite her cheerful words, Delia was no more encouraged than the children who had quickly become so dear to her.

~

On Friday morning after they'd returned from dropping the girls at school, Jake had said he would meet Delia and his nieces by the creek for the picnic around four o'clock, about the time he would finish up a meeting with Red about Horizon. Red wanted him to meet a jockey, and the jockey had to meet Horizon. Jake also said Delia could take the girls to Velvet Brooks after school to prepare for the picnic. The girls wanted to see the horses too.

According to Delia, the staff and her family loved seeing her charges. It also would give her a chance to find a quilt she wanted to bring for the picnic and time to arrange a surprise she'd mentioned.

The meeting with the jockey had gone well. Something to celebrate during the picnic. But why did he feel so glum? He had finally found a jockey who agreed to ride Horizon for the season ahead, and one with an outstanding racing record.

Scratching behind his ear, he forced himself to admit he shouldn't have done that blasted foolish thing yesterday. Kissing Delia! He'd let his emotions from spending a wonderful week with her get the better of him. Then again, had he not seen longing and hope in her chocolate eyes after the surprise in her expression had waned?

At the time, it had seemed like the right thing to do. He couldn't deny he'd fallen head over heels, hopelessly in love with her. Every single time she smiled at him, his heart melted. And in truth, he longed to draw her into his arms and kiss her properly. But had he acted impulsively, only to be cast aside, left to contend with a broken heart? Had he opened himself up to rejection? He'd experienced plenty of that in his lifetime, and he'd rather not experience more of it if it could be helped.

But it could not be helped. He was, indeed, irrefutably drawn to Delia Lyndon.

Leaning over the stall door inside the barn, he reached out to pat his horse on the nose. "You've got a chance now, Horizon. We've found someone to ride you, and you'll need to make friends with him."

Too bad Delia wasn't with him to share the moment, but he would see her shortly at the picnic. He could tell her the good news about finding a jockey, and then what? Say goodbye to the woman who completed him? The woman who made him and the girls laugh and smile so much? The woman who believed in his dreams?

~

Delia glanced at the timepiece on her white blouse while standing in the music room with Jake's nieces, clustered around the piano bench where Gladdie demonstrated a song for them. Almost time for the picnic. She needed to find Nathaniel Hartley, one of the farm's extra hands. She intended to ask him to lug the corn hole game from the barn out to the picnic area ahead of time. Corn hole had become a family favorite at Velvet Brooks. Hopefully, Ruby, Ella, and Mary would enjoy it as much as she and her sisters did.

"Girls, if you'll stay here at the piano with my sister, I have a surprise to arrange for you, but you must listen to everything Gladdie says. Am I understood?" She gave them each a stern look.

The girls nodded. Ruby spoke for the three of them. "We'll be good."

"Splendid. I'll only be gone about fifteen minutes. Thank you for watching them, Gladdie." Mama had gone with Pa to run some errands in town, so she was relying on her sister.

"Sure. We'll see how the girls do with their singing skills." Gladdie began asking the girls about their favorite songs, and Delia hurried outside toward the barn.

Once inside the barn, she caught sight of Red speaking to Jake, and when Jake spoke her name, curiosity got the better of her. She ducked back outside and leaned against the door out of sight, straining to hear the discussion.

"I knew I couldn't hide the ache in my heart from you.

You're too perceptive, Brickman." Jake's voice continued. "Yes, I admit I've fallen for Miss Delia Lyndon, but I don't believe a fine lady such as her would have anything to do with a fella like me. I'm just a stable boy from the Adirondacks."

Delia's mouth dropped open at hearing the same words Pa had used in the library, coming from Red Brickman to Jake. But hadn't Jake said it was for the best if Leonora returned? Perhaps he hadn't meant it the way she'd assumed.

"And I'm just a glorified stable boy," Red's voice responded, a little louder than Jake's. "I think you're selling yourself short, Jake."

Jake had fallen in love with her? He had feelings for her, after all?

~

"I don't know, Red. Miss Lyndon seems like she's from a whole different class than me." Jake stared at Horizon, but he cocked his head to one side. Would Red tell him more?

"Miss Delaney, yes, she's a fine lady, but as a newcomer to these parts, you have an air of mystery about you. And a mighty good business idea." Red chuckled as he patted horse flesh. "Plus, this steed here, he's gonna take you places. He's a champion. In fact, you're a champion, Jake Williams. Don't let anyone tell you otherwise. If it were me in your shoes, I'd tell Miss Delia how I feel."

"Shucks, Red. Everyone knows you're one of the finest trainers Kentucky has to offer, and working for one of the top horseracing families in the state. I did some checking around to confirm all of this before I accepted Mr. Lyndon's offer to train Horizon. Even if all you say about me is true, Delia's involved with that Sullivan fellow." Doubt leaked into Jake's voice.

"That Sullivan fellow don't have nothin' on you but Daddy's

money." Red reached for a pitchfork nearby. "Born with a silver spoon in his mouth. She don't need his money. Miss Delia got her own money. There's a mighty fine dowry for the man who marries a Spencer-Lyndon daughter."

"I have enough left from the sale of my sister's property that I don't need Miss Delia's dowry either. It's not much, but it's enough. We'll be comfortable." Jake stepped forward to grab the extra pitchfork sitting against the wall, his chest expanding with hope. "But are you sayin' that Sullivan boy hasn't proposed yet?" He started helping the trainer clear the floor.

"That's exactly what I'm tryin' to say. Well, he proposed once, and they got all the way to the altar, but she ran away. Rode off into the distance on Midnight Sunburst. Left Charlie Ford without a ride home." Red paused before adding, "They are a bit fickle with each other, if you ask me. On and off again like a fly on a horse's tail."

Jake blinked at this stunning news. He'd run away, too, knowing what he did about the Sullivan third son. It only confirmed to him that Delia wasn't meant for Thaddeus, after all.

"Well, that aside, I'm crazy for her. She's so pretty, shy, sweet like honey, smart as a whip, and..." Pausing his shoveling, Jake rubbed his chin. "*Demure* is the word."

"Yes. A real fine lady."

"She's always looking away, hiding those pretty brown eyes from me. I'd hate to do anything to hurt her. It seems as though she has a solid future ahead by marrying into the Sullivans, at least financially."

"Maybe, and maybe not. I think she'd be much happier with someone like yerself." Red tossed a load of manure on the end of his pitchfork into a pile behind him.

"Still, I'm not sure I should come to Lexington and start off by stealin' another man's girl, making an enemy of one of the wealthiest families in the area. And sometimes...I can still hear the echo of rich guests at the Sagamore saying, 'Hey, you, stable boy, saddle my horse.' Hard to forget things like that, you know?" Jake emptied his pitchfork and shook his head. "Not to mention, I already made an enemy of that Sullivan fella when I spilled red punch all over his shirt at the Lyndons' dinner party."

A cough from around the corner caused Jake and the trainer to turn, looking toward the main entrance of the barn. They'd both heard it, but Red shrugged and turned back to the task at hand. He didn't seem too concerned, so Jake wouldn't worry either.

"And then you asked his girl to spend a week at your farm, bonding with your nieces." Red chuckled. "He's likely simmering. A little competition will spur him on. He'll be asking her to marry him again real soon. I wouldn't wait too long to tell her you love her if I were you."

"But we've only just met. Won't she think I'm rushing into things?"

"You won't know if you don't ask." Red gave him a pointed look.

Jake tossed a pitchfork of hay into the pile behind them. "You may be right. You've given me much to consider."

Almost time to meet Delia and the girls at the picnic. He'd finish the stall and then be on his way. And later on, when the girls were tucked into bed, he needed to revisit the idea of making a proposal of marriage to Miss Delia. Sure, they hadn't known each other for long, but he didn't think he could bear the idea of losing a chance with her. Lately, he'd taken a lot of chances. Why not one more?

~

elia pressed a hand to cover her mouth. Demure? He'd called her demure and had said her eyes were pretty. What a sweet thing to say!

But when Jake had mentioned the punch spill, she'd coughed and there had been a bit of a pause. She was sure they were going to step out of the barn and discover her presence, but they hadn't.

She began tiptoeing back toward the house, holding her hand over her heart as she considered the pain and sorrow in Jake's voice when he'd spoken of the resort patrons who'd called him a stable boy. Yet Jake had somehow learned to swallow his hurt. Or maybe he'd given it to the Lord. In any case, he'd managed to shrug it off and keep going forward with his life. He'd discovered a way to become a confident man regardless of the past, a man willing to take risks. Not only a confident man, but a humble one. She saw it in the way he reached out to others and asked questions before making his final decisions, and also in the way he submitted to God by believing in the power of prayer.

If only she could find that kind of confidence and strength. She quaked in her shoes sometimes when she entered a room full of strangers.

Far enough away from the barn, she picked up her skirts and fled, setting her eye on the veranda. If she could make it there, perhaps she could have a moment to recover.

Beginning next week, she'd see much less of Jake. Her heart sank at the thought. He'd be training Horizon with Red on the racetrack at Velvet Brooks—but at five o'clock in the morning, an hour when she usually slept. She'd be lucky to wave to him now and then if she happened to see him when she went on her morning horseback ride around seven or eight.

The words he'd spoken about her...they brought equal parts comfort and confusion.

Reaching the veranda, she stopped to lean against one of

the columns and catch her breath before facing the girls. Her heart beat faster because she now knew without a shadow of a doubt, Jake had feelings for her. But would he pursue her?

He spoke truth. A marriage to Thaddeus would give her financial security and unite two of the strongest horse farming families in all of Lexington, maybe all of Kentucky. Jake stirred something in her, though, something powerful like a waterfall or a mighty rushing river. Where would it lead?

What if he proposed during the picnic? What would her answer be? She needed to find Martin and ask him to convey her message to Nathaniel about finding the corn hole game so she had a little more time to gather her composure. She didn't dare walk in on the men after hearing Jake pour out his heart to Red.

She certainly had options now, with Thaddeus likely to propose, and Jake contemplating a future with her. She only had to know her heart.

CHAPTER THIRTEEN

A pony is a childhood dream. A horse is an adult treasure.
—Rebecca Carroll

Delia thanked Willamena for preparing ham and cheddar cheese sandwiches on freshly baked rolls. She'd also made a potato salad with bacon crumbles, a dozen pickled eggs, a peach cobbler, and lemonade. The girls followed Delia toward the creek, and she smiled to see their uncle sitting at the base of a tree near their picnic site, waiting for them, a book open in his lap.

On closer inspection, she realized he read from a tattered and worn Bible, its leather edges and binding frail from use. He set the book aside to help her spread the quilt and serve the meal, but Delia's eyes kept returning to his Bible. Jake reminded her of her father and her maternal grandfather, Reverend William Spencer, a retired preacher. Both had frequently read from the Holy Scriptures. Delia held them in great admiration for it, knowing they absorbed divinely inspired and infallible truths.

The girls plopped down on the quilt, and soon they'd prayed and eaten their fill of delicious foods. Jake must've eaten a half dozen of the pickled eggs. And he'd asked for a second helping of peach cobbler. The girls had loved the sandwiches. And Jake had told her of his good news. He'd finally found a jockey for Horizon.

Delia explained the corn hole game to them after the meal, but Ruby had grasped the concept at once. Ella and Mary followed her to toss the little burlap bags filled with dried corn kernels into the holes on the elevated board Nathaniel had set up.

"Thank you for all the help you've given us. I've made a small deposit into your bank account in town so you can't say no, as I know you would if I try to hand you a bank draft." Seated beside her on the quilt, Jake gave her some wooden plates as she returned items into the picnic basket. She opened her mouth to protest, but he continued, holding up his hand. "No, I insist you be paid properly. Besides, the girls and I love the new kitchen curtains. I know you also finished most of the wallpapering for the one bedroom. You've saved me hours of aggravation. The girls and I couldn't have gotten through this week without you."

"I'm glad you like the curtains and the wallpaper." Delia sighed. "I suppose Pa told you I had an account at Sullivan Savings & Loan."

"Right you are." Jake grinned while they watched his nieces take turns tossing the little bags of corn toward the holes in the board. "I've never seen this game before. They really seem to like it. Why do they call it corn hole?"

"The little bags are filled with corn kernels. The popularity of the game is spreading like wildfire in Kentucky. Pa says some German immigrants brought it here. Some say Ohioans had it first, and others say Kentuckians did." Delia placed the crock of lemonade into the basket and closed the lid. "But I think we had it first."

"The girls are certainly enjoying it," he remarked. "They are taking turns without arguing."

Ruby came running over to the blanket, shading her eyes from the sun as she pointed toward the long line of fencing on the other side of the drive enclosing one of the Velvet Brooks pastures. "See how many horses are all around this place? Uncle Jake, I want you to teach me to ride. Not just a pony. A real horse, like that one!" Ruby pointed to a sleek chestnut mare.

"We'll see." Jake smiled with a knowing twinkle in his eyes. "I think it may be a bit too soon for you to ride a thoroughbred, but let me think on it. I do remember taking a strong interest in horses when I was about your age." He tapped her on the nose gently.

"Please, please, Uncle Jake. I know I can do it!" Ruby clasped her hands together in praying fashion.

Jake sat up straighter. "I did say I would think about it. You have my word."

"Thank you," Ruby replied, satisfied for the moment. She turned and ran back to the corn hole game with her sisters.

Delia kept her voice low. "I was about her age when I learned to ride, too, graduating from a pony to a thoroughbred. I started out with some trail riding and advanced to showmanship jumping shortly after. I still have some of my ribbons and trophies from the competitions. Bring her over when you think she is ready, Jake. I'd be more than happy to work with her. If she starts riding soon, she could be ready for the Velvet Brooks Vintage competition."

"Thank you for the generous offer. I do plan on starting her sisters out with a pony first, but Ruby talks about some riding lessons she had back in Richmond on a pony." Jake leaned closer. "I've thought about a name for our farm. Lottie Belle, after Charlotte, with an 'e' on Belle, for beautiful. Ma always called my sister 'Lottie Belle' as a child."

Delia clasped her hands together. "I love it. It's perfect."

"Do you think so?" He smiled at her joy.

"I do, and I know you'll have a wonderful future there, but I must admit, I'll miss taking care of the girls each morning, brushing their hair, driving with you to take them to school, holding sweet Mary in my lap, reading books to her, having breakfast together..." Her voice trailed away.

"Washing dishes, scraping wallpaper, slaving over a hot cook stove." He chuckled, but then he looked down, frowning. "It's no place for a lady like you, Miss Delia. You should be writing your stories, helping at the library, hosting those parties of yours..."

If only he knew she didn't sit around like a princess in a castle. "Life isn't always grand at Velvet Brooks. I work hard to help keep our home nice. Sometimes I even muck out the stalls, lay fresh hay inside them, water the horses, exercise them, brush them, oil and polish the saddles." She lifted her chin. "I've even been known to scrub the floors now and then. And in Pa's absence, to help handle certain business matters."

Jake's brows furrowed. "I'm sure you do a great many things at Velvet Brooks, and all with grace and style. I didn't mean to imply otherwise. You're a fine lady, Miss Delia. The finest I've ever personally known."

Delia's cheeks warmed again as she swept her lashes down. "Thank you, Jake." Then she glanced over at him. "And you, sir, are a fine country gentleman."

He chuckled, rubbing his chin for a moment. "A fine country gentleman.' I guess I hadn't thought of myself like that before. I believe you are the second person to classify me as such."

She couldn't tell him she knew Red had indicated something similar to him only a short while ago, but she found herself doing her part to encourage him. Would he have enough confidence to tell her about his feelings for her? Did she want him to? Yes, she did.

"Taking in three children while starting a new business venture and racing horses is an enormous undertaking. I'm sure you'll feel better once you've found a cook and a house-keeper." She could only hope he would see himself the way she and others did. "Your household will be running smoothly. And soon, Horizon will begin winning some races. You'll see. Everyone will know who Jake Williams is, and very soon. And I meant what I said—I'll miss spending more time with you and the girls."

Jake wore a sheepish grin, but it dissolved, a stern look replacing it. "Are you going to submit those stories to the *Lexington Gazette*?"

"I might. I've been thinking about it. Perhaps under a pen name."

"I think you should use your own name. Everyone should know these are your stories." He fished around in his shirt pocket and produced a newspaper clipping, handing it to her. "I saw this in the local newspaper. There's a twenty-five-dollar prize for any writer who submits a short story, a poem, an arti-cle, or an essay if accepted by the senior editor at the *Lexington Gazette*. They're offering the prize every month for submis-sions. Let me know when your first story is published, will you?"

"You seem awfully confident about someone choosing to publish my scribbles, but I've never won anything." Reluctance and doubt wavered in her voice as she glanced at the clipping, her hands trembling. "I tried to win the debutante of the year, but one of the Sullivans always seemed to win. And I tried out for a leading role in a Jane Austen play and lost it to a Sullivan as well."

He scoffed. "Sounds like the Sullivan pocketbook has been working behind the scenes."

"I hadn't thought of that before, but I suppose it is possible." Delia furrowed her brows.

Had Harold Sullivan made donations to her finishing school to secure titles and roles for his daughters and nieces? Her losses in those situations had caused her days and weeks of agony. Had she known he may have paid the administrators in exchange for the prized positions, she might not have agonized so much. No wonder Veronica had shrugged it off so easily when her turn had come to enter society as a debutante and she hadn't earned the coveted titles or roles either. Her older sister had likely known Harold's monetary influence and position in society reached far and wide. Stunned, she hardly heard Jake's words.

"You won't know if you don't try. If they don't accept your first submission, keep trying until they accept one. And I'm curious about something else. Why do you like this Thaddeus Sullivan fellow? Though I beg you to forgive my impertinence for asking."

"Maybe I will take your submission advice, but I can't answer the second question today. It would take me too much time to explain, and we have three other sets of ears present. But I, too, am curious about something. You have never told me what it is you like to do in your spare time, although I've answered that question for you." Maybe she could distract him from the topic of Thaddeus.

"Me?" Jake turned toward her, brows going up. "Let's see. When I'm not riding or taking a holiday to take in a horse race, I like fishing, boating, and reading. Uncle Caleb, the one I told you about before, spurred me along in my studies. Along with my parents, he helped me cultivate a love for books, but there were only so many I could bring from New York on the train. I did manage to bring most of my sister's books from Richmond and my brother-in-law's medical books. I have a few of my favorites from home here, too, and I very much enjoyed the books you brought me."

"Did you finish reading all of them?" She turned back from a glance at the girls with an arched brow.

His lips twisted into a grin. "Devoured them. Already returned them too."

"Father has a well-stocked library if you wish to borrow any books, and of course, we have the growing library in Lexington." A shout drew her attention as Ella and Mary both tried to pick up the same canvas bag. "What do you say we join the girls? I challenge you to beat me at corn hole. The best score of three tosses each shall be the victor." Delia jumped to her feet and pulled him up from the quilt, making him laugh as she led him to the game where his nieces swarmed around them, squealing with joy to have them join in the fun. "All you have to do is toss these bags of corn into the hole worth the most points. Lucky for you, I don't have good aim."

"Ah, then maybe I have a chance of winning since I haven't any aim either." He stood nearby with a raised brow as she accepted a handful of the bags from Ruby.

Delia took a considerable amount of time getting into the perfect position and practicing her aim by swinging her arm. She finally tossed a sack toward the board, and landed it in the center hole for fifty points. She jumped up and down, squealing and laughing at her good fortune, and on her first try in quite some time.

Jake narrowed his eyes and shook his head, a smirk on his face. "Pshaw!" He waved her victory aside, but his smirk turned into a sly grin. He extended his hand for another bag of corn kernels as Ruby slapped one into his hand. "Prepare to weep," he teased, winking at Delia.

She chuckled and tilted her chin upward.

Undaunted by her impressive first throw, he pretended to

wind his arm up like a baseball pitcher before tossing his bag well beyond the board, making them laugh. On his next throw, he jumped up high as he tossed the bag and earned his first score of fifty points. Ruby wrote down the number using some chalk on the slate Delia had given the girls and calculated each player's total points.

"This is good for her arithmetic." Jake winked at Ruby as she rolled her eyes.

Delia's turn came back around, and she scored another fifty points, stepping into the lead. "Now you see one of the many benefits of the game, not to mention the exercise." She nodded in Mary and Ella's direction as they ran toward the board, scrambling to see who could pick up the most bags.

Jake nodded, rolling up his shirt sleeves before his turn. "I see. An excellent game, indeed. They will sleep like rocks tonight."

"Indeed." Delia crossed her arms over her chest. "May I remind you, sir, this is your final throw?"

He scratched his head with a silly grin, pretending to have forgotten his strategy. "Oh, is it my turn?"

"Please just throw the bag, Uncle Jake. We're waiting for our next turn." Ruby emulated Delia, crossing her arms over her chest too. She tapped one foot on the grass.

Jake's face grew serious, and he squeezed his brows as if concentrating. He began winding his arm up like a pitcher again, making the girls laugh. Then he jumped up high and landed another center hole.

He made a show of bowing, and the girls, including Delia, clapped with glee. She hadn't laughed this much in ages. Next, Ella brought her a bag for her final throw while Ruby tabulated the score, although Delia suspected they'd lost count somewhere along the way. She tossed the bag and closed her eyes, only opening them at a squeal from Mary.

Ella jumped up and down. "Fifty points, Ruby. Did you write that down?"

Ruby looked up from the slate. "Miss Delia is the winner. She has one-hundred-and-fifty points."

"And what does the winner receive?" Jake gave Delia a sideways glance.

Delia wavered. "When my sisters and I played, usually the person keeping score decided."

"I get to decide?" Ruby grinned, tapping a finger on her face. Her eyes brightened. "That's easy. Miss Delia wins a kiss from Uncle Jake."

Ella nodded and clapped her hands in obvious approval.

"Kiss!" Mary echoed, clapping her hands to mimic Ella.

Looking around at their faces, how could she or Jake protest? Not only that, but why did it hold so much appeal? Delia chuckled nervously, but her brow arched. Would Jake resist this tempting turn of events? Or would he withdraw as he had before?

Jake grinned, gazing at Delia. "In that case..."

He stepped to her side in a swift moment before she could protest. Not that she would. For some wonderful reason beyond her comprehension, she desired his kiss.

"Ready?"

Was he asking her permission, like a gentleman? Oh my, yes! Was this really happening, or was she imagining it? She nodded, unable to find her voice, not even for the smallest squeak in response.

Wrapping his arms around her, he whispered, "Let's make this unforgettable." He leaned her back into a dip she could only describe as perfectly swoony...and then lowered his mouth to hers, planting a passionate kiss on her lips. Her giggles disappeared entirely as, for one blissful moment, she reveled in the joy of that kiss.

When he pulled her upright, he had rendered her speechless. Regaining her composure, she smoothed her skirts and searched his eyes. He returned her gaze with an equal measure of surprise and affection. She could certainly get used to this kind of attention.

And...oh dear. Sweet little cheers, squeals, and girlish laughter rose to their ears. They had witnesses. Three very talkative, joyful, small, but, quite possibly, powerful witnesses.

Had the kiss only been in fun, or was it the beginning of something more? Would he ask her to marry him the next time she saw him?

And what about Thaddeus? That was another very big *oh dear*. Surely, the girls wouldn't reveal this secret—at least for now.

CHAPTER FOURTEEN

I'm not afraid of storms, for I'm learning how to sail my ship.
—Amy March in *Little Women* by Louisa May Alcott

Jake left the picnic with a spring in his step. Was he walking too fast for his nieces to keep up? His long strides were perhaps a might too much for three little girls. But then, his whole world seemed to have sped up, including his relationship with Miss Delia Lyndon. Had not Boaz redeemed Ruth? More than anything, he wanted to redeem Delia from Thaddeus Sullivan. Not to spite Thaddeus, but to give Delia everything she deserved and spend the rest of his life loving and serving her.

Red's advice and that kiss had told him all he needed to know. The way she'd looked into his eyes as he held her. He stopped in his tracks, waiting for the girls to catch up as they bounded toward him and the front porch of Lottie Belle.

He stooped down to pick up Mary, swinging her into his

arms. "Ruby, take Ella by the hand. That's it. Hurry along, girls. We've much to do this evening."

"Are we going somewhere, Uncle Jake?" Ruby took Ella's hand in hers and skipped until she caught up to him, Ella running alongside her.

"Yes. We're going to town. Get your coats on. It may be dark before we are back." He climbed the steps to the porch. He stopped before the door, turning around to face his nieces while a plan began to form in his mind. "Wait, girls. Let's sit down here and have a little talk."

When they'd taken a seat around him on the top porch step, and with Mary on his knee, he took in the expectant faces, all turned on him. He offered a silent prayer for a little extra help from above.

"Let me ask you a question." Jake patted Ella's hair and then winked at Ruby. He tapped Mary on the nose. "How would you feel about...I mean, if I...how would you like...?"

Ruby put her hands on her hips. "Just spit it out, Uncle Jake."

He laughed, his shyness disappearing. "How would you feel if I were to ask Miss Delia to marry me?"

His two older nieces offered wide smiles, hope filling their eyes. Their smiles turned to enthusiastic nods.

Ruby toyed with one of her braids. "I think it would be wonderful. We like Miss Delia. We'd be a real family, like it felt this week, except for when she had to go home in the evenings."

Ella's face squinched, and she tilted her head to one side. "Does this mean she'll be our mother?"

Jake took a deep breath and then released a long sigh, his thoughts turning to his sister. "Sort of, though no one can ever replace your mother. But I think my sister, your ma, would approve of Miss Delia filling in as a sort of mother figure. And it did feel as if we were a family this week, and if Miss Delia says yes, it would probably feel like that every week."

"So, she might not say yes." Ruby's gaze turned downward.

"Well, we won't know if I don't ask. And we may need to give her plenty of time to think about her answer. But in the meantime, I'm going to need a wedding ring, and maybe a very nice dinner arrangement." He scratched behind his ear. "I'm thinking something romantic, a dinner for two. Perhaps right here on the front porch tomorrow evening after you are all tucked in bed. Your nanny will be home by then, so you can have an early dinner with her in the kitchen. And I'll invite Miss Delia to a private, *quiet* dinner." Had he placed enough emphasis on the word *quiet*?

Ruby nodded and her lips curved up. "I think your plan is good."

"Just good?" What could a nine-year-old see that was faulty about his plan if she only considered it good?

Ruby cocked her head to one side. "You need flowers. You should send her some roses. That's what our pa did when he wanted to tell Ma he loved her extra special. We can help set the table for you. But Uncle Jake, maybe the nanny should do the cooking."

Jake chuckled. "I agree. Miss Delia deserves something extra special. Now I'll hitch up the team while you fetch your coats. We'd best hurry. Time's a'wastin'..."

The girls scrambled inside while he headed to the barn, whistling a tune. He simply had to rescue Delia from her beau. Last week had left his heart full to the brim with love, joy, and happiness. Had she felt it too?

Ruby had described it best when she'd mentioned the word *family*. Did Delia hold the same love in her heart for all of them? It was an *all* kind of thing, for certain. He had a home to offer, his protection, faith to guide them, a heart full of love and admiration for her, and three little girls who would adore her. Would it be enough to win her hand?

If he didn't take a chance by asking her to marry him, he'd never know.

~

Later the evening of the picnic, Delia found a spot on a bench in the rose garden to ponder the answer to Jake's question about why she liked Thaddeus. If she could figure that out, perhaps she would know what to do about the romantic opportunities before her. Jake intrigued and attracted her, but she still had a special place in her heart for Thaddeus.

Thaddeus knew horses and everything about racing. Their families had much in common. And he had rescued her from awkward social situations or unwanted attentions on several past occasions, on top of courting her with gifts and romantic outings.

Mama came out onto the rear porch with a large bouquet of flowers in her hands. Red roses? Joining Delia on the bench, her mother handed her the bouquet. "These beautiful roses are for you from the florist in Lexington, just delivered a few moments ago with a note. I didn't read it, but I am guessing they are from your Thaddeus. Look how exquisite they are. I can only imagine how much he paid for them."

"Oh, my goodness. Such a grand bouquet of blooms!" The second in under a week. "They are glorious, aren't they? There must be two dozen here." Delia took in the scent of the blossoms, wrapping her arms around the enormous arrangement. "I'll read the card later."

Mama rested her gaze on some of the daffodils in bloom in the flowerbed across from the bench. "I think Thaddeus has missed riding with you in the mornings since you've been caring for Jake's nieces. Speaking of them, how did the picnic go? Did the girls enjoy the corn hole game?"

"They loved it. Ruby knew how to play. She said her parents used to play it with them in Richmond before their passing. She wants to learn to ride horses, but Jake isn't sure she's ready. I told him to bring her over when he feels she is and I would help her learn some things about showmanship riding. I'll miss helping them out each day."

"Maybe your time with Jake and the girls has spurred Thaddeus on." Mama tipped her head toward the bouquet. "Judging by those roses."

"Maybe so." Delia nodded, unsettled, but without being able to explain or admit it to her mother. Why did it excite her less than it might have before she'd met Jake?

Her mother rose with a contented sigh. "To be young, the whole world ahead, and in love again. Well, I'm heading upstairs to turn in early and read. Sleep well, dear, and I'll see you in the morning."

"See you in the morning." Delia watched her mother leave and turned her attention to the card nestled in the roses.

Opening the envelope, she read the card tucked amongst the fragrant blooms. *Dearest Delia, please dine with me tomorrow evening. I'll pick you up at seven. Yours truly, Jake.*

The flowers were from *Jake*? He intended to take her on an outing?

A smile played on her lips at the prospect. But, oh dear, Thaddeus would call on her tomorrow too. Would offering him tea in the parlor be sufficient? Could his earlier offering of daffodils indicate that he planned to finally ask her to marry him again?

And where would Jake escort her to dine? It sounded as if when he left their picnic, Jake had hitched up the wagon and gone to town to order flowers. What else might he have planned? She could hardly wait to find out.

Delia's stomach tightened. She had to figure out what her answer would be. She had to answer Jake's question about why she and Thaddeus were together.

Her mind rushed back to a moment at the piano when Aunt Eliza had cornered her, in the room facing the very garden where she now sat. Had she been about twelve? Just returned from a birthday party for the Sullivan twins, excited about the fact her party dress had matched Mary Louise's. When her aunt had asked if she'd enjoyed the party, she'd babbled about the many wonderful gifts Percy and Mary Lou had received, the delicious cake, and the matching dresses she and Mary Lou had worn. She couldn't recall exactly why her aunt had been at Velvet Brooks, or how it had come about that Mary Lou had a dress to match hers, but she could recall those words her aunt had spoken. "My dear niece, I don't care how many ponies your pa buys you or how many pretty dresses you wear. You don't hold a candle to the Sullivan girls, and you never will."

Aunt Eliza's smug and cutting words showed how little she thought of her own family, and particularly her own niece. How dare she make such a proclamation, and behind the back of Eleanor Lyndon, her own sister! Did her aunt dislike her sister's children because she had never married? Mama had said Aunt Eliza didn't consider herself pretty enough to attract a husband, but her aunt's self-esteem issues, or her marital status, didn't excuse the matter in her mind.

Delia had learned to forgive Aunt Eliza over the years, but why did she still feel like the inadequate twelve- or thirteen-year-old girl on the day her aunt had delivered the crippling blow, rending her heart? Aunt Eliza's statement had echoed in Delia's mind until some days, she thought she might drown in it.

Why did she still care? The words had been spoken long ago. But how did one forget such harsh words spoken with such vile cruelty? She'd certainly tried, reminding herself of the old saying about sticks and stones, but she'd not grown a backbone thick enough to repel Aunt Eliza's words. Not while living in Veronica's shadow, nor while living in the shadow of the fashionable Sullivan girls at every turn.

Even Gladdie always had a vivacious and bubbly personality, the darling and happy baby of the family—at least, until Clay stole her happiness. Delia prayed Gladdie would recover, and it couldn't happen soon enough. Her younger sister grew stronger with each passing day, but still, as the middle daughter, Delia didn't have Veronica's sass or confidence or Gladdie's joyful nature. Unsure of what she had to offer the world, she hid among the books in the library and beneath large hats, averting her eyes from strangers.

She heaved a sigh and looked toward the tree line becoming less visible in the dusk, blinking tears away. The back door closing made her jump.

Martin approached with her shawl in his hands. "Here you are, Miss Delia. Your mother asked me to bring your shawl. Would you like me to put those flowers in water for you?"

Delia recovered quickly and accepted the shawl, exchanging it for the bouquet of roses. "Thank you. Yes, if you could put the flowers in a vase and set them in my bedroom, I would very much like to wake up to see them in the morning."

The butler surveyed the roses, holding them at a distance with both hands. "Certainly, miss. Such beautiful roses. I've heard Churchill Downs is going to make a horseshoe-shaped wreath of roses for the Derby victor."

"Someone at Mother's dinner party mentioned the horseshoe wreath of roses. They're calling it the 'Run for the Roses' now. I can hardly wait to see how Gold Dancer, Glory, Midnight Sunburst, and Horizon will perform at the Phoenix Stakes and the Derby. Hard to believe Pa is entering three horses this year, and Jake told me Pa has set up a campaign for his horse. I'll be cheering them on, and Thaddeus's horse, too, of course, Bluegrass Blaze. Five horses we know and dearly love." Symbols of her current confusion.

He nodded. "I've already purchased my tickets. Don't stay out too long. We can't have you coming down with a chill." The butler hurried away, likely anxious to retire after a long day's work.

It amazed her how their employees operated in the background, churning out tasks almost effortlessly, it seemed. She could only describe her life as beautiful...most of the time. She loved Velvet Brooks and her childhood. The farm meant a great deal to her and to all of the Lyndon family. Three generations, beginning with her grandfather, Colonel Lyndon, had worked hard to build it. How Mama managed so many aspects of its household workings made her marvel, as did how Pa kept the farm turning a tidy profit. One day, it would fall to her and her sisters to continue the success of Velvet Brooks. Maybe that was why her parents wanted her to marry a Sullivan.

Everything the Sullivans touched turned to gold.

A match between the Lyndons and Sullivans would result in a powerhouse generation of horseracing royalty.

And there it was—her reason for wanting to marry Thaddeus. Even deeper than the affection for him their shared memories had created. If Thaddeus chose to marry her and make her a Sullivan, his love for her would finally disprove and dispel her aunt's unkind estimations.

Gladdie stepped into the garden wearing a grin a mile wide, the third person to interrupt Delia's thinking session. Her sister scooted onto the bench beside her, smoothing her skirts as she settled in, pulling her shawl close.

"I thought you'd gone to bed early like Pa and Mama. Why are you grinning like a Cheshire cat?" Delia glanced over at Gladdie.

"Maybe I happened to step inside your bedroom to admire some vibrant daffodils and happened to read a certain note from a certain Sullivan gentleman. And then I saw some red roses from a certain gentleman named Jake."

"You're positively rotten." Delia laughed softly as she shook her head.

"I know I am, but aren't you excited? You know this means Thaddeus and maybe Jake are likely going to propose tomorrow evening." Gladdie's smile exuded glee and genuine happiness for her. Then her brows furrowed. "What are you going to wear?"

"I have no idea what to wear," Delia admitted.

"You should wear your best white dress, the one with the blue sash. You *are* going to say yes, aren't you? It's the second chance you've been longing for, unless Jake Williams has turned your head."

"I admit, Jake has turned my head, but Thaddeus and I have a history deeper than the Grand Canyon. I've waited for months for this moment, and I hardly know Jake. Do I really want to throw away all I have established with Thaddeus?" Not to mention, the influence and position becoming a Sullivan would afford. She could become a benefactress to all sorts of causes.

"Then it's settled. You'll be so happy. I can visit you at Sullivan Hill, and we'll have tea every day in a glorious mansion."

"It's not settled. I plan to keep praying." She had prayed endlessly about her dilemma without hearing an answer. Yet she refused to give up. She wound one of her curls around her finger. "I'm not leaving this bench until I'm sure."

"If God wants you to marry Jake, the Lord will find some way to get your attention." Gladdie sighed. "I do believe our newcomer is a godly man with a solid work ethic."

"I agree. Jake is a godly man. Maybe it's what has me rethinking everything. Thaddeus has faith, too, but he's quiet about it. He's more likely to talk about a horse than God."

"True." Gladdie chuckled and rose. "Good night, Delia. Don't sit out here much longer. I'm going upstairs to get under the warm covers with a good book." Her sister hurried away.

Gladdie had put her finger on one of Delia's biggest concerns. Jake appeared to have a much stronger faith than Thaddeus. As impressive as that might be, she couldn't wait for him forever to profess his feelings for her. She'd waited on Thaddeus long enough. If she let much more time pass, she took a chance on becoming a spinster like Aunt Eliza. Would her heart turn into something ugly? Would she despise everyone as her aunt seemed to?

But with Jake, yet a stranger in comparison to her beau, she would have not only his great love and admiration, but the love of those three little girls, giving her purpose—as well as the prospect of having her own children. Their household would be large from the onset. Hadn't she always wanted a big family?

And with Jake, she had a feeling his love would free her to do things she had never imagined before, such as pursuing the publication of her writing. Hard work and sacrifice might accompany a life with Jake, but with the household managed properly, she could see great contentment in store.

Would he pursue her, or would he continue to find her situation too complicated because of Thaddeus and his family?

She sighed beneath a dark, silent sky full of stars. Why shouldn't she marry her childhood sweetheart, knowing it could give her peace for the first time in years? But why did the idea of marrying Jake seem as though it could free her from the Sullivans altogether and bring an end to years of torment? Two different futures stared at her, and with both in reach, what did the Lord want her to do?

CHAPTER FIFTEEN

There is no fear in love; but perfect love casteth out fear:
because fear hath torment. He that feareth is not made perfect
in love.
—I John 4:18

Saturday, April 4, 1903

At five-thirty in the morning while the girls were still asleep, Jake leaned over the rails of the one-mile oval racetrack at Velvet Brooks with Mr. Lyndon at his side, a stopwatch in both of their hands as Brady Danford, astride Horizon, leaned in low over the mane to bring him into the homestretch for the final quarter mile. The new jockey and Jake's horse moved as one, making it clear that Horizon had warmed up to Brady since yesterday's introduction.

Horses had instincts, and he deducted from their current performance that the horse would enjoy working with his rider.

Perhaps they could indeed obtain a victory despite the short time of training left on their schedule. Racing day approached, and all he could do now was follow the plan Mr. Lyndon had mapped out with Red Brickman and pray for the best results.

When horse and rider passed the quarter-mile marker, Jake consulted his stopwatch. "Three seconds better than yesterday."

Mr. Lyndon nodded approvingly, squinting in the gleam of the early-morning sunrise. "If Horizon keeps up this kind of performance, he should do well at his debut."

Jake cleared his throat, mustering all of his courage for the delicate topic on his mind. "Before the day gets away from us, there's something I'd like to ask you, Mr. Lyndon." Jake removed his hat, turning toward Delia's father. Worst case scenario, her pa might say no.

"Sure, what is it, son?" Mr. Lyndon nodded toward Red Brickman, who then signaled for the next horse and jockey to step into place to begin a practice race. Then he leaned toward Jake.

Jake's shoulders relaxed a tad. It did help some that he'd called him *son*. Best to dive right into it. "Mr. Lyndon, I'd like to ask for your approval and blessing before I ask Delia for her hand in marriage. I realize there's another fella in the picture, and I'm unsure of your arrangement with him. Not to mention, since I haven't known her for very long, I have no idea if she'll say yes. But sir, although it's been a whirlwind, I've fallen deeply in love with her."

Silence passed before Mr. Lyndon turned to face him instead of the track, though he had kept his ear bent toward Jake. Was he going to tell him to remove his horse from the property? Ask him to keep away from his daughter? Jake held his breath for what seemed an eternity, but in reality, consisted of merely seconds ticking by.

Mr. Lyndon looked down as he removed and straightened his cap, likely digesting Jake's words. Then he put it on again and pushed the brim upward. "Yes, there is another fella in the picture. He's been dragging his feet, if you ask me, and to some degree for reasons unbeknownst to me, I think my daughter is too. They've a long history. Not all of it smooth, as you know." He rested his hand on the rail. "Despite that, as you've settled into our community, Mrs. Lyndon and I have thought that you and Delia might make a fine couple. If Delia says yes, you'll have our blessing. I wish I could tell you I knew she'd say yes, but in truth, her heart remains a mystery to me. In fact, I find women in general a complicated and beautiful mystery."

Jake chuckled. Had her pa really agreed? He had! He should refrain from dancing a celebratory jig. Instead, he aimed for something more dignified. "A complicated and beautiful mystery. I agree with you there. Maybe it's what I love so much about Delia. And thank you, sir. Having your blessing means a great deal to me. I risk making an enemy of Thaddeus Sullivan. That aside, I do hope she'll say yes. You'll be among the first to know when and if she does."

Delia's pa smiled warmly and shook hands with him, a twinkle in his eye. "Sometimes enemies can't be avoided. In the end, the important thing to Mrs. Lyndon and me is that our daughter is happy, loved, protected, and settled in a secure marriage. And on that note, I'll see you later. I promised my wife I'd be at the breakfast table before seven, and our farm manager still wants me to look at a horse that may need veterinary care. Probably ate something that disagreed with him while grazing. I look forward to hearing how this works out with our Delia."

Jake nodded. "I do too. Thank you again, sir."

Mr. Lyndon headed toward the big horse barn to meet up with Hank Parker, the man who kept meticulous notes regarding each horse on the property. Jake breathed a sigh of relief. There went one of the finest horseracing minds he'd ever met, perhaps in all of Kentucky, and someone he could continue to learn from if he stayed on his good side. Step one of his long list of things to do before the day was out could be crossed off. Now, he had to show up in style and win Delia's heart with an extra romantic proposal.

Maybe after he cooked breakfast for himself and the girls, they'd make a stop at the farm up the road selling a team of horses and a nice roomy carriage he'd seen. Big enough to transport four or five passengers from the train to Lottie Belle, it sure would come in handy for a country inn like he envisioned. Would Delia approve?

And he had to pick up Nanny Philips at the train station and convince her to cook something amazing for tonight's meal on the front porch where he would pop the question.

Please let her say yes, Lord. Could You be giving me a whole new life and a wife too?

∼

"Delia! There you are. Wake up!" Urgency in Gladdie's voice startled Delia out of slumber.

Where was she? Oh yes. Father's library. She'd fallen asleep on the sofa near the fireplace.

"At least you are dressed properly." Gladdie sighed, crossing the room and stepping behind Pa's desk to peer out one of the front windows through the lace panels hung between forest-green velvet drapes. "Your guests are here."

Groaning, Delia recalled her decision not to sleep last night to prevent any bad dreams from clouding her judgment when Thaddeus arrived. She'd tutored some children that morning, helping them with their reading lessons. And now, she could hardly keep her eyes open. If only she could tell him to come again in a few more hours so she could go back to sleep.

Sitting up on the sofa, she yawned, stretching her arms above her head. "Did you say 'guests'? Who did Thaddeus bring with him? A chaperone? We have no need of a chaperone. There will be plenty of servants and family around. We're probably just having tea in the parlor."

"Jake."

"Jake is early?" Delia blinked. Was it seven o'clock already? Oh goodness, she really must shake herself awake.

"No, silly goose. Thaddeus has arrived in his motor carriage. I think Jake has arrived on his horse. Let me look again." Gladdie turned back to peer through the window.

"Jake didn't have to ride Horizon across the street." Delia began smoothing her dress and patting her hair into place.

"It's not Horizon. Jake has arrived in a fine carriage, pulled by two beautiful black stallions." Gladdie continued to stare out of the window. "Both men are carrying flowers. They are at the door, about to knock."

"Oh. Jake needs a fine carriage to pick up guests at the train station for his boardinghouse, whenever it opens. Perhaps he rented or purchased it." Delia rose from the sofa. She hurried to the little oval mirror near the doors leading to the hall which, thankfully, remained closed. Martin could seat the gentlemen in the sitting room while she made herself presentable. She wore the white lace dress with the blue sash, the one her sister had recommended. Glancing in the mirror, she pinched her cheeks for color.

"They are staring each other down now. Oh dear..."

"What?" Delia glanced at her sister in alarm.

"Thaddeus has stepped in front of Jake, pushing him back from the door. And now Jake has stepped in front of him. And now Thaddeus is pushing Jake aside." Gladdie issued each statement with the urgency of a commentator at a horse race. "I do hope Martin hurries to answer the door, but they haven't knocked yet." Gladdie sighed with relief. "Ah, there is Martin opening the doors before Thaddeus punches Jake or Jake punches Thaddeus. He must have heard them arrive. It's a good thing Pa and Mama went to town. This is all very unexpected."

Delia grimaced. "Indeed. Perhaps I should have sent a note around requesting Thaddeus come a good deal earlier."

Martin knocked on the library door and peeked inside, informing Delia he'd led Jake to the dining room and Thaddeus to the sitting room.

"Thank you, Martin. Will you serve tea for Thaddeus?" Delia arched her brow.

"Not for Jake, ma'am?"

"On second thought, yes, tea for Jake, too, but we'll be leaving shortly for dinner." As soon as she could get rid of Thaddeus. How terrible that sounded, but alas. She was in a dire predicament. Jake expected her to dine with him. "In case it takes a while to speak with Thaddeus, it may be a good idea to serve them both tea."

"Very good, ma'am." Martin closed the door to complete his mission.

Delia spun around to face Gladdie. "I need your help."

"I'll say." Gladdie chuckled, a hand on her hip.

"Could you—?"

Her sister interrupted, holding up a hand. "Entertain Jake while you speak with Thaddeus?"

Delia gulped, nodding.

"Say no more. I will do my best. And I do hope you can hurry Thaddeus along since Jake will be waiting."

Delia frowned. "I can only try. Thaddeus probably won't stay long. He is always gallivanting off to visit his friends, but I confess, I am entirely unsure of his intentions."

This was a disaster, but if she could stay calm, perhaps she could remedy the matter with a little finesse and tact. Could she have an excuse ready? She could perhaps admit to having dinner plans without offering details, but then he'd already seen Jake. Maybe she could feign illness. A headache?

"Who will you greet first?" Gladdie tilted her head to one side.

"Jake." She had to at least greet him, if only briefly, but then she would give Thaddeus her full attention first.

"All right. Lead the way, Miss Popularity." Gladdie gestured toward the door.

"Popularity is overrated, trust me. It only has me in a complete dither." Delia drew in a deep breath, and opening the door, peeked into the hall. No sign of either guest. "The coast is clear."

She led them into the hall. They crossed to the dining room.

Delia drew in another quick breath. Now was not the time for the shakes. She needed to emulate the confidence her sisters possessed.

Breezing into the room, she smiled. "Hello, Jake." Delia bobbed a quick curtsy. It seemed like the thing to do. "I'll just be a moment...or two...and then I'll return for our outing. Gladdie has offered to pour tea for you in my absence."

Jake, standing with his hands behind his back and looking handsome in his best suit, bowed his head. "Of course."

Delia shot a helpless look toward her sister, and leaving her to pour tea once Martin arrived with a tray, she ducked into the hallway again, turned left, and headed for the sitting room.

She sailed into the sitting room, doing her best to remain poised. "Thaddeus, how nice to see you. I received the beautiful daffodils you sent. Thank you so much."

He stopped pacing between the two sofas facing each other and immediately dropped to one knee, holding a bouquet of brightly colored spring blooms toward her. "Delia..."

Was he truly on bended knee? Why didn't her heart flutter as she had always thought it would when this moment finally arrived? Nonetheless, she drew near to him, allowing him to take her hand in his, accepting the flowers with her other hand. She breathed in the scent, admiring the velvety and colorful petals of snapdragons, hyacinths, and tulips.

But then the door creaked open behind them. Delia glanced over her shoulder to find Martin entering the room with the tea tray.

He stopped in his tracks. "Oh, pardon me..."

"It's all right, Martin. You may set it anywhere." Delia lifted her chin, doing her best to maintain a soft voice and the kind of calm and dignity her mother would under any awkward circumstances.

Thaddeus shifted on his knee with a slight grimace.

Martin deposited the tea on the table beside the armchair where Mama normally served tea from near the fireplace. He scurried away as fast as a flea landing on a cat.

"Now, where were we?" She offered a weak smile, returning her attention onto her beau.

Thaddeus cleared his throat and began again, wobbling a little. "Delia, sweetheart, I've come to propose again. I know it didn't work out exactly as we'd planned the first time around, but this time, I am convinced we will find happiness together. Do say you'll marry me, and as soon as possible. I am besotted with you and cannot wait much longer to hold you in my arms forever."

She swallowed hard. What could she say to convince him she needed more time? If he truly loved her, wouldn't he wait? But before she could respond, Thaddeus began patting his suit, searching for something.

"Oh, and I have your ring." He reached inside his suit pocket and produced the ring she'd once worn so proudly, until that dream. He slid it onto her finger.

With her mind flitting about, trying to determine how to convince him to wait for her answer, she couldn't comment about the changes he'd made to the ring yet, but the new pearls clustered on each side did cause her brow to arch in surprise. Pa always said honesty was the best policy. She took a deep breath. "Thaddeus, I've waited for this moment for a long time. It means a great deal to me that you trust me again enough to ask me to marry you, and I need you to trust me a little more, to give me just a bit more time to think this over."

There. She'd said it honestly, and from the heart.

His mouth dropped open, and disappointment flashed through his eyes. At least he hadn't asked about Jake's presence in the house. Not yet, anyhow. Was that anger that made his chest puff out as he rose from bended knee?

"How much more time, Delia?" Thaddeus raked a hand through his hair.

"I...uh...I don't know exactly. Not too terribly long." How could she calm him? "Come, let's have a cup of tea together and discuss whose parlor we might marry in if I say yes." She spun away from him.

"I don't want tea, Delia. I want you. We can marry at Sullivan Hill's parlor or right here at Velvet Brooks before summer's end." Thaddeus reached for her hand, pulling her back into his arms. He searched her eyes. "It's Jake, isn't it? He's gone and confused you."

She bit her lower lip. She wasn't ready to discuss Jake with him.

"I saw the red roses he brought you when we were on the porch."

More red roses? He must've been holding them behind his back earlier. Delia flushed.

"Red roses are given to women for reasons of love, Delia, not to thank someone for tending the children, if that's what you're going to tell me. He's going to propose, isn't he?" Thaddeus scowled, his brows furrowing.

"I don't really know. I've only briefly said hello to him. But if he does propose, don't I have every right to consider the best possible situation for me, Thaddeus? You have dragged your feet for a very long time, and if you think about it from my perspective, I'll be placing my life and entire future into someone else's care if I marry. It's an enormous decision for a woman." Delia bit her lip and lowered her gaze. Would he understand?

No. When she peeked up at him through her lashes, tremendous disappointment still filled his eyes. To be expected. She drew herself up taller and squared her shoulders. "And I'm certain you don't want me to rush into this now that you have finally proposed and then have me end up running away again..."

Thaddeus sighed. "All right. I will wait for your answer. Just don't keep me waiting forever. I do hope you like the engagement ring and that you'll wear it."

"I shouldn't accept this until I decide." She began removing the ring.

He placed his hand over hers. "No, I want you to wear it. Keep me close to your heart until you decide."

"All right." She smiled, looking at the ring again. "I did notice you've added a cluster of pearls to each side. I like it very much. It's beautiful."

His hands on her forearms, he gave her a quick peck of a kiss on the forehead. "I'm very glad you like it. I'll probably see you next at the race. We can sit together."

"That would be nice. I can hardly wait to see how Bluegrass Blaze does."

The mention of his horse made him perk up a bit. "I'm very sorry to rush away, but I am expected to attend the Lexington Jockey Club meeting this evening. All sorts of things to do for the big race, and my father wants me at his side. There is some talk about ensuring the bookmakers are taking a fair cut and no more of the money wagered than deserved due to accusations of corruption. I'll probably see your father there. You understand, right?"

"Oh, yes, of course. I've heard about these concerns. Pa is very passionate about making sure everything is above board and completely honest. I'd forgotten about the meeting. I understand." She smoothed the lapels of his suit. "It's important that these issues are handled properly."

"Thank you. I'm glad you understand." Thaddeus strode toward the door. He turned and blew her a kiss and then exited, closing the door with a thud that made her startle. Was some part of him angry with her delay? And no doubt, the fact he was leaving her in the company of his competitor added to his disgruntled mood.

All in all, despite the flash of anger she'd seen in his eyes and the slam of the door, he'd taken her utter ambivalence rather well. Better than she'd expected. He hadn't stayed for tea, but that was for the best. Concerns about dishonest and greedy bookmakers had begun to cause a growing anti-racing sentiment across the entire country. And now she didn't have to feign an illness. She was free to join Jake for dinner.

But a glance down at the ring on her finger made her bite her lower lip. Why didn't having this symbol of his love and his proposal make her heart soar as it once had? Though it was nice to see the ring upon her hand, *nice* might not be enough to capture her heart this time. And lately, she grew weary of Thaddeus's unpredictable temperament in contrast to Jake's even-keeled nature.

Presently, she had little time to consider the proposal. Another gentleman waited, and Gladdie would be running out of small talk by now. Probably best to set the flowers aside. She laid them on the end table. Clearly, having two suitors had its share of problems. Perhaps she should wear the ring on her other hand instead of her ring finger.

~

The roar of the motor carriage starting and then rumbling away with Thaddeus behind the wheel set Delia's nerves at ease. She breezed into the dining room with as much confidence as she could muster and a smile playing on her lips. "Good evening, Jake. Thank you for waiting. Are we ready for dinner?"

Jake rose from his seat, reaching for the bouquet of red roses Thaddeus had mentioned which were lying on the table. He looked so dapper in his suit, his hair pulled back into its usual ponytail tied with a leather cord. Where did he intend to take her in his new carriage? Would he propose too?

Delia turned toward Gladdie. "Thank you for pouring tea."

"You're welcome. Have fun at dinner." Her sister gave Delia a teasing smirk as she rose from the table and dashed away, leaving Jake standing at his seat.

He smiled warmly, fidgeting with his tie. Did he look a mite nervous?

She stepped toward him, clasping her hands playfully, her brow arched. "So...where are we going for dinner this evening?"

Did she really have him all to herself now? Visions of the passionate kiss they'd shared at the picnic flashed through her mind. Would he kiss her again this evening?

He cleared his throat and held out the roses. Oh dear, more flowers. "I thought we might dine in the privacy of my front porch, just the two of us. I know it's not a fancy restaurant, but you'll find I've had three charming little assistants."

Ruby, Ella, and Mary had helped him prepare a romantic dinner for two? What could be more delightful? "Oh, Jake. It sounds perfect." She breathed in the scent of the red roses.

"And these are lovely. Thank you. I'll just set them aside and get my hat and a wrap."

Moments later, she admired his new team of horses—two black stallions. He helped her into the carriage, and while he settled into the driver's seat beside her, she donned a pair of gloves, turning toward him. "Have you thought of names for them yet?"

He shook his head. "I may need some help there."

"I hope you didn't go to the trouble of purchasing them simply to take me across the road in style." She peeked over at him with another arched brow.

He gathered the reins in his hands and snapped them gently, urging the horses forward. "No, they're on the list, remember? But I did want to make this evening special."

She had trouble thinking of things to say on the short drive, so she made polite small talk, thanking him for the flowers he'd sent after the picnic. Why did her heart beat so fast?

When he'd parked the carriage in the drive before his house and helped her down, he led her to a small table on his front porch. She smiled, covering her mouth with her hand, her heart melting. The girls had done a splendid job. They'd spread the table with a white linen cloth and placed an arrangement of wildflowers in a tin pail for the centerpiece. Two candles flanked the pail, and although the silverware wasn't perfectly aligned, they'd made a valiant attempt.

"The girls made the place cards and drawings for you." Jake welcomed her to be seated with an outstretched arm, then drew out and held her chair.

She situated herself, taking in the covered plates, tent cards at both places, and the stack of scrolls—their drawings? And something smelled delicious under the covers on those plates.

"Oh, my goodness! This is so wonderful, Jake." Her eyes misted at seeing their names penciled in on their place cards, embellished with drawings of flowers. Hers read, *Miss Delia,* and his, *Uncle Jake*. The three scrolls, each tied with pink ribbon, waited beside her place setting.

He took the other seat, and she searched his eyes once he settled. "This is delightful. Did you do the cooking, or Nanny Philips?"

"Nanny Philips made us roasted chicken, stuffing, mashed potatoes, gravy, and spring peas." His brows formed an arch. "I hope you like everything."

Delia grinned, taking note of the basket of rolls and an apple tart nearby. "I do. I love everything you mentioned. I can't imagine I'll be able to eat all of it, but I will surely enjoy trying. That's quite a lot of cooking for someone who also took a train journey today. She'll be expecting a raise."

Jake laughed, but he covered her hand with his. "Shall we eat before it grows cold?"

She leaned toward the drawings. "Should I open these scrolls first?"

He tilted his head to one side. "Those are for later, I think. I'm told they go along with a very important question I'd like to ask, but I'm saving that until after we've eaten. I'll say a blessing, though."

"All right." With a thrill of excitement, she bowed her head, and he gave the Lord thanks for the meal and for bringing her into his life.

Delia swiped a tear from her eye and then followed his lead, removing the cover on her plate to reveal a delicious home-cooked feast. A happy tear, but it wouldn't do to shed tears on such an occasion.

Some soft, jazzy tune reached their ears as they began to eat —perhaps a record playing from a Victrola? She glanced over her shoulder and caught sight of the window nearest them, open a few inches. Had he purchased the Victrola, or maybe borrowed one? Goodness, he'd thought of everything. Even the sun setting in the distance seemed to cooperate, the sky painted in hues of peach, pink, and purple.

They chatted about how much the girls had enjoyed the picnic, Horizon's progress at the track, how the horse was warming up to his new jockey, and how delicious the meal tasted. Someone kept up with changing the records so romantic music never failed to swirl around them. Nanny Philips, perhaps? Surely, the girls were tucked into bed.

When it grew a little darker and they'd finished eating, Jake lit the candles. She'd never been more thankful for the large oak tree shielding them from the road, but no one passed by. She hadn't seen any little faces peeking out of the window at them either.

"And now, for my question. And then we'll dance, I hope." Jake pushed his chair back and rose from his seat, pulling a little velvet box from the inside pocket of his suit jacket. He opened it and placed it on the table where she could see a diamond ring flanked by two emeralds sparkling in the flickering candlelight.

Delia sucked in a soft breath.

His expression solemn, he knelt, and on bended knee, took her trembling hand in his. "I know we haven't known each other for very long...but I feel as if I've known you a lifetime after our week together at Lottie Belle."

Delia clasped her hand over her mouth, smiling. He had risen to the challenge, casting his concerns over her beau aside.

"I haven't yet told you how much I admire and love you, Delia. But I do. I love you more than the air I breathe. More than all that I own and all that I am. I can only hope you feel the same about me or will one day come to feel the same. Please say you will marry me. I will look after you, love you, guard you, and protect you all the days of my life. We can have as long or as short a courtship as you wish. Only say yes. Say you would like to build a life and a family with me—and my nieces, of course. I should mention, I did seek permission from your pa, and he said it would be up to you but has granted his blessing."

Delia's mouth felt permanently stuck open. She hadn't expected any of this to happen so soon in their short relationship. "Oh, Jake, I...I don't know what to say."

Jake rose and took his seat. "I didn't think you would have an answer yet. I'm aware you enjoy many benefits of life at Velvet Brooks. And this would be a life of hard work, but I will do everything in my power to give you the comforts you are accustomed to. In time, we will reach a similar point at Lottie Belle. I've been working on my budget. We could employ a cook and a housekeeper at first. Later, when we have regular customers, and if Horizon or our future horses do well on the track, perhaps a farmhand, a groom, and another housemaid. We will need plenty of help. Running a country inn is demanding."

She drew in a breath to respond, but he held up a hand. If only she could tell him she didn't mind if their life included hard work. Some dreams were worth fighting for, the way her family worked hard for theirs.

"No, do not answer me now. I know this is a surprise, and I must give you time to consider. Take the engagement ring, wear it, think about all I have said. Let me know when you are ready to tell me your answer."

"Oh Jake, I really shouldn't accept this until I'm sure..." Just as she'd told Thaddeus.

"No, hush. I want you to have it. I hope it fits." He slid the ring on her finger. It fit perfectly. He didn't seem to notice the ring Thaddeus had just given her which she'd moved to her other hand. What would she do with two engagement rings? Wear them both as the gentlemen insisted until she came to a decision?

He kissed her hand. Jake had melted her heart, as had his sweet nieces. He had given her much to consider.

"Thank you for giving me time to consider your proposal. I need to pray about everything." When he nodded, she relaxed and gave his hand a gentle squeeze. "Time to open the scrolls now?"

"Yes. They enjoyed making these for you." His warm smile, reaffirming his patience, helped ease more of her tension.

Gingerly, she reached for the first scroll. Mary's drawing, illegible, made them both smile. "I confess, I have no idea what Mary has drawn. Do you?"

He shook his head. "No idea. Maybe it's a flock of chickens."

She chuckled softly. How was it that Jake made her laugh so much?

Ella's drawing was of a little house with a family of five stick people, with her name at the bottom.

"Aw, look, Jake." She pointed to the heart Ella had drawn.

He placed his hand over his heart.

She opened Ruby's scroll next. It was more of a letter with a flower drawn beside the words she'd written. It read, *Just say yes, please. With love from Ruby.*

She sighed. "You're right. These go with your question, and they are so very sweet." Delia's eyes misted again. How would she decide? And how could she ever say no to Jake...or Thaddeus?

The record changed and a new tune began to play.

Jake grinned. "I like this song." He rose and held out his hand. "May I have this dance?"

Taking her hand, he pulled her onto her feet and led her to one side of the table. There, she leaned her head on his shoulder, breathing in his musky cologne, enjoying the way his strong arms held her close as they slow-danced to the music.

Two songs later, Jake tilted her chin upward. "May I kiss you, Delia?"

"Yes," she whispered without hesitation.

He kissed her softly on the lips, gently, and thoroughly. Oh dear. She melted in his embrace.

Delia had done what her parents had said, and she indeed had options as a result, but knowledge concerning the best choice for her future evaded her. And why couldn't she hear God's voice, directing her? Being with Jake seemed so right, but she desperately needed to know the Lord's answer lest she flee from her own wedding again.

CHAPTER SIXTEEN

I can make a General in five minutes, but a good horse is hard
to replace.
—Abraham Lincoln

Saturday, April 18, 1903
The Phoenix Stakes Race, Lexington Association Track

"Mama talks of little but the fact you have two proposals to choose from." Veronica sipped her hot tea as she and Delia observed a preliminary race from a clubhouse table near the windows at the Lexington Association's racecourse. The two of them had chosen to eat separately to have some sisterly time to discuss the decision Delia faced. Their parents, along with Gladdie, their spinster aunts, and the Spencer and Lyndon grandparents, enjoyed a leisurely lunch in a family dining room located in a different part of the clubhouse. "She would prefer you to have accepted one of your suitors by now, but she certainly doesn't want you to make a habit of running away on your wedding day."

A few weeks had passed since Delia had received the two marriage proposals.

Delia rested her chin on the palm of her hand and leaned forward. "What would you do?"

"If it were me, I'd go on a holiday away from everyone until I could clearly see who my heart missed more and for what reasons."

Delia arched her brow. "But where?"

"I don't know, but it's an enormous decision. I want you to be happy in a thriving marriage and family, as I am with Edward and our little Edward Junior." Turning to look out the clubhouse windows, Veronica slowly rose to her feet, biting her lower lip, her eyes glued to the track.

Their conversation forgotten in the excitement of the current race, Delia glanced out the window as a hush filled the room. A dozen horses and their riders thundered toward the clubhouse turn in hopes of crossing the finish line first. Delia easily spotted Pa's horse taking the lead as Charlie Ford, wearing Velvet Brooks's pink-and-yellow colors on his bright silk shirt, leaned over Gunpowder Fury's mane, urging him onward. Delia stood with her sister as some of the other guests in the ladies' dining area clustered around the windows for a better look.

The race for four-year-old horses proved Veronica's favorite bay still had the blood of a champion coursing through his veins. In an astonishing forty-five seconds, Gunpowder Fury crossed the finish line by a nose-length lead on a horse named Wild Walter. Veronica cheered, jumping up and down, and Delia joined in her happiness, both throwing their arms up in the air, elated at the victory they had witnessed.

"Pa will be so happy about this," Veronica said on an exhale as they settled into their seats to finish their luncheon.

"Yes, he will. Especially since Glorious Day Dreamer won his race today too. Wouldn't it be grand if Gold Dancer wins his?" Delia smiled to think of it.

Wild Walter came from Shady Oaks Farm in Tennessee. The owner, Mr. Ebhart, would be disappointed, but he would also respect a Lyndon win. He'd trained some of his horses at Velvet Brooks in his early days, before his farm had grown to its current size. After the horses slowed into a trot, Wild Walter's jockey reached between the horses to shake hands with Charlie Ford. Sportsmanlike conduct meant everything at the races, and Pa had taught his daughters to appreciate those kinds of gestures.

After finishing their luncheon of beef consommé, tomato cucumber salad, and half of a glazed meatloaf sandwich, Delia and Veronica joined Pa and the rest of their family in their box in the stands for the main race of the day, the Phoenix Stakes, which held the biggest purse for its winners. In the third row, Gladdie sat between Grandma and Grandpa Spencer, having volunteered to help Grandma Spencer navigate the crowds and tend to any needs she might have, which usually included helping Grandpa Spencer too. Perhaps fetching a cup of lemonade or reading the stats on the horses aloud to them from the program...

On the front row in the Lyndon box, Mama sat next to Pa, Jake, and Thaddeus. Pa chatted with both men as well as their grandfather, Colonel Lyndon, seated farther down the row beside Grandmother Lyndon. Aunt Eliza and Aunt Ida talked with Edward in the second row, and when Veronica sat next to her husband near their aunts, Delia's stomach churned. Aunt Eliza had reprimanded her earlier in the day in front of her family, saying Delia shouldn't run away from her choice of a groom this time. Her only saving grace was that Thaddeus and Jake hadn't yet arrived in the box when the remark had been made, long before their meals in the clubhouse.

The two men would expect her to return to the seat on the end of the front row between them. With Jake on one side and Thaddeus on her other, she could smile and do as Pa had said —make them earn her affection. When she reached her seat, they both stood until she had settled.

"Can I get you anything before the main race begins, Delia?" Thaddeus offered.

"Would you like some lemonade or popcorn, Delia?" Jake offered a warm smile.

Delia looked from one to the other. "I'm fine, gentlemen, but thank you." While it did bolster her confidence a bit to have her two suitors vying to please her, the main race was about to start. And although she'd somehow managed to accomplish what Pa had encouraged her to in having them earn her favor, shouldn't she try to keep the peace between them and diminish tensions while they waited on her decision? She turned her attention to the program in her hands, studying the competition entered in the day's feature race.

Charlie's pink-and-gold silk jersey stood out below. Jake's new jockey, Brady Danford, astride Horizon, wore a lime-green and blue silk jersey. In the middle of the horses, she recognized one of the Sullivans' four jockeys wearing their purple and white. Counting Thaddeus's entry, the Sullivan Hill horse farm had entered at least five horses in the day's races. She had to pay attention to distinguish them since each of their jockeys wore different patterns in their shirts but the same Sullivan colors.

When the gun shot sounded and the flag waved, the horses took off. Delia fought her tension as the powerful steeds began the race, their hooves thundering toward the clubhouse turn. A hush fell over the spectators. Fans resisted the urge to cheer too soon. Races could change drastically in the final stretch.

When the horses finished the clubhouse turn, she lifted a pair of binoculars to her eyes, watching with breathless anticipation as Horizon and four other horses fought for the lead going into the final turn. The crowd began cheering wildly, and Delia rose with everyone else in her box.

Coming out of the turn, for a few seconds, Bluegrass Blaze and Gold Dancer ran neck and neck, slightly ahead of Horizon and some other horse she didn't recognize. In that glorious moment where everything shifts in a race, blue and lime-green silk flashed as Brady shot forward on Horizon. The stallion had clearly decided he wanted to win the race, and win the race he did, by at least four or five lengths in a stunning finish. He brought the entire crowd in the stands to their feet. Gold Dancer came across the line second, and Bluegrass Blaze finished third.

Her family cheered, but she couldn't help noticing when Thaddeus's fists came down on the rails when his horse took third place. Elated about Jake's victory, she didn't have a second to spare in disappointment. In horseracing, one had to simply enjoy the outcome. She'd pegged Horizon from the start, knowing his spirit showed the courage of a champion. She nearly threw her arms around Jake, but with Thaddeus at her side, too, she curbed her enthusiasm.

"I'm so happy for you, Jake. I knew Horizon could do it," Delia said sweetly when the cheering subsided. And there wasn't much she could do about Jake wrapping his arms around her and lifting her off her feet. He made her laugh. He twirled her around and then set her down to offer a more respectable hug to her mother.

"Well done, Jake," Mrs. Lyndon said, a smile on her face.

"Red will be thrilled. He's down there heading toward the winner's circle to join Brady," Pa said. "Congratulations, Jake. What a remarkable finish!"

"Thank you for all of the help you've given me at Velvet Brooks, sir," Jake replied, shaking hands with her father.

"Congratulations, Jake," Thaddeus offered, also shaking

hands. He patted Jake on the back like a good sport. Thank goodness for his sportsmanlike conduct, despite the understandable disappointment in his eyes. Gold Dancer had finished in second place, so she could relate on some level.

"Time to head to the winner's circle. It's customary for those involved in training the horse to accompany the winner, so I'll proudly join you and show you the way. I know a shortcut we can take." Pa led Jake out of the box. "Your trophy will look nice displayed at Lottie Belle."

"I can't wait to tell the girls. Ruby will be so happy." Jake thumped Delia's father on the shoulder.

As she turned toward Thaddeus, Delia's spirit sank at the resentment flashing in his eyes while he glanced at Jake and then at her. How much of Thaddeus's gentlemanly congratulations were a show for her sake? Would he sulk all the way to the Kentucky Derby? Or just until she agreed to be his wife?

CHAPTER SEVENTEEN

Where in this world can man find nobility without pride, friendship without envy, or beauty without vanity? Here where grace is laced with muscle and strength by gentleness confined. — "Ode to the Horse" by Ronald Duncan, created for Horse of the Year Show

SATURDAY, APRIL 25, 1903
LOTTIE BELL FARM, LEXINGTON, KENTUCKY

Pounding on Delia's bedroom door startled her from a sound sleep into a frightful waking state. She sat up on one elbow, her eyelids heavy as she tried to force them open. Her monthly tea and hat-trimming party had taken its toll. She'd gone out of her way to invite a few extra ladies, helped Willamena bake apple tarts and cranberry orange bread, and the event had left an enormous mess in the dining room to clean. It'd taken her hours to return the room to normal and help with washing the dishes since Frances had an outing of her own to attend and Grace had her hands full with other chores. She'd fallen into a deep sleep hours before, but now she blinked in the darkness, wondering why someone pounded on her bedroom door.

"Fire! Everyone, wake up! Fire at Jake's farm!" Delia recognized Pa's voice. More pounding on her door. Then on Gladdie's door. "All hands on deck! Delia! Gladdie! Wake up!"

Fire? At Lottie Belle? No! Delia struck a match to light the oil lamp and read her clock. Shortly after two in the morning. Technically, Sunday morning, but Saturday, the middle of the night to her. *Lord, have mercy. Please don't let anything happen to Jake or those sweet little girls.*

She threw her covers aside, then grabbed her robe, putting it on as she flew out into the hall. Still tying the belt, she nearly collided with Gladdie, whose bedroom faced the front lawn of Velvet Brooks. She turned to the side to avoid the collision, slipping past her sister to the window.

Delia lifted the shade and spread the curtains wide open. Flames engulfed Jake's barn, dancing across the rooftop, each spike of the fire reaching higher toward the night sky. She froze for a few seconds, taking in the horrid sight. Her dream! What she now beheld was an exact replica of her dream, the one that had shaken her to the core, causing her to flee from Thaddeus at the altar. *Horizon!* Was Horizon at Lottie Belle or at Velvet Brooks tonight? Was Jake somewhere amid those flames, trying to put the fire out?

"My dream! My horrible dream..." Delia clasped a hand to her mouth as tears pooled in her eyes.

Gladdie, peering over her shoulder at the sight, put her arms around Delia's shoulders and gently but firmly turned her around. "We have to help Jake. Horizon is safe, here at Velvet Brooks, but we'll make sure on our way over to the barn. Get dressed as quickly as you can. We'll need to bring washtubs, buckets, or big pans from the kitchen. Anything to carry water from Jake's well."

Delia nodded wordlessly, stunned. She hurried across the hall, obeying Gladdie's quick commands.

Times like these, she wished her parents would allow a telephone at the farm. Jake didn't have one either. The Sullivans did, though. Maybe they could call the fire department. Had the Sullivans seen the flames yet? The fire lit up the sky, and surely, someone would have seen it, but not if they all slept soundly at Sullivan Hill.

Delia dressed as fast as she could ever remember dressing, but it seemed it took her forever to slip into an old work dress, apron, stockings, and boots. She hurried downstairs to the kitchen, Gladdie on her heels. Pa had awakened everyone. The whole household, half of them dressed in night clothes, headed across the street with pots and pans, buckets, and anything they could use to carry water.

Delia ran to the barn on the left of the property. She had to see Horizon for herself. After flinging the barn doors open with all of her strength, she ran down the wide aisle half out of breath to his stall. When he looked up, lifting his nose and casting sleepy eyes in her direction from the bed of thick hay where he lay safe and sound, she breathed a sigh of relief and ran for Cornflower Road.

There she quickly caught up to the others and learned Nathaniel Hartley, their farmhand at Velvet Brooks whose cottage faced Lottie Belle, had seen the flames first. He'd alerted those living in the cottages on the northwest side of the back forty to gather buckets and head to Jake's farm. Then he'd made a run for the main house to alert Pa. After, he'd gone toward Rose Glen, waking Edward and Veronica.

Among the first to arrive at Lottie Belle, Delia and her family found Jake frantically pumping water at the outdoor well.

Nanny Philips, Ruby, Ella, and Mary huddled on the front porch, watching the flames consume the barn, burning everything in their path. The little girls looked on with wide eyes, terror on their faces, still wearing their nightgowns, wrapped in shawls.

Jake turned to face them, surprise written on his face. "I sure am glad to see all of you!" He took a moment to breathe in deeply. Then he quickly brought them up to speed, looking at each of their faces as he spoke, seeming to draw upon a strangely calm reserve. "We're all fine. I turned out my new team and the cow. I'd already returned the other horses from Mr. Lyndon to Velvet Brooks. For now, the chickens are a safe distance away in the henhouse. Horizon is safe at Velvet Brooks, thank the good Lord. I managed to get the wagon and the new carriage out, along with some of my tools and tack, but whatever is in there now is lost. It can be replaced, and that ol' barn was worthless, anyways. If you could all just help put the fire out...then we could find my stock."

Pa took charge with a nod, organizing a line from the pump to the barn. Edward and Pa took turns pumping water into the containers and passing them along. Delia, Gladdie, Mama, Willamena and Hank Parker, Grace and Carter Mitchell, Red Brickman, Nathaniel Hartley, Frances Ellis, Martin Everly, and the new young stable hand, George Pittman, worked for a long time in the line. They passed the buckets along, splashing water on every flame they could reach. Jake and Red took the most risk, running toward the flames. Veronica held little Edward in her arms, huddled near the porch with the nanny to comfort the children, watching them work, but unable to help with her newborn to look after.

It terrified Delia to see Jake and Red running inside the barn to douse the flames. They couldn't reach those on the roof. Large parts of it had begun to cave in and crash to the ground, finally causing them to stop going inside. Instead, they tossed water along the perimeter.

The fire reached a part of the barn where Jake's stores of hay crackled. The flames devoured the dry tinder like a ravenous wolf, spitting out sparks and embers ascending into the sky as the fire reached new heights. Jake's seed would be gone, too, and Delia's heart sank for him. Hay burned faster than the wooden walls. With much of the roof gone above the stores of hay, the fire crackled and roared, eating its way through the precious supplies.

Veronica volunteered to return to Velvet Brooks, hitch up the team, and head to the Sullivans to use their telephone to call the Lexington fire department. Pa agreed, but Mama abandoned her spot in line, stepping closer to the porch.

"No, you stay with my grandson, Veronica. Besides, I can see your presence is calming for Jake's girls and Nanny Philips. I'll go in your stead. I'm not much help here. I can barely keep up lifting those heavy buckets of water, and there's no safer place for a baby than in the arms of his mother when it comes to a fire." Mama's voice sounded firm, and Delia knew Veronica wouldn't argue. Her sister could not ride for help easily with a baby to look after.

The flames continued dancing around the barn walls as Harold Sullivan and his son Percy arrived on horseback. Delia looked for Thaddeus and his older brother, Henry, to emerge from the darkness shortly behind them, hopefully accompanied by their employees and the Sullivan women, but no one else followed.

The time for questions would come later. They continued to work at a steady pace, passing water along in every sort of container available, even as more areas of the barn slowly collapsed, piece by burning piece, each worn timber falling to the ground. But a few minutes after Harold and Percy had dismounted and joined the line, Red stepped out of it to catch his breath.

He bent forward facing them, leaning his hands on his

knees and breathing hard, staring oddly at Harold. "Where are them other two Sullivan boys, Harry? And all of the staff and servants? We sure could use their help about now."

Thaddeus's father kept passing buckets and pans of water, barely glancing at Red. "I sent Henry to Richmond on business a few days ago. Thaddeus left Lexington on the four o'clock train this afternoon to join him. Didn't he saddle up and ride into town at about two or three o'clock this afternoon, Percy?"

"Yes, sir, he did, Pa," Percy answered, a grimace on his face as he passed a particularly heavy bucket of water along the line.

"And your farm employees? I know you have a whole bunch who live at Sullivan Hill." Red's eyes glared with disgust at Thaddeus's father.

Pa stopped pumping water, exchanging places with Edward. Breathing heavy, he listened, but he didn't try to stop Red's line of questioning. They all wanted answers.

Harold paused after passing a bucket. "You want me to leave and wake them all up? I told Mrs. Sullivan to send everyone she could, but maybe she couldn't rouse more help this time of night. I left as soon as Mrs. Lyndon arrived. I brought Percy because he's our only son at home right now, as I have explained."

"I would've thought you'd have rounded up more folks yourself." Red barked out the accusation.

Delia frowned as the tension mounted. It wasn't like Thaddeus not to mention leaving town, but perhaps he figured she needed time and space to make her decision after the awkward scene at the race. Though Mama had pressed her to give him an answer by the Kentucky Derby, Pa had said to give no answer if she couldn't abide by her word. And Harold Sullivan owned a hotel in Richmond. Maybe Harold had sent his sons to handle something to do with his fancy inn. She'd seen the outside of it a time or two when they'd visited Uncle Wade

Spencer, her maternal grandfather's brother, and his relations who lived in Richmond.

A few moments passed after Red's exchange with Harold before Jake stepped out of the line to catch his breath. He stood between Red and Harold. "It's all right, Harold. I appreciate you and Percy coming. This bonfire seems worse than it is, everyone. The way I figure, God must plan on givin' me a new barn. Why don't we sing 'Amazing Grace'? It could be a lot worse than it is, and we have begun to put a dent in those flames."

Folks stared at Jake as though he'd lost his mind. Didn't Red have good reason for behaving as mad as a hornet? Harold hadn't used good sense. They could hardly blame him, though, at this early hour.

Jake wiped some of the soot from his face with the sleeve of his shirt before adding, "At least no one is hurt. The animals are on the loose but safe. We are blessed today, dear friends."

Singing instead of bickering—Delia liked his idea. Pa nodded too. They only needed to encourage the others who seemed afraid to lift their voices. But if one of them would start singing, the others would surely join.

"I'll start us off with the right pitch," she said, standing up straighter to sing properly and hit the right notes. She paused from passing a bucket to offer the correct melody for the first few notes, allowing her voice to ring out as loudly as she could so they could all hear above the crackling flames and popping noises coming from the barn.

Why not sing? They all lived in the countryside for a reason. Here, the best place in the world, where it didn't matter if one wanted to play the piano at midnight or belt out a tune under the stars at three o'clock in the morning while one's barn burned to the ground. With no townsfolk to complain about disturbing the peace, they had only God and the angels of heaven for a witness.

The others joined Delia's voice in song almost from the first few notes, and when the second verse concluded, they heard a horse approaching. Mama appeared riding one of Velvet Brooks's horses, Nutmeg, and galloped into their midst. At the clopping of more horse hooves and perhaps the rumble of wheels behind her, Delia squinted into the darkness. Was that Caroline, Mary Lou, and Tilly coming up the drive in a Sullivan carriage only a short distance behind Mama?

"You all sound like angels come down from heaven," Mama said as she pulled in the reins. She dismounted. "Caroline and her girls are bringing sustenance and refreshment. Her cook and kitchen maid made sandwiches. Hot coffee and cold water too."

Jake stepped out of his place in the line and paused before Delia as the others released sighs and smiles of relief at the thought of refreshment. While they appeared distracted by the arrival of the Sullivan ladies, he leaned in close and placed a hand on her shoulder, reigniting a spark of attraction between them, even with their faces smudged with soot and ashes. "Your presence here tonight will not be forgotten, Delia. I can't tell you how much I appreciate it."

"Of course, Jake. You know I would do anything to help. I'm so glad everyone is all right. The barn can be replaced. People and animals cannot." She stretched her aching back from the hundreds of buckets she'd passed along.

"God is good," he responded before jumping back into the line, leaving her marveling about his ability to find good in tragic circumstances.

"Hush! Do you hear that?" Red said, holding up the line.

Straining her ears, Delia listened. The ringing of alarm bells in the distance began to close in on them. The fire wagon from Lexington finally approached. When the enormous tank of water pulled by eight horses trundled into Jake's drive, everyone cheered. Finally, those who had expertise in putting out fires brought them relief, along with a fresh team of men.

Carter and Nathaniel, enthused by the arrival of help, took over for Pa and Edward while they went to find Jake's stock. Delia's back and feet ached. Her soul longed for a good cry, but Jake didn't let his barn burning to the ground bother him.

She joined Leonora Philips and the other womenfolk near the porch and the refreshments as the firemen went to work, smothering the remaining flames and embers with a forceful stream of water, using a long hose on areas of the barn they couldn't reach.

Ruby, Ella, and Mary looked sleepy, their hair tousled and eyes heavy. Nonetheless, they climbed into her lap all at once, throwing their arms around her neck. Mary clung to her the most, eventually intertwining her chubby, warm little fingers with Delia's. Leonora thanked her for coming to their rescue, but weary from the long night, they didn't exchange many words. Perhaps they would meet under better conditions in the future.

She continued to marvel at Jake's optimistic nature as the embers smoldered and the little girls curled up beside her. The man had a gift of encouragement deep within. She had almost begun to nod off when someone handed her a cup of cool water and a ham sandwich. Her parched throat drank up all of the water in seconds. Tilly, Thaddeus's sister, handed her another cup, and Delia thanked her, drinking it all down too. She ate her sandwich slowly, watching the men at work.

When she'd finished, she turned to Leonora. "I think they have things well under control. The fire is almost out. Would you like help putting the girls back into bed?"

After receiving a favorable reply, Delia set her plate aside and carried little Mary inside the house. She followed Ruby, Ella, and the nanny upstairs. They tucked the sleepy girls into their beds, and after Leonora said good night, thanking her again for helping them, Delia tiptoed outside.

As she emerged onto the porch, Pa and Edward were

returning from the east side of Jake's farm with his cow and the new team. They could all go home when the men finished eating. The half-dozen firemen had nearly extinguished the remaining embers, soaking them until only smoke rose eerily over the area where the barn once stood. Veronica mentioned something about taking Edward Junior home soon, and Delia heartily agreed.

"Here's some coffee with cream and sugar." Mary Louise gave Delia a steaming tin cup.

"Thanks, Mary Lou," Delia replied. Thaddeus's sister moved along to help someone else, leaving her to sit beside her sister while Mama and Caroline passed out plates of food.

"I'm so glad Edward Junior slept through most of it." Delia spoke in a low voice, not wanting to wake her nephew. She leaned closer to her sister, peeking at his angelic face. "How's he doing?"

"I know he's too little to know what's happening, but it is a terrible sight to see someone's barn burning down."

"I'm a little concerned about Jake's girls witnessing all of this," Delia admitted.

"Children are resilient. Eddie toddles about all day, falling, bumping into things, and then he is on his feet again the next minute, on to explore something else." Veronica smiled down at the baby in her arms. "I think his girls will be all right, and they'll have learned about the dangers of fire."

"True. I hadn't thought of it that way. I wish I knew how all of this started." Delia frowned.

"Me too. I hope Jake can get to the bottom of it," her sister said, her eyes heavy as she glanced in the direction where the barn used to stand.

Jake thanked them all at one time, undoubtedly knowing they had each begun to succumb to exhaustion. Delia could hardly wait to crawl back under her quilt and clean sheets. She didn't even care if she had smudges on her face and hands, or ashes in her hair. If they hurried and didn't talk too much, they might have time to wash their hands and faces before falling asleep with the sunrise.

They walked toward home, the only sound their footsteps crunching over dirt and gravel. No one dared to speak a word lest they wake the world. With the stars still visible as dawn peeked over the horizon, Delia limped across Cornflower Road with her parents and sisters, the farm's employees dragging slowly behind them. Mama rode on Nutmeg at a slow pace, the mare's hooves clomping more quietly than usual, as if she knew her steps should whisper. Veronica and Edward waved before turning right to cut through the barns and corrals toward Rose Glen.

Covered in ashes, blackened by soot, and all undoubtedly aching and weary, but bound heart and soul, knit together as one, not one among them would go home untouched by the flames they'd witnessed at Lottie Belle. Surely, God's grace had shined upon them that night. The fire had brought them together, reminding them what they could do when they joined to help a friend and neighbor in a time of trouble.

Only, Delia had a sinking feeling in the pit of her stomach. Something truly sinister at work had attempted to destroy Jake and his bright future, one that might also belong to her if she accepted his proposal.

CHAPTER EIGHTEEN

The wise man's eyes are in his head; but the fool walketh in
darkness: and I myself perceived also that one event happeneth
to them all.
—Ecclesiastes 2:14

May 1, 1903
Lottie Belle

Where did that incessant pounding noise come from? Jake
shook himself awake. More pounding. What time was
it? A glance at the clock on his nightstand revealed it was nearly
six o'clock on Friday morning. Time to get up soon, anyways.

The pounding continued as he tossed the covers aside and
swung his feet to the floor. He dressed quickly and stumbled
his way downstairs, still buttoning his shirt, blinking at the
sunlight streaming through the windows. Nanny Philips,
wearing a duster over her nightgown, her hair a fright in some-

thing ladies called rag curlers, had reached the door ahead of him. He heard her mention Brady's name and exchange a few words with whoever had knocked.

She glanced at Jake. "It's someone from the sheriff's department. Inquiring about Brady Danford." She invited the police officer inside the entry hall before turning toward the stairs. "I'll finish dressing, wake the girls, and start breakfast."

"Thank you, Nanny Philips." Jake cleared his throat and pulled his suspenders up on his shoulders. "Is everything all right, Officer?"

"Sorry to disturb you at this early hour, but I understand Danford is your jockey and was expected to ride in the Derby this Saturday." The officer's brow hovered low.

Jake nodded. "That's right." Why did he have a feeling more bad news was about to reach his ears?

The police officer sighed, concern evident in his somber expression. "He was attacked late last night and left for dead in an alley in Lexington. From what we understand, two men approached him and beat him up pretty good. Someone discovered him and led us to the scene of the incident. He's been admitted to the hospital and kept insisting we contact you. I pass this way on the way home, and since my shift has ended, I agreed to notify you."

"Is he going to be all right?" Somehow, the race on Saturday didn't matter so much anymore. Would Brady live?

"I think he'll recover, but I don't know what the doctors will find. Maybe some broken ribs. And looked like a broken nose." The officer offered a sympathetic expression and shook hands with him. "He wanted you to know right away. Kept mumbling something about how he didn't think he could ride in the Derby."

Jake followed him outside onto the front porch. "The least of my concerns under the circumstances, but so good of him, and you, to let me know. Thank you, Officer. I'll head to the hospital as soon as possible."

He lingered as the officer walked to his horse, swung up into the saddle, and left Lottie Belle. He could really use a good cup of strong coffee about now. His barn had been rebuilt with the help of folks like the Lyndons, the Sullivans, and others in the community, and he sure did enjoy the view of the new building in the morning sunshine, but who had attacked Brady?

Strangers? Happenstance, or something more menacing? Someone who didn't want him to ride Horizon in the Derby? If it hadn't come on the heels of his barn being burned to the ground, Jake might not have thought much of it.

Had Thaddeus Sullivan been behind these incidents? It wouldn't surprise him, but he couldn't very well go making such accusations. No, he'd have to trust God to help him sort through this.

First things first. A cup of coffee. A visit to Brady to make sure he was all right despite his injuries. Then he'd withdraw Horizon from the Derby. Jake sighed and turned to go inside. It couldn't be helped. How could he find a jockey before tomorrow?

He'd pay a visit to Mr. Lyndon, who might want to go to the hospital with him. He'd also know what should be done to withdraw his horse. Horizon, Diamond Comet, Glory, and Gold Dancer had all been loaded onto the early-morning train under Red Brickman's watchful eye by now, headed to Louisville ahead of the race. Charlie and the other jockey Joseph Lyndon sometimes used, named Thimble, would have ridden on the train with Red. By now, they had left without Brady, probably dismayed that Horizon wouldn't have a jockey to help him acclimate to the Churchill Downs track. And now, he'd have no one to ride him in the most important race of his career.

M

artin interrupted Friday morning's breakfast to announce Jake's arrival, and the arrival of George Pittman, their new farmhand. Clasping a warm cup of coffee, Delia opened her eyes wide at this unexpected pleasure. Why did the sight of Jake make her heart leap for joy? In fact, why didn't Thaddeus come around a little more often of late? Busy getting ready for the Derby, like everyone else.

"Come in, both of you. Please, join us. Care for some coffee, a plate of hot cakes, perhaps?" Mama spoke from her seat, a cup of steaming tea in her hands.

Pa had just picked up his copy of the newspaper, but he set it aside. "What a nice surprise. Yes, do join us. Martin, if you'd fix them a plate."

Jake shot a weak smile in her direction. She returned his silent greeting with an affectionate smile, but something was wrong. Something gravely serious. She exchanged a glance with her sister. Gladdie saw it too.

Jake and George, also wearing a somber expression, followed Martin to the empty seats across from Delia and her mother. "I encountered George on my way here, and in sharing the news I have to tell you, he said he also has something on his chest that we should know. I have to withdraw Horizon from the Derby. Someone attacked Brady."

"What?" Pa's brows furrowed. "Withdraw Horizon? He's already boarded the train along with our other horses, and Brady should have boarded with Red, Charlie, and our other jockey, Thimble Daniels." Carter would be there, too, helping look after their horses once they reached Churchill Downs.

Thimble was just as small as Charlie and Brady, and his name reflected it. The jockey sometimes rode for Pa, and since Pa had entered two horses for the Derby and Glory in a race for two-year-old horses, they'd surely need Thimble and couldn't spare him for Jake.

Delia could hardly fathom this news. In fact, it took her a few seconds to close her mouth. Brady, attacked? By whom? "Poor Brady! How could this have happened?" First Jake's barn, and now this.

Jake brought them up to speed with what little he knew. Then he turned to Pa. "I thought you might want to join me in visiting him at the hospital after breakfast. I'm sure it would encourage him, and I'd like to make sure he's going to be all right. See if there's anything we can do for him."

Pa massaged his temple a moment. "Yes, I'd like to visit Brady with you."

"That's horrid that someone would do such a thing. And how are we going to find another jockey while he recovers?" Mama's teacup clanked in its saucer. "And by tomorrow?"

Gladdie stared at the orange in her hands as she removed a segment. "We should visit him next week too—Mother, Delia, and me. After Jake and Pa go. And send him letters of encouragement until he has recovered. See if he has any family we can look in on."

"I could bring him a book, perhaps..." Delia's voice faded.

Pa leaned forward, angling toward their farmhand. "George, tell us what's on your mind."

George hung his head. "I'm real sorry I didn't come to you sooner, Mr. Lyndon, and especially to you, Mr. Jake. But when I ran into you this morning, passing by the barn when I led Nutmeg outside for a bath... Anyways, Mr. Jake told me what happened to Brady. It made me mad as a hornet. I knew I had to come forward."

All eyes turned toward George, who looked down briefly. A lanky young man, he possessed youthful freckles on his nose that hadn't faded yet, darker from his work outside. Somehow, though, those freckles gave him an honest appearance, along with the denim overalls he usually wore.

Pa nodded. "Go on."

George swiped some hair from his brown eyes and plunged forward. "The night of the fire, I saw Thaddeus Sullivan beside Jake's barn, riding his dapple-gray horse. I was on my way home from Briar Tavern. He couldn't have taken the four o'clock train, you see. It was just maybe half an hour before I figure the fire must've really started going strong. Maybe about one o'clock in the morning. Plenty of time to have set that fire and then disappear. He looked a little woozy to me. Maybe he'd been drinking. I know you might think I was, too, but I only had one cup of ale that night. You have my word."

"I see. This is disturbing news, indeed. Mr. Sullivan swore Thaddeus had already left for Richmond." Pa drew in a deep breath and then released a sigh.

Delia bit her lower lip. This couldn't possibly be true.

Jake stared at the plate of bacon and hot cakes Martin set before him. Had he lost his appetite too?

George had turned nineteen and perhaps enjoyed the occasional mug of ale with friends his age, though he had no reputation for fabricating tales or being a drunkard. But Thaddeus simply wouldn't have done such a thing. George had to have mistaken him for someone else, but who? Perhaps George had more to drink at the tavern than he recalled.

Thaddeus did often ride a dapple-gray horse. That fact she could not argue.

"Just one thing bothers me. Why did you wait this long to tell us?" Pa leaned back in his seat, but he kept his gaze on George.

"No one likes to cross a Sullivan, sir."

Pa grunted. "I can understand that. The Sullivans are a mighty force in these parts. Are you willing to sign a statement should Jake decide to pursue the matter with the police, or in case anything else strange happens?"

"I am, sir, if that's what you and Mr. Jake would like me to do." George glanced at the plate Martin set before him, but he waited for Pa's and Jake's answers.

Pa looked at Jake, who nodded.

Her father addressed George. "Yes. Right after breakfast. I'll have you draft a statement in my library, and then sign and date it." Pa picked up his fork. "Jake and I will also head to the Lexington Association Track after we check on Brady. We'll find someone to ride Horizon."

"But how, with the race tomorrow?" Gladdie's tone didn't inspire much hope.

"To be honest, I'm believing for a miracle. Eat your breakfast, everyone." Pa, still holding the fork, reached for some maple syrup.

Jake's eyes only briefly met Delia's. All any of them could do was pray for Brady and try to digest the blow George had delivered concerning Thaddeus. Delia refused to believe it. Maybe Brady knew the men who'd attacked him and this whole matter could be cleared up—except for the fact no one knew how Jake's barn had burned to the ground.

While Pa and Jake drove to town, Delia closeted herself in the library, alternating between pacing, prayer, reading a few pages in a book, attempting to add stitches to her embroidery, and taking a few sips of chamomile tea to soothe her nerves. Occasionally, her gaze drifted toward the desk drawer where Pa had placed George's statement.

Gladdie and her mother joined her in the library after a while too.

A few hours later, Jake and Pa returned, bursting into the room with hope in their eyes.

Pa informed them they'd found Gabriel Bolton, the one everyone called "the angel jockey with wings." Folks called him that due to not only his name but his outstanding racing record. Since the horse he would have ridden in the Derby had to withdraw due to a minor ligament injury, he had agreed to ride Horizon.

Jake picked Delia up and swung her around. "We're going to the Derby, after all!"

Delia laughed as he spun her before setting her back down. Were her cheeks red?

Gladdie jumped up and hugged him too. Mama clapped, and Pa squeezed her, making her laugh.

"I'd better get home to the girls. I've been gone longer than expected. Nanny Philips will be anxious by now." Jake glanced toward Delia. "I feel better that we've seen Brady too. He's going to live, but he's sore. He won't be able to ride for a long time."

"I'll walk you to the door." She followed him out into the hall. "Will you be riding with us on the train tomorrow into Louisville?"

Jake retrieved his hat. "Yes and looking forward to it. A chance to sit with you, sweet Delia."

She looked down, shyness overwhelming her. "See you tomorrow, then. I'll say a prayer for Horizon and Gabriel, and for Brady to heal."

"Thank you." And with that, Jake stepped outside.

A twinge of sadness at his departure surprised her. If she married him, they would never be separated by Cornflower Road ever again. But she found it awfully hard to arrive at any decision with so much chaos swirling around them.

She returned to the library, taking her seat on the sofa. Setting the book she'd tried to read previously on her lap, she found she was unable to open it, and a contemplative mood fell over her. Gladdie sat on the other end of the sofa with some needlework, and Mama, with her own needlework, in a rocking chair near the fireplace. Grace occasionally came by with a fresh pot of hot tea, and the aroma of roast beef permeated the household as Willamena prepared dinner.

Pa, seated in his favorite chair, turned to her. "I know you must be as concerned about Thaddeus as the rest of us, Delia. I can't help but wonder if George consumed too much strong drink at the tavern. We've known him and his family for years. Attended the same church together. I gave him a chance of employment at Velvet Brooks and a cabin to live in here on the property like most of our other workers have because I trust George as much as I do Thaddeus, having known them both from birth. Maybe the two ruffians who beat up Brady have something to do with the fire. Maybe it's all coincidental. Maybe the one incident has nothing to do with the other. One thing I do know—the truth has a way of coming out."

"How is Brady? Did Jake take it awfully hard?" Delia reached inside a pocket in her skirts and found a lace-edged handkerchief to dab the corners of her eyes as they threatened to mist.

"He's in bad shape. Two broken ribs, a broken nose, a broken wrist, and a black eye. And yes, Jake took it very hard. But as you saw, he is determined not to let it deter him, for Brady's sake. Brady said he'd very much like a job to come back to when he recovers. And Jake has decided not to miss this chance for Horizon. And for all of us, too, since we trained him here."

"I'm glad he isn't giving up." Delia bit her lower lip. "For Brady's sake too."

Horizon simply had to go on. It would encourage Brady, even if only to read about the race in the papers after the fact. They had to show his attackers that nothing could stop God's plans for Jake, Horizon, and Velvet Brooks.

Why did she have a terrible ache in her heart? Could Thaddeus have something to do with these setbacks for Jake? The

Lord kept bringing him to the top in spite of them, but the incidents remained troubling, indeed.

CHAPTER NINETEEN

We have almost forgotten how strange a thing it is that so huge
and powerful and intelligent an animal as a horse should allow
another, and far more feeble animal, to ride upon its back.
—Peter Gray

MAY 2, 1903

CHURCHILL DOWNS, LOUISVILLE, KENTUCKY

Usually nothing could dampen Delia's joyous mood for
the Kentucky Derby, but like Jake and the rest of her
family, because of the strange circumstances leading up to the
event, she had to rally her spirit more than usual for the twenty-
ninth running of her state's beloved horseracing day named
after the famous Epsom Derby in England. The train ride from
Lexington to Louisville, followed by a ride in a trolley to reach
the racecourse, did much to invigorate her senses. She was
thankful for beautiful summerlike weather—seventy-four
degrees and sunny—but she kept her fan at the ready.

Wearing her widest-brimmed hat, Delia, her two suitors, and her entire family prepared for the main race of the day as they sat in a private box located near the new clubhouse at Churchill Downs. She, along with most other Kentuckians, considered it one of the most exciting days of the year. And once again, she found herself seated between Thaddeus and Jake, eager for the "Run for the Roses" to begin. A purse of six-thousand dollars had drawn a fine number of horses to enter the main event.

All day long, trolleys and trains had brought spectators to and from the racecourse, along with a steady stream of wagons, buggies, and carriages. And everyone wore their finest. Delia looked out over a sea of hats. Thousands of people had come from all over to participate in the day's events, including Missouri, Tennessee, Ohio, Indiana, and Illinois. From the east, the Derby had begun to attract racing families from New York, Maryland, and New Jersey. They milled about with picnic baskets in tow, everyone in a celebratory mood. Many who were members, like her own family, had opted for a meal in one of the clubhouse dining rooms.

When Delia rose along with her family and the crowd for the traditional singing of "My Old Kentucky Home," her heart swelled with pride. By the end, hardly a dry eye was left to gaze across the track at the colorful flags waving over the stables.

Since the race was restricted to three-year-old thorough-breds, male or female, horses only had one chance in their life-time to win the Derby, one of the factors making the race so prestigious. How wonderful the prospect of Diamond Comet and Gold Dancer having a shot at those roses—not to mention Bluegrass Blaze and Horizon. And later on, Glorious Day Dreamer would have a chance in another race.

Thaddeus seemed more anxious than usual, tapping the arms of his seat. Why couldn't she relax and think of something to say to him? Had paranoia and tension set in, toppling their relationship? She ought to worry about such matters tomorrow and enjoy the day.

Colonel Lyndon, Delia's grandfather, leaned forward from the row behind and patted Jake on the shoulder. "Now that you've broken your maiden, it will be interesting to see how Horizon does today. So sorry to hear about Brady. I read about it in the newspaper. Front page news. Terribly alarming."

Jake wore a befuddled expression, so Delia leaned toward him. "Breaking one's maiden means your horse or its rider has won for the first time."

"Ah, yes. I remember my Uncle Caleb using that expression a time or two." Jake twisted around in his seat to offer a smile and nod toward her grandfather. Mumbling so only Delia could hear, he added, "Yes, it will be especially interesting with a new jockey."

She patted Jake's hand, offered an empathetic look, and whispered, "Gabriel is good. He'll know what to do."

At least Jake didn't scowl at Thaddeus, but the two gentlemen refused to look at each other today. Beyond nods upon Thaddeus meeting them in the clubhouse for dishes of a gourmet-styled burgoo, her two suitors had barely acknowledged each other.

"No bug boys here today." Grandfather Lyndon patted Jake on the shoulder again.

Delia's brows rose. Maybe his hearing wasn't so bad, after all. And she, too, had taken note of the front page article about Brady in the *Lexington Gazette* that morning. In a roundabout way, Grandfather meant to reassure Jake that Gabriel was experienced. Only, a glance at Jake revealed he was lost.

Delia leaned toward him again, raising her voice a tad so he could hear over the murmur of the crowd. "He means no apprentice jockeys will ride today. Only those with the most experience."

Jake smiled, sitting up straighter. "Praise the Lord for that."

Pa leaned toward them from their left. "How's the going today, Thaddeus, Jake?"

Jake wore another blank expression. Delia cupped her hand over her mouth and whispered, "He's asking the condition of the racing surface, in your opinion. You might reply by saying fast, good, muddy, or sloppy."

"A fast track today, sir," Jake answered. He mouthed a *thank you* to her, and she smiled.

Thaddeus concurred with a nod and shifted in his seat. Why was he so quiet today? Still sulking about the Phoenix? Or perhaps because she hadn't given him an answer yet? Or did he grapple with a guilty conscience? No, it simply couldn't be true. Could it?

Grandfather Lyndon raised his voice for Delia's father to hear, along with everyone else in their box. "Joseph, I ran into my old friend, Colonel Ezekiel Clay."

Delia could recall stories about Colonel Clay serving in the war with her grandfather. She couldn't, however, recall if they'd been on the same side or in opposition to each other.

"And how are things at Runnymede? I would imagine he has a horse or two competing."

Runnymede was one of the oldest farms in Kentucky. Delia looked over her shoulder to see her grandfather nod toward Pa.

"Not today, but he's particularly excited about a new foal named Agile, born last year." Grandfather Lyndon reached over to pat Veronica's hand. "After I told him about the birth of my great-grandson, we traded stories about our walking canes. It's what folks do at our age—at least until Delia marries and gives us another grandchild."

"See what we have to look forward to, darling?" her mother teased Pa.

"Walking canes?" Pa nudged and winked at Delia. "Or grandchildren?"

Delia rolled her eyes.

Jake patted her hand comfortingly, a wide grin on his face. No doubt, he would be happy with more children, too, someday, and the thought made her warm inside.

Thaddeus, at her other side, didn't blink an eye. Had he even been paying attention, or was he somewhere else?

And then the gunshot reverberated through the air and the horses were off and running. When a frontrunner Delia didn't recognize led the pack of horses, Delia leaned forward. A hush fell over the crowd. All eyes were glued to the track, giving her goosebumps as hooves thundered past.

The horses circled around the oval and headed for the final turn. Everyone in her box rose. Delia raised her binoculars to her eyes and spotted Horizon, Gold Dancer, Diamond Comet, and Bluegrass Blaze. In that order, and it brought a smile to her face to see them taking the lead of all the horses on the track.

Bluegrass Blaze edged forward ahead of both horses.

Thaddeus hollered, "Go, Bluegrass, go!"

But then Horizon took the lead.

Jake yelled, "Go, go, go!"

Delia, caught between them, remained silent.

Horizon remained in the lead by a nose length. Gold Dancer edged ahead of Bluegrass Blaze. Diamond Comet dropped back and probably wouldn't recover, but he might have a shot at fourth place. The other three horses were nearly neck and neck as they came around the final turn. Delia's mouth dropped open, but she couldn't find her voice.

Horizon and his rider must have sensed their competition. Gabriel leaned in low over his mane and gave the command with a stroke of his riding whip to the horse's rear. Jake's horse broke into an astounding pace, easily taking the lead by a furlong.

Behind Horizon by an eighth of a mile, Bluegrass Blaze edged ahead of Gold Dancer but then fell back as Gold Dancer eased ahead.

While those two fought for second place, Gabriel permitted Horizon to breeze across the finish line to a cheering crowd. Gabriel raised his right arm. Gold Dancer crossed next, followed closely by Bluegrass Blaze. Then Diamond Comet. Gabriel, bouncing along astride Horizon to cool down the horse's muscles, waved to the crowd, which continued cheering.

Thaddeus gripped the railing with clenched fists. Delia's heart ached for him.

Jake's elation quickly spread to everyone else in the box, including Delia when he put his arm around her, jumping up and down for joy. Her father's exuberance was evident, too—naturally, since three horses trained at Velvet Brooks had finished in the top four. An incredible statement for the legacy of the Lyndon family. Delia allowed the joy to wash over her soul as she jumped up and down alongside Jake. Horizon had done it again. How sweet the victory tasted.

Only, a glance at Thaddeus's dour expression revealed the contagion did not reach him.

And this oddity kept Delia awake at night with a great deal of consternation, including the question no one dared ask. Was he somehow behind the fire and the attack on Jake's jockey? Surely not, in spite of his sour temperament. Delia simply could not find it in her heart to believe it. She would set out to prove him innocent if necessary. He might be a tempest in a teapot, but he was no criminal.

Or was he? Either way, she would learn the truth.

~

May 4, 1903
The Lexington Livery

"If you could just tell me if Thaddeus Sullivan checked his horse in before four o'clock on Saturday, April the twenty-fifth, I would be ever so grateful, Mr. Benson." Delia offered her sweetest smile and even batted her eyelashes for the livery owner in Lexington. She hated having to ask the question she posed, but if Thaddeus had left on the four o'clock Saturday train, wouldn't he have checked his horse at the livery? And if it could prove his innocence, why shouldn't she ask?

Jake and Pa waited outside, having dropped them off with the hope she and Gladdie could charm Mr. Benson into giving them the information they needed.

"I don't know, ma'am." The stocky livery owner hesitated, scratching his beard. "Those records are private. I don't feel right about showing them to anyone."

Mr. Benson turned back to remove a saddle from a horse someone had recently returned. Delia glanced at Gladdie. Her sister shrugged. What else could she say to gain the owner's cooperation? The man lugged the saddle to a spot in a row with other saddles draped across a rail. Delia followed him, Gladdie on her heels. After positioning the saddle, he opened some leather polish and began giving it a shine.

Delia stood back out of his way. "I didn't think you'd want me to go to the trouble of involving a constable or the sheriff. I guessed you would prefer we keep the matter between us…"

The owner put the lid on the polish and gave her a sideways glance, returning to the horse. She and Gladdie followed.

Delia simply had to get to the bottom of this for herself. Surely, her beau would never take things so far as to burn down Jake's barn. He might have a naturally competitive streak. Yes, he sometimes liked to argue. But he loved horses and his good standing in the community far too much to do something so vile and evil as risk the lives of Jake, his nieces, Leonora, all those who helped extinguish the flames, and Jake's stock. She didn't know if Thaddeus realized Horizon usually boarded at Velvet Brooks, but she couldn't imagine him trying to set fire to the beautiful horse. She had to find proof to clear his name.

Hence all the reasons Delia now stood before the livery owner with Gladdie at her side.

Mr. Benson began brushing the recently returned horse which waited patiently for his afternoon feeding. "I do appreciate the fact you haven't sent the constable or a sheriff around. I'm in no mood to answer their questions."

Delia smiled, smoothing her skirts. Perhaps Mr. Benson had come to his senses. If she promised to keep her mouth shut, maybe he would permit her to see the records or provide the answers to her questions. She had done all she could to defend her beau. Now she needed proof—evidence he had gone to Richmond long before someone had set fire to Jake's barn. If she couldn't obtain it here, she might have to urge Pa and Jake to drive them to the train station to view those records.

The livery owner continued brushing the horse, sparing a brief glance at her and Gladdie. "Well, I suppose you are Colonel Lyndon's and Reverend Spencer's granddaughters, after all, and everyone around here respects your pa. Joseph Lyndon has done much for our racing community. What exactly do you want to know again?"

"If you could just confirm exactly what day and time Thaddeus Sullivan boarded his horse. It should've been on a Saturday, April the twenty-fifth, before catching the four o'clock train to Richmond," Delia explained.

Mr. Benson set the brush aside and led the horse into his stall, closing the half door. "All right, ladies, right this way."

They followed him to his desk in a corner of the livery. He flipped through a ledger, turning the pages through each day of the week until he found the entry. Pointing to it, he read aloud the notes he'd written. "'Thaddeus Sullivan boarded a dapple-gray mare on Sunday afternoon at three o'clock, April the twenty-sixth.' I do recall he said he was taking the four o'clock train to Richmond, but it was on Sunday afternoon, not Saturday."

Delia's mouth dropped open as he turned the ledger around so she could inspect the entry for herself. "Are you absolutely certain, Mr. Benson? Is it possible there is a mistake with the date you have written here? Couldn't it have been Saturday, the day before?"

He shook his head. "I know this is accurate for several reasons. First, you can see how the entries are made as the customers arrive. All of these entries above this are the other customers in order. Secondly, I didn't want to be here on a Sunday, but my last helper left without much notice. I haven't hired anyone to fill his position yet, so I haven't had a day off in a while, but I remember thinking how it was getting close to closing time when he came in. Thirdly, I asked Thaddeus if he had entered a horse in the Derby and if he'd return in time for the big race in Louisville. He said yes and that he'd return from Richmond to retrieve his horse within three days—on Wednesday the twenty-ninth. He picked up his horse on Wednesday afternoon. See my entry here." Mr. Benson flipped to a different page with all of his Wednesday customers. "He paid for three nights and four days of boarding on Sunday when he brought the horse in. I require advance payment, as you know."

Delia nodded. They had boarded horses with him before whenever they took a train to Richmond or Louisville.

"Another thing, we had a nice chat about my new machines on Sunday. He likes motor carriages and is thinking about purchasing one. But it was definitely on a Sunday afternoon before closing. You can see I only had four other customers after Thaddeus before Monday morning. We are always slow on Sundays, and I close at five o'clock sharp."

Delia and Gladdie leaned forward to inspect the entries he

showed them. Sure enough, Thaddeus had arrived to board his horse on Sunday, the day after the fire at Lottie Belle. He indeed returned on Wednesday the twenty-ninth, with plenty of time to have hired someone to injure Brady.

"I just don't understand," Delia murmured, shaking her head as she stared at the ledger entries in disbelief.

Gladdie patted Delia's hand and took over from there. "Thank you so much for your time, Mr. Benson. I'm sure you have many other things to do. You've helped us a great deal. We'll be on our way now."

Delia followed Gladdie from the barn, stepping outside to climb into the carriage where Jake and Pa waited for them. By the time Delia settled in beside Jake on the front seat and Gladdie settled in beside Pa in the seat behind them, she'd begun to recover her wits a little, but she still believed Thaddeus couldn't have facilitated the mysterious events.

"Well, what did you discover, Detective Delia?" Jake's brow arched, and he shot her a curious glance while holding the reins.

"I'm still in disbelief," she confessed, but she quickly brought them up to speed about their discovery, adding, "Sadly, it places Thaddeus in the area at the time of the fire and the time of Brady Danford's attack, but it is all circumstantial evidence and doesn't necessarily mean he committed these horrific acts. While we have a witness placing him at your barn, it is still one man's word against another's. George could have mistaken someone else for Thaddeus in the dark, especially if he had too much to drink."

"Good work, Detective Delia." Pa reached forward to pat her on the shoulder. "I know it wasn't easy to ask those questions about Thaddeus, but I think it was best we let you ladies ask rather than Jake and me. We would have seemed heavy-handed, and he might have insisted on a warrant. That could take a lot of time, and a judge might not have granted one easily."

"I agree, Pa," Gladdie said. "Delia is a natural at sleuthing. I wish you both could have seen her at work. She said all the right things and applied exactly the right amount of pressure to gain Mr. Benson's cooperation."

"Nice job, both of you. As I told George, I suggest we keep this new information under wraps until Jake decides if he wants to press charges," Pa said. "I don't know what to think, either, but the evidence does seem to be mounting."

Jake snapped the reins, the carriage lurched forward, and Delia's stomach churned. She wanted only to be home, but that would take another forty-five minutes. She had tried to convince Pa and Jake of Thaddeus's innocence, but she, too, began to wonder about the implications.

Jake's back-to-back victories in Lexington and Louisville put him and his horse on the charts, and for obvious reasons, Jake's interest in marrying Delia added to motives for Thaddeus.

"How has Thaddeus been behaving since he returned from Richmond, Delia?" Pa interrupted her thoughts. "Have you seen much of him, other than at the Derby? How did he seem to you?"

"No, I haven't, but I spoke to him on Derby Day. He said he's been busy trying to train Bluegrass Blaze and help Henry hire some new staff at the hotel in Richmond, but perhaps it is for the best." Delia adjusted her hat. "These incidents make everyone suspicious of him, and the strain of it might cause us to argue. I still remain convinced he would never do anything of the sort, but if he isn't behind these incidents, then who is?"

Would someone harm Horizon or Jake's new jockey before their next race at Pimlico? Could Jake and his nieces be in any danger?

CHAPTER TWENTY

A man on a horse is spiritually, as well as physically, bigger
than a man on foot.
—John Steinbeck

"Thank you for seeing me again today, Delia. You looked quite shaken this afternoon when we returned from our investigation." Jake offered his arm to her as they strolled beside the four-board fences and corrals at Velvet Brooks. He'd said he had something important to tell her, hence the reason she'd agreed to the stroll. Not that she minded the opportunity to spend time with him.

"You're welcome. It's always nice to see you, Jake. I believe I've recovered from the news we learned at the Lexington Livery. I'm still convinced Thaddeus has a perfectly good reason for the delay in his departure for Richmond. Surely, someone can exonerate him concerning these matters and confirm his whereabouts the night of the fire. And I keep praying someone will come forward and prove he had nothing to do with the attack on Brady Danford." The demi-train of Delia's peach gown trailed over the bluegrass as they observed Horizon grazing in the distance to their left. Straight ahead, they could see Jake's new barn on his property across Cornflower Road. With its fresh coat of white paint, the barn looked nice in the foreground of Jake's Victorian house.

Jake sucked in a deep breath and turned his face away. "I'm learning about bluegrass since my arrival in Kentucky. They say it is full of nutrients which strengthen the bones of horses."

"It's nutritious, the horses seem to love the way it tastes, and it holds up well for sod despite frequent grazing. But I'm sure you didn't come to tell me what I already know. However, before you do tell me why you are here, I must ask how Ruby, Ella, and Mary are doing. In the crisis surrounding these mysterious events, I confess, I forgot to ask earlier today."

He chuckled. "You are perceptive, Delia. No, I didn't come here to discuss bluegrass. And thank you for inquiring about my nieces. They are doing well, but they ask about you frequently, especially Ruby."

"That's very sweet. I need to visit them soon."

"The main reason I came to speak with you is because I wanted to let you know, I have come to a decision regarding Thaddeus Sullivan. I have decided to press charges against him for the burning of my barn. At minimum, I expect the sheriff will open an investigation."

Aghast, she stiffened and looked away, trying to hide the disappointment surely crossing her face. "I do wish you would reconsider."

"I believe this is the right thing to do," he insisted. "I wanted to tell you myself so you don't hear about it from the newspapers or anyone else secondhand. And there is something else, but I'm not sure I should mention it."

"What is it?" She searched Jake's blue eyes, realizing she

would never be able to decide about marrying either of them until she found the truth about the attacks on him.

He leaned over the fence, resting his elbows on the top rail. He wore his long blond hair in its customary ponytail tied with a length of leather cording. How small she felt beside a man of his height as they studied the horses in the corralled meadows beneath the brilliant sunset which cast a pink-and-orange glow on everything. What else could've gone wrong? If only they could be free of the series of disasters so he could think of kissing her once again.

His jaw clenched and his cheek muscles grew taut. "Someone has started a rumor claiming I injected Horizon with an Adirondack serum to win the Phoenix Stakes and the Kentucky Derby." He paused, releasing a heavy sigh. "Folks are saying it is a mixture made from red and white clover extract and a mint family herb extract known as bee balm. All abundant in upstate New York, where folks know I come from. Some say the bee balm herb gives horses a burst of strength. Even if it were true, these are all natural substances. But the rumor makes it sound as if I cheated somehow. And not only this, but I worry that it could tarnish your father's name and all he has worked so hard for."

Closing her eyes, Delia shook her head, lamenting Jake's suffering. Would no end come of these sordid tales? She covered his hand with her own. "I'm so sorry. How did you find out about it?"

"When your pa and I were outside in the carriage waiting for you and Gladdie to come out of the livery, Mr. Breckenridge spotted us. He had just come out of the tack shop with a new harness for one of his horses. He said everyone has heard the rumor, and he wanted me to be aware of it. I don't take kindly to someone spreading lies and slander about my name all over town, inferring I am a dishonest, cheating sort."

Delia's mind raced, searching for something comforting to

say to lift his spirit in the face of so much adversity. "Surely, folks know Horizon is training here at Velvet Brooks and that my father would never allow cheating of any kind. We all know he's won his races fair and square. I don't think they'll believe such an accusation once they've considered it."

He didn't offer a reply, but his eyes narrowed as he set his face like flint. Her heart ached for Thaddeus, wrongly accused of so many criminal actions, but it also ached for Jake.

"I appreciate the fact you're letting me know about pressing charges in advance. I hope I'm not wrong. I still believe Thaddeus could never do those things, and I hope they find the real culprit. I find it all so unsettling." Under her breath she added, "Just like my dream..."

"Shall we turn back toward the main house?" He stood up straight and offered his arm.

Delia took it with a soft smile.

Before they could reach the veranda, Thaddeus approached from the west and the neighboring estate belonging to his parents. Riding a bay horse, he dismounted as they drew closer, tying his mount to the hitching post on the opposite side of Jake's horse.

Thaddeus didn't say anything, but his face stiffened at seeing her on Jake's arm. When Delia and Jake stood about five feet from him, her two beaux glared at each other.

Jake drew himself up taller. "So...you've burned my barn to the ground, hired two men to beat up my jockey, and now, you've spread false rumors around town against me, adding slander to your list of crimes."

"Step aside, Delia. I don't want you hurt in the crosshairs. Let's settle this right here, Jake Williams." Thaddeus put his fists up and stepped closer.

"Thaddeus! Gentlemen, there is no need to resort to a fist-fight." Aghast, Delia looked from one to the other.

Jake took her by the hand and led her to the veranda,

depositing her on the bench. "Stay here, Delia." He crossed to the drive and swung a fist so fast, it made her head spin, walloping Thaddeus in the eye.

Thaddeus roared, clutching his face as the punch landed. The force of the blow sent him stumbling backward into the hitching post, narrowly avoiding a fall. His horse whinnied, tossing its head and snorting.

Jake coiled like a spring, ready to strike again. Thaddeus, still holding his eye, glared at him, his face flushed with anger. Delia sobbed, burying her face in her hands. How had they turned into fierce adversaries, locked in a battle of pride and rivalry?

Thaddeus managed to regain his balance. He straightened his coat and adjusted his hat, taking a deep breath. "Is that the best you can do, Jake?" His voice dripping with mockery, he sneered.

Delia had leapt from the bench to get between them as Jake grabbed Thaddeus by his shirt collar and fancy silk tie, aiming a fist at his face, ready to deliver another blow when the front door of Velvet Brooks opened. She couldn't see who'd stepped out onto the veranda at first, but her mother cried out, pleading with them to stop. A moment later, Pa and Martin dove between the men, pushing them apart.

Mama pulled Delia toward the house as carriage wheels crunched on the drive. Mrs. Sullivan! Mama's hand on Delia's arm remained firm. "Delia, come inside. Go upstairs to your room, and do not come out until I come for you or send someone for you. Thaddeus and Jake, go home. Martin, I'll be in the sitting room, and after you show Mrs. Sullivan inside, please bring tea on my best tea service at once. Mr. Lyndon, I'll need your help. Please accompany me."

Mother's commanding tone caused everyone to spring into action, including the two men who'd brawled only moments ago. They scrambled onto their horses, breathing hard. Thaddeus's eye was already turning black. He and Jake rode away in different directions.

Inside, Delia lifted the hem of her gown and dashed upstairs, then she hovered around the corner at the top of the staircase, unseen to those below, straining her ears.

"I'd like to see Mrs. Lyndon at once—*and* that daughter of hers who has caused all of this trouble," Mrs. Sullivan said to Martin as he led her down the hall toward the sitting room.

"Yes, ma'am. Right this way, ma'am." Martin's reply floated up the staircase as Delia wiped tears from her cheeks, still shaken by the fight between her two suitors. Mrs. Sullivan blamed her! Nonetheless, she did as her mother instructed, remaining hidden from view.

Sinking to the floor in a pile of skirts and tears, Delia leaned her head against the wall. She could discern only a few words from the sitting room among the bevy of concerns Mrs. Sullivan unleashed and the murmured replies from Delia's parents.

About twenty minutes later, footsteps echoed in the hall below. Then the front door slammed shut, and she listened for the carriage to pull away. As Delia peeked around the corner to view her mother standing in the hall below, Mama spun around and let out a Kentucky holler. "Delaney Mae Lyndon!"

"Yes ma'am?" Delia emerged on the top step.

"Pack your trunk. You are going to New York to visit your Aunt Mae on the next train headed east. For a few weeks... maybe a month. I'm sure your father's sister will be delighted to provide you with a quiet place of refuge, far away from Mrs. Sullivan."

Aunt Mae? Veronica had suggested a trip to clear Delia's head. And her sister spoke highly of their estranged aunt, though Delia had met her only briefly when Aunt Mae came to Velvet Brooks for Veronica's wedding. First, she had a few concerns. "Why? You and Pa don't blame me for all of these incidents, do you?"

Mama put her hands on her hips and looked up at her. "No, I certainly do not. In fact, I'm beginning to think it was a Godsend that you didn't marry Thaddeus yet. If he turns out to be the culprit behind all of these mysterious events, I don't care if he's the son of Queen Victoria herself. He wouldn't be a wise choice for a husband. But if you aren't here and this nonsense continues, maybe Mrs. Sullivan will begin to see you have nothing to do with any of it."

Pa nodded as he came to stand behind Mama. "I agree with your mother. Jake told me he is going to have the sheriff open an investigation. Maybe by the time you return, we'll know the truth. Let us know when your trunk is packed. I'll give you a ride to the train station."

"But my work at the library...they're counting on me," Delia protested, descending the steps, pausing halfway. "One of the usual assistants has been sick a lot lately, and Miss Daphne told me they are shorthanded and behind. She asked me to come three days next week instead of only two. Not to mention the students I tutor on Saturdays, and the monthly deliveries of books I make."

"We'll have to stop on the way and let them know you'll be in New York. As for your students, we can ask Gladdie to fill in for you. Mrs. Sullivan is returning in three days for your answer to Thaddeus's proposal, and you can't be here. I won't have her insisting on a rushed marriage." Mama shooed Delia back up the staircase. "And for heaven's sake, don't dawdle. I don't want you to miss the last train. Be sure you pack your cloak. I'll send Grace up to help you."

"All right. Can you send Frances too?" Delia turned around before reaching the top step, keeping a hand on the railing. "And did Mrs. Sullivan see the fight between Jake and her son?"

Mama shook her head. "No, but I'm sure she'll hear all

about it. And no, you can't have help from Frances. She must pack as well. She'll accompany you on the journey as your ladies' maid and companion."

"I'll need to stop at the post office on the way." Delia would explain why later...if anything came of the short story or the poem she'd worked up the courage to submit for publication.

Relief enveloped her that she wouldn't have to face Mrs. Sullivan, nor would she have to see Thaddeus after his fight with Jake. On the other hand, she wouldn't be able to help find evidence to defend Thaddeus. But Jake pressing charges against him and the ensuing investigation would surely bring truth to light. And being in New York would give her the time she needed to sort things out in her heart and mind.

CHAPTER TWENTY-ONE

All Scripture is inspired by God and is useful to teach us what
is true and to make us realize what is wrong in our lives. It
corrects us when we are wrong and teaches us to do what is
right.
—2 Timothy 3:16, NLT

MAY 7, 1903
MANHATTAN

Aunt Mae peered at Delia through her lorgnettes as she
held them to her eyes. "Let me get a good look at you. Do
sit up straighter. It won't do to have my niece slumping when
we drive through the most fashionable neighborhood in
Manhattan, now, will it?"

As the carriage driver shut the door behind her, closing out
the noise and bustle of the train station, Delia pressed her back
against the seat of her aunt's carriage and sat up straighter, rear-
ranging her skirts. "Yes, ma'am—I mean, Aunt Mae."

Frances sat beside Delia, familiar with the journey from the train station to Aunt Mae Wilson's home. On the journey here, she'd given Delia as many details as possible, especially about her aunt's strict routine since Frances had served as a maid and companion during her sister Veronica's visit to Manhattan.

"You look almost identical to Veronica, but I see you are lacking her confidence. We shall remedy that matter at once. You must remember you are a Lyndon, and you represent my family. Hold your chin up, girl. Sit up straight and be somebody." Aunt Mae clucked while patting her silvery white topknot. Had her hair turned whiter than the last time Delia had seen her?

She did as her aunt required, stiffening her spine.

"That's better. Now, I do happen to know a thing or two about your predicament," her aunt said as the carriage lurched forward, driven by a team of rather large beasts of burden.

"You do? I mean, yes, of course. Mama said she would send a telegram and a letter."

"And I have received both in advance of your arrival since the mail train makes fewer stops. Since you are named after me, Delia Mae Lyndon, I freely admit, I am looking forward to our time together. I do hope it will turn out to be a pleasant visit, but I have some expectations which will be adhered to while you are here."

"Yes, Aunt Mae." Delia dipped her head.

"For one thing, you won't be seeing much of New York, so I suggest you take a good look around as we make the drive toward my home. Of course, we'll take a drive each day during the afternoon promenade around Central Park. And I've decided we'll attend one of the Metropolitan Opera performances. The only other thing we will do—except attend church on Sundays, of course—is a luncheon at the Waldorf. You'll need an evening gown for the Metropolitan performance. I assume you brought one."

"Yes, Aunt Mae, I did."

"Very good. You shall spend the majority of your time with me in solitude, reflection, and prayer so you can weigh the true desires of your heart. We will also pray the guilt or innocence of this Thaddeus Sullivan will come clear in the time you are away. Near the end of your visit, we will attend the race at Pimlico in Baltimore, the Dinner Party Stakes. Well, that was the big race at Pimlico when I was about your age and attended with my father, your grandfather Colonel Lyndon, and my brother, your dear father. They kept the Dinner Party Stakes and added a race, naming it the Preakness Stakes, after a horse by that name proved himself on the track. I remember it quite well, but we'll save that for another day. As I understand it, your pa, Jake, and Thaddeus will meet us there along with their jockeys, a groom, and your pa's trainer. By then, we shall trust God's will is evident. When we return to New York, we will do a little shopping to purchase your trousseau and a wedding dress. It won't be as extravagant as what I purchased for Veronica because I am told there is the risk of you running away. But I expect if you choose correctly this time, that won't happen again. Then off you will go to plan the details of your simple but elegant parlor wedding. Either way, this will be settled once and for all. Have I made myself perfectly clear?"

Delia gulped. Aunt Mae was so like Delia's father—so certain of herself that she expected the Almighty Himself to sit up and take notice. "Yes, Aunt Mae. But what if I can't hear the Lord's voice in this matter?"

Aunt Mae guffawed. "Well, then, sing to Him, child. He inhabits the praises of His people. And now let me inform you of my social expectations..."

Delia listened as her aunt prattled on about her various house rules. While she found her aunt's plan rigid, it might also prove helpful. The majority of her time would be spent in peace and quiet, reflecting. Perhaps she could finally grasp what the Lord wanted her to do with her future.

"Since we have church tomorrow morning, it will be an early night. And I'm sure you are famished and exhausted from your long journey."

Her aunt's words rang true. Delia couldn't wait to have a hot meal of something other than the lighter fare the train offered. A good night's rest would do her wonders, and then she had best sing praises to the Lord as quickly as possible.

~

Delia thoroughly enjoyed the leisurely pace of the next few days with her aunt, and especially their outings, including one to see *Madame Butterfly* at the Metropolitan Opera House. To her delight, her aunt pointed out the boxes owned by the Vanderbilts, the Astors, and J.P. Morgan. Wearing an evening gown in a shade of forest green, Delia reveled in seeing the golden damask stage curtains, the sunburst chandelier over the auditorium, and the proscenium arch inscribed with the names of famed composers such as Mozart, Beethoven, and Verdi.

Her aunt surprised her, taking her for dinner during the hour-and-a-half-long intermission at a French restaurant near the theater, where they feasted on Oysters Rockefeller for an appetizer followed by a salad of lettuce and cucumbers with vinaigrette. Her aunt ordered the chicken Florentine for them, served with roasted carrots and a crusty bread her aunt referred to as a baguette. For dessert, Aunt Mae selected a new dessert called pêche Melba, consisting of peaches served with raspberry sauce over a scoop of vanilla ice cream. The restaurant's delicious food surpassed dinner at home.

The tragic ending of the opera performance gave Delia much to think about. Aunt Mae introduced her to a few of her friends as they left her private box, but Delia certainly wouldn't remember any of their names since her aunt hurried them to the carriage, telling her she had a second surprise.

"Where are we going?" Delia asked, glancing at her time-piece pinned to her gown. "It's already ten o'clock in the evening."

"I'm taking you to my favorite Italian bakery for more ice cream. Unfortunately, the dessert we tried earlier has not satisfied my craving for something sweet, but this particular bakery serves one of my favorite desserts—a scoop of Italian gelato with tiramisu ladyfinger cakes."

"Oh, how delicious!" Delia exclaimed, a smile spreading across her face.

Her aunt's driver navigated their open carriage through the traffic while the city glowed with gas lamps on street corners. The sidewalks seemed constantly alive with inhabitants bustling along, enjoying the nightlife. Dozens of restaurants, hotels, shops, museums, tall buildings, and theaters lined every block. Now and then, a motor carriage honked a horn or buzzed past them, its engine roaring. Carriages, cabs, and electric trolleys darted in every direction.

When they settled at a table inside the bakery with all sorts of confections on display in its glass cases, Aunt Mae fixed a hopeful expression on her. "Did you enjoy the performance?"

Delia clasped her hands together on the table. "I did. Thank you for taking me to see it."

"You sound hesitant." Her aunt stirred the cup of hot tea she had ordered to accompany their dessert.

"I'm not a huge fan of stories which end in tragedies. I feel anguish deeply, and my heart aches for Madame Butterfly. But the play makes me think about how important it is to marry a man who will truly love you."

"Yes." Aunt Mae tilted her head to one side. "I hope you marry someone like my husband, your Uncle George. I know you probably barely remember him, but he faithfully loved me alone throughout our marriage. He always made me his priority, looking after all of my needs. He put me above his own needs and desires. He prepared for my future, too, leaving me an independently wealthy woman when he passed."

Delia considered her aunt's words and the play while she ate the gelato quietly, watching through the restaurant's window near their table as various couples passed by on the busy street. Some of them walked arm in arm, and others held hands. Some laughed, and others walked briskly, side by side, in a hurry to be somewhere. She tried to picture Jake in the city and found she could not, but she could see Thaddeus enjoying the busy atmosphere.

"Have you spoken about faith with your two beaux?"

"Many times," Delia answered, not surprised by her aunt's question. Aunt Mae spoke of prayer and her Scripture readings frequently.

"Which of these two men in your life has a stronger faith?" Her aunt's brow arched, curiosity in her eyes.

"Thaddeus doesn't like to speak about his faith much, but he will discuss it if pressed. We grew up in the same church, but Jake applies his faith in life to everything. I believe it is because Thaddeus doesn't need his faith as much as Jake does, having to raise his three little orphaned nieces and start over in life in a new state after the loss of his sister."

"Faith says a lot about a man. A man must be humble and recognize his need for God. If he relies on his family, friends, position, or his riches, it can all be taken away in an instant. But the Lord is there forever if a man is committed to follow Him." Her aunt gave her a knowing look. "I can see you being a mother to those three little nieces. And maybe having some of your own children too. Do you think it's possible God has called you to that role?"

"I suppose it could be possible. I enjoyed my week with

them when he needed an emergency nanny." Delia reached for her tea. "Becoming a mother figure to Jake's nieces has crossed my mind a few times."

"And you say Jake is from upstate New York in the Adirondack Park..."

"That's right. Green Island on Lake George. He worked in the stable for the resort there," she reminded her aunt, though she'd mentioned it earlier in her visit.

"Jesus was born in a humble stable," her aunt said. Delia nodded before her aunt continued. "And you said he owns a champion horse and is building an inn in that old Victorian across the road from Velvet Brooks."

"That's all true, while Thaddeus lives in a mansion with many servants."

"And if you marry Thaddeus, you'll live at Sullivan Hill with all those servants. I remember the estate. The Sullivans have always had something a bit wrong with them. They are uppity folks, but I realize you've grown up with Thaddeus. You must like him an awful lot to go back to him after running away from him. Wasn't he upset that you jilted him at the altar in front of all of Lexington?" Her aunt shifted in her seat, and her brows furrowed.

Delia grimaced. "Yes, but he has forgiven me. He understood it was all because of that dream I told you about."

"Oh, yes, the fire dream." Her aunt ate another bite of her gelato. "And then you saw a fire at Jake's. Definitely a connection there."

"I've thought so too. But all that aside, it's Thaddeus's mother who has had trouble forgetting I was a runaway bride."

"I can understand that. A mother would hurt for her son and the family reputation." Her aunt sighed. "Well, if it were me, I think I'd be happier without the mother-in-law and without sharing the mansion with the Sullivan family."

"He offered to build us a little house apart from the

mansion, but I think I'd enjoy living in it, at least for a few years." Remorse instantly flooded Delia. Was her desire for status and wealth a weakness, blinding her to the truth about Thaddeus?

Aunt Mae's lips pinched together, hinting at concern. "It seems to me you'd be much happier with Jake. He will need and appreciate you, based on what you mentioned about the praise he lavished on you for helping him with his nieces and the house. Sounds as though he will treat you like a queen."

Delia sat back and blinked at her. "Do you not think Thaddeus would as well?"

"Thaddeus will never be happy being a third-born son living in the shadow of his father's success, his older brothers, and under his mother's thumb. I hate to say it, but from what little you've told me, I believe it would be an uphill battle all the way for happiness if you wed your childhood sweetheart. As for those mysterious incidents you mentioned, it really does sound as though Thaddeus will stop at nothing to have you and has lost his mind with jealousy over Jake's proposal to you. Though maybe I've got it all wrong." Aunt Mae shrugged. "Perhaps it's someone else entirely who is sabotaging Jake."

Delia had stiffened. "Yes, but who? He doesn't seem to have any other enemies, yet I don't think it's Thaddeus. He can be feisty, but he's not a criminal."

Her aunt shook her head, her eyes wide. "It's important you have a healthy view of things. Perceptions aren't always a reflection of the truth. I could tell you stories about the Sullivan ancestors. I'm surprised your father hasn't mentioned old Ned Sullivan."

"Ned?"

"Yes, Ned. Some distant cousin or uncle who used to live in the area. He shot a fellow on Main Street who came to Lexington in the early days to open a bank and give Sullivan's Savings & Loan some competition." Aunt Mae waved her spoon around as she spoke. "And then one of the Sullivans paid off the sheriff, so they never pressed charges. Ned got away with a cold-blooded murder in broad daylight and then moved away."

Delia's eyes widened, and her mouth dropped open.

"Then there was Susie Sullivan, Ned's daughter. She ran off with some dirt-poor farmer and left Abel Sullivan with four children and no mother. He raised all four of them and married some other woman. Then Susie wanted to come back, and of course, it was too late for that. Did I mention Ellen Sullivan? Another cousin, but before your generation. I went to school with her. She ran off to Europe with some fellow and never came back."

"Oh, dear me, I don't think Pa told me any of these stories. Mama didn't mention any of them either."

"My father, Colonel Lyndon, your grandfather, used to talk about these stories with my mother every now and then. I guess at the time Ned shot that fellow, I wasn't even born yet. Over the years, I learned a lot by listening. Now your pa, my brother, he would get bored and fall asleep, so he probably doesn't remember some stories I've heard that I won't bore you with." Aunt Mae stifled a yawn. "I'm getting sleepy myself now. We should be on our way home."

Delia reflected upon the stories her aunt had shared on the drive home. Apparently, Thaddeus had a number of previous relations with a considerably dark past. Did they have some sort of generational curse? Faith in Jesus could break such a bondage, but not if Thaddeus hadn't truly placed his trust in the Lord.

~

elia enjoyed the daily carriage rides through Central Park, Sunday mornings at church, and lunch with Aunt Mae in one of the Waldorf Hotel dining rooms, but by the day after the visit to the opera house, she had only a few days left to pray about her future and come to a decision. The race at Pimlico approached all too fast. Settled in her bedroom at her aunt's home, she perused all of her Bible studies and notes.

She'd attempted to write out the pros and cons about Jake and Thaddeus. She'd read her Bible, studying stories of famous couples in the Bible such as Ruth and Boaz, Mary and Joseph, Abraham and Sarah, Isaac and Rebecca, and Rachel and Jacob. She made lists about the most noteworthy attributes and problems of each couple. She tried to draw parallels from the various characters to the two men in her life.

She'd knelt in prayer each day, waiting for the Lord to speak to her heart. And she sang praises as much as possible. Not too loud, of course, but frequently. Finally, she heard the Lord speak in a whisper, directing her to read James 4:3. She flipped her Bible open to the verse. *Ye ask, and receive not, because ye ask amiss, that ye may consume it upon your lusts.*

She knew exactly what the Lord meant and that she must repent.

As if her heart and ears had opened, she recalled her thoughts in the garden the night before Thaddeus and Jake proposed. Thoughts about wanting to marry Thaddeus in order to have the status and wealth to accomplish benevolent works. Benevolent works might be good, but to marry Thaddeus mainly because of this desire constituted wrong motives in God's eyes. She'd also wished she would never again have to wear hand-me-downs. God wouldn't want her to marry Thaddeus if too much of her wanted to do so to fill her desire for status and elegant new dresses.

And finally, she'd worried about not living up to Aunt

Eliza's expectations when she should care more about what God thought of her. Did she have a chasm so deep in her heart from Aunt Eliza's cruel words that she had been trying too hard all of these years to prove her worth? And all because a woman had spoken unkind words out of her own barrenness more than a decade ago?

Aunt Mae had said, "Perceptions aren't always a reflection of the truth." The Sullivans seemed to succeed at creating perceptions that frequently weren't true. Every family had its share of secrets, but if infidelity and murder ran thick through the Sullivan bloodline, perhaps she didn't want to marry a Sullivan, after all.

Had her perceptions been so skewed that she hadn't been able to see all the love and honor Jake offered her? If God was leading her to marry Jake, she should heed the call.

The Lord directed her to John 10:10. *The thief cometh not, but for to steal, and to kill, and to destroy: I am come that they might have life, and that they might have it more abundantly.* The Lord didn't mind if she had nice things, but He had come to give her so much more—joy, peace, love, good health, and faith, for instance.

The Holy Spirit, the teacher of all things, brought another verse to her mind, reminding her to keep the Lord at the center of her heart, mind, and actions. *Seek ye first the Kingdom of God and His righteousness, and all these things shall be added unto you.*

If she valued her relationship with the Lord and expanding His Kingdom more than her desire for anything in the world, He would take care of all of her other needs. She should be content with whatever the Lord provided and what He gave her the strength to create—such as she did at her hat-trimming teas, where she ministered to the women in her social circle. The Word instructed followers of the Lord to be content in all circumstances.

Who do you want me to marry, Lord?

She strained to hear His voice. Not that she hadn't asked Him a hundred times already, but had she truly opened her spiritual ears and eyes to hear the truth before?

Trust me. I will show you once again, just as I have shown you once before.

Receiving an answer brought her up short. The dream? Perhaps He *had* tried to show her before. Perhaps the Lord had sent her the dream as a warning, showing her Thaddeus would set fire to Jake's barn. Her first instincts had caused her to flee from Thaddeus, both because of the dream and the nagging deep in her heart about marrying him for the wrong reasons. Perhaps she'd had just cause to flee, though she hadn't met Jake yet. At the time of the dream, she hadn't known she saw his barn burning. Perhaps her spirit had known.

CHAPTER TWENTY-TWO

The essential joy of being with horses is that it brings us in contact with the rare elements of grace, beauty, spirit, and freedom.
—Sharon Ralls Lemon, famous horsewoman

MAY 16, 1903
BALTIMORE, MARYLAND, PIMLICO RACECOURSE

The day of the race at Pimlico finally arrived. Delia held her hat firmly to her head as she looked around, taking in the stands, the yellow Victorian clubhouse with its green shutters and a balcony wrapping all the way around it, the stables, and the dirt track. Everyone wore their most fashionable clothing, all wanting to be seen in attendance at the event dating back to the days of George Washington himself. Carriages, steam railways, and electric trolleys brought fans to the oval track, aptly called "Old Hilltop" since it overlooked Jones Falls.

Aunt Mae had received a telegram a few days prior to the Preakness Stakes race, inviting them to meet Pa in the clubhouse at Pimlico for lunch at noon. Arriving on a train from Kentucky with their horses a day early, he'd also said to reserve a table with the maître d' to accommodate a party of about ten. Hence, Delia, Aunt Mae, and Frances—who had accompanied them on the train to Baltimore—situated themselves at a round linen-covered table with Pa, Red Brickman, and Jake. Charlie Ford and Gabriel Bolton wouldn't join them before the race since they had to watch their weight.

Thaddeus had registered Bluegrass Blaze for the same race as Horizon. Pa had said that should any of the Sullivans show up, he expected them all to be on their best behavior. When Thad still hadn't arrived by the second course, Aunt Mae clucked her tongue. She leaned toward Delia and whispered, "One would think he would at least join you for the meal, but perhaps he doesn't realize you are here yet. Then again, with an investigation underway, perhaps it is for the best."

With Jake seated on her other side, she could only nod in agreement. Nonetheless, they feasted on a four-course meal while she fought down her nerves. They still had a number of races to sit through for the next hour and a half before the day's featured race, leaving them plenty of time to linger over a delicious meal.

She had nearly finished her roast beef tips when a waiter delivered a message to Jake. He unfolded the note and read it, a look of grave concern appearing on his face.

She leaned forward, placing her hand on his. "What's happened?"

"Carter sent this note from the stable. Horizon has gone missing. He said to tell no one lest we be disqualified and meet him at the stable at once." Jake's brows furrowed as he handed the note to his right so Pa could read it for himself.

"The culprit who has it in for Jake strikes again," Red

Brickman said through a tense jaw. He tossed his linen napkin onto his dinner plate.

Pa finished reading the note. "Try to stay calm, everyone. We don't want anyone to get wind of this, or Jake will be out of the race. With officials crawling all over the stables, I don't know how we'll be able to hide the fact that Horizon's gone missing."

Aunt Mae placed her hand on her ample bosom. "The bigger question is, how do we find him in time for the race?"

"I can't help thinking the same rat who lives near Lottie Belle has followed us to Pimlico." Red raked a hand through his hair. "I shouldn't have left Carter alone to look after Horizon. This is all my fault."

Delia gulped. This time, she had to admit the truth of what Red inferred. Thaddeus, the common denominator and the one missing from among them, appeared to have struck in both Lexington and Baltimore.

"No, it's not your fault." Pa kept his voice low. "The horse can't be too far away. We both saw him less than an hour ago at the stable."

"So let's all go look for him, as Carter asked," Delia suggested softly.

"Good plan," Pa agreed with a curt nod.

"Let's hurry. Every moment wasted could cost us our chance at victory." Jake scooted his chair back but remained seated, reaching for Delia's hand. "But let's pray first."

Everyone bowed their heads, closed their eyes, and clasped hands around the table. Jake led the prayer in a husky, strained whisper. "Dear Lord, we need You to do what seems impossible and help us find our missing horse in time for the race. In Jesus's name we pray, knowing You hear us and are sending us victory in this very moment."

They stood in unison and filed out of the dining room, all of them on a mission. The clock was ticking, and they needed a miracle.

~

"And you're sure he's only been gone about half an hour?" Pa repeated.

Carter nodded. "I left the stall to get a cup of coffee. That took ten minutes. I'm real sorry, Jake. I should have waited for Red. I did as the protocol says. I put a Pimlico stable hand here at the door to guard him, but when I came back with the coffee, the attendant was gone. I haven't seen him since."

Delia cocked her head to one side. They'd all peeked in the stall at least three times, but no horse appeared. Only an empty bed of hay remained. On her right, an official headed their way with a clipboard in his hands. "Quick. Shut the stall door," she whispered. "Someone's coming."

Jake followed her glance and closed the stall door. Then he positioned himself in front of it. Red joined him, crossing his arms over his chest.

The official stopped at the neighboring stall first. He looked through the open top half of the door at the horse and checked something off his list before moving to Horizon's stall. The groom exchanged a greeting with him. The official stepped up to Delia and their group.

"And how's Horizon doing today? Ready to race?" The official's brows arched and he winked at her.

Delia returned his smile. "Yes sir, he's ready for the race."

The official nodded toward the stall, a pen poised in his hand. "Can you open the top half of the door? I need to see him myself. Part of the rules and all."

"Oh, no, we can't let anyone disturb his nap. You'll have to return later." Delia clasped her hands behind her back and offered her sweetest smile. "If he doesn't get an undisturbed nap, he doesn't race well. Strict rules of our trainer, Red Brick-man. You can see the notes on our entry form. The judges are aware."

The official gave Delia a sideways look. Then he grinned and nodded. "Reminds me of a horse I had once. I understand. I'll check back later."

When the man had moved on to the next row, they all breathed a sigh of relief.

"That was a close call." Jake wiped sweat beads from his forehead with the back of his hand.

"Quick thinking, Delia." It was Aunt Mae's turn to wink at her.

"We should find a bay horse to put in the stall until we return," Red muttered under his breath, obviously mindful of the fact other grooms stood around in the same row, most of them inside their stalls with their horses except for one at the far end who wandered in and out of the row.

A wiry fellow wearing a red-and-black plaid shirt with a slightly balding head stood to their right, in the direction the official had come from. He didn't wear a Pimlico uniform or badge, nor did he carry a clipboard. He didn't wear a groomer's badge either. He paced every so often and kept glancing in their direction, narrowing his eyes as he looked at them.

She had a hunch about the fellow and crossed to his side. "Excuse me, sir. Perhaps you could help us out. Have you seen any strange characters lurking about this row today?"

"Maybe," he replied.

"Perhaps you could speak to my friends about it." She beckoned him toward Horizon's stall.

He followed, but he hung back a little, a sheepish and disturbed look on his face.

Delia bit her lower lip. "This gentleman thinks he may have seen something out of place today. Isn't that correct, sir?"

The fellow looked to his right and then to his left. "How much does my information matter to ye?"

"I do love a good mystery." Aunt Mae opened the clasps of her purse. She withdrew a twenty-dollar bill and held it up. "Does this refresh your memory?"

He smiled and snatched the bill. "I do know where he be." He pointed to Horizon's empty stall.

Delia sucked in a breath.

"Can you lead us to him?" Jake's brows lifted, his expression hopeful.

"For a price." The fellow's tone was coy, and he kept his hands jammed in his pockets.

"Can you tell us how you know?" Pa crossed his arms over his chest, his lips pressed into a firm line. "And how far is it from here?"

"It's a twenty-minute hard ride. I know because the fella who paid me to take him where he be now gave me a hundred dollars and said meet him here by a certain time and he'd pay a hundred dollars more when the task was complete. Well, I been here since the certain time, and he ain't here."

Aunt Mae opened her purse again. She held another bill up, but this one she kept close to her heart. "I have a fifty to give you now if you'll lead us to him. None of us are from this area, and it'll be faster if you're with us. I'll give you another fifty if you'll help us get him back here in time for the Preakness Stakes. And, when we return, I'll give you yet another fifty if you show us the man who asked you to make him disappear in the first place."

The man stared at the bill clutched tightly to her chest. He appeared to ponder the offer for a few seconds. Then he nodded. "All right. You got yerself a deal. Ye can call me Harvey."

"Very well, Harvey. Follow us to my carriage. We'll have to move fast. I'm parked outside the gates in the sea of carriages."

Aunt Mae turned toward their trainer and tilted her chin up so the brim of her hat didn't obstruct her view. "Red, why don't you stay here with Jake and Carter, in case that official returns? Delia and Joseph will go with me. On the way there, my niece and brother can fight over who'll ride him back in time for the race."

❧

Half an hour later, after a harrowing rush to the parking area, and another harrowing search for her aunt's carriage, and an even more harrowing drive over hills and dales according to Harvey's directions—with Pa driving because Aunt Mae's driver had been taking a break when they found the carriage—they arrived at a farm in the countryside where Horizon grazed in a corral behind a barn.

Pa had struck a deal with Delia. He would drive the carriage, and she would race the horse back to Pimlico. Some discussion had taken place on the way to the farm over their worries about Horizon's stamina for the race. And all they could do was pray over the concern. It was the only chance the bay and Jake had.

With each passing minute vital to their success, she wasted no time climbing down from the carriage and dashing over to Horizon. Only, her efforts to hurry were nearly in vain. Harvey had to rummage around in the barn to find the saddle. A few minutes later, he brought it out, and Pa helped Delia saddle Horizon. It didn't matter that she'd have to ride astride rather than sidesaddle like a proper lady. Jake depended on her getting Horizon there with enough time left to recover whatever stamina the horse could muster and go on to win a huge race.

As Delia urged Jake's stallion beside the carriage, Pa settled back inside the driver's seat. "I'm not going to ask any questions, Harvey. But I sure would like to know who owns this farm and where the owner is at this precise moment."

Delia didn't have time to waste. "Pa, let's go. I paid close attention on the way here, but I expect you'll be right behind me in case I lose my way."

He snapped the reins to urge the team to her aunt's rented carriage forward. "Hold on to your hat, Mae. There's no time to lose if we don't want to miss the race."

Her aunt did as Pa advised, and Delia patted the magnificent horse. She could only pray God would supply the beautiful steed everything he needed. "Give me all you've got, Horizon, and save some for Pimlico. Godspeed, okay, boy?" The horse offered her a snicker of a neigh. Friskier than usual, Horizon seemed happy to see someone he recognized. Trusting he understood the mission, she dug her knees into his haunches and, snapping the reins, hollered, "Yaw!"

Horizon took off like an eagle. She leaned forward, low over his mane, as they passed the carriage. Pleased with his speed as they gained momentum, Delia prayed she and Horizon wouldn't make any wrong turns. Adrenalin pumped through her. God had given them half of their miracle in finding Jake's horse. Now they only needed the second half. Knowing the Lord had designed a victory, she didn't think too hard except to thank Jesus and revel in the midst of the miracle, enjoying the unfolding of it. They had less than thirty minutes to reach Pimlico in time for Horizon to line up with the other horses.

∾

Delia rounded the corner into the row where Jake, Red, and Carter waited by Horizon's stall, breathing a sigh of relief to see their smiles on her approach. Horizon's hooves clopped on the ground loudly, echoing down the row, drawing attention. She tried to remain natural and nonchalant as if racing him wildly to the end of the rows of stalls belonged to their usual warmup routine. She'd already determined if an official stopped her, she would merely say she'd done her part to warm him up for the race, acting as if she'd been riding inside the stable yard for some time.

"Ah, you're a sight for sore eyes, Delia," Jake said breathlessly as she dismounted. After patting Horizon, he pulled her close. He held the lead with one hand and her with his other, tipping her backward and lowering his mouth to hers, reminding her of the kiss they'd shared at the picnic with his nieces. My, what a kiss! This one made her lightheaded. Her knees went wobbly too. She didn't want it to end, but she also needed to breathe.

She hadn't expected his appreciation to take such a passionate and romantic form, and it left her flushed, her heart beating even more rapidly than from the exertion of the ride.

"How much time is left before the race? We've been riding hard for almost a full thirty minutes." Dizzy from his kiss and struggling to make her wind-blown self presentable, she'd lost all track of time. "That's if you count the twenty minutes of country roads and ten additional minutes to get through the gates."

Red cleared his throat, reminding Delia others were present as she attempted to re-pin her hat in place.

"We start lining up in ten," the trainer answered. "We knew if anyone could do it, you could."

"Well done, Miss Delia," Carter said, a wide grin on his face. "Ah, here comes Gabriel now."

Had they witnessed their kiss? Heat warmed her cheeks.

"Thank you. It was definitely a team effort." She patted the horse. "He needs some water and a cool down walk. Do you think he'll be all right?"

Carter nodded, taking the lead from Jake. "Let's go get some water, Horizon."

"Who's with Gold Dancer?" What a shame that in all of the events leading up to this moment, she hadn't had a chance to look in on their own champion.

"Charlie is mounting up now. We've been checking on him." Red turned as Gabriel approached. Jake offered the jockey the short version of their predicament.

Gabriel patted Horizon. "I thought he looked sweaty. He's taking it like a trooper. We'll do our best in the race."

"It's all we can do. May God be with you both," Jake replied, hope evident in his eyes as his jockey led his prize stallion down the row.

Pa and Aunt Mae, with Harvey in tow, hurried toward them.

Delia turned to the man whose kiss made her heart race. "Jake, will you escort me to the clubhouse balcony so we can watch the race together?"

Jake's anxious glance slid between her and his trainer.

"We got this, Jake. Go watch the race." Red waved. "I'll walk with Gabriel and Horizon to the starting line."

Nodding, Jake smiled at her. "Yes, I'd be delighted to join you."

After the long walk to the clubhouse balcony from the stables, Delia spotted Thaddeus there, looking around—presumably for them. He adjusted his fedora and attempted to loosen his tie as they navigated the crowd, moving closer to him.

"That's him!" Harvey pointed, elbowing Aunt Mae.

Delia stopped in her tracks, laboring to catch her breath.

"That's who?" Her aunt's eyes darted about beneath furrowed brows.

"The man who paid me to make your horse disappear."

Delia followed his gaze to Thaddeus—the common denominator between the sabotage attempts in Lexington and Baltimore, just as Red had inferred. Her heart sank, and she wrapped her hand tightly around Jake's.

"That's Thaddeus Sullivan," Pa informed Aunt Mae in a low voice.

Aunt Mae gasped. "I think I remember seeing him at Veronica's wedding. In fact, he used to run around Velvet Brooks with his siblings and your daughters, as I recall. I barely recognized him." Turning to Harvey, she opened the clasp of her pocketbook and held out the other fifty. "You can relax, Harvey. We won't bother you for any testimony or police statements. His father is filthy rich and will only attempt to pay off anyone who stands in their way, but all the same, we are thankful for your honesty in this despicable matter. And you've done well to right your wrong by helping us retrieve our champion horse. I believe you may consider yourself fully paid now."

Harvey tucked the final fifty-dollar bill inside his shirt pocket. "Thank you kindly, ma'am."

"Thank you, Harvey. And thank you, Mae. You've helped us a great deal." Pa nodded toward an open spot on the balcony near the railing. "Let's watch the race from over here. If Thaddeus sees us, we'll ignore him. I'm too angry for words."

"That makes two of us." Jake's fingers tightened over Delia's. "It's going to take a lot of extra prayer and forgiveness to get past everything he's done. We'll need to confront him at some point. He'll just keep doing this sort of thing if he thinks he can get away with it."

Delia squeezed Jake's hand back, feeling faint. She hadn't wanted to believe Thaddeus capable or guilty of such actions, but now the truth set her fully free from so many lies. The Sullivans were not the end-all-be-all answer to everything. Waves of disappointment washed over her. God had been trying to warn her for a long time. And in His mercy, she now knew she could never marry Thaddeus Sullivan.

She gazed up at Jake when they settled near the balcony

railing with a fine view of the track. They would stand for the race along with the other clubhouse members and guests. "Try not to let his actions ruin your enjoyment of the race or the sport. He has shown his true colors, but not everyone behaves as he does."

He pulled her closer to him with an arm around her waist. "Does this mean you'll be accepting my offer of marriage, Miss Delia Lyndon?" Jake's blue eyes locked on hers.

Heat again rose to her cheeks. "Yes, Jake Williams. It certainly does."

He picked her up off of her feet and held her close in his arms, causing Pa, Aunt Mae, and other bystanders who overheard Jake's question to smile and nod in their direction. Delia didn't care. She was too happy to be with the man she now knew God wanted her to marry. No more wrestling over the decision of who she would spend the rest of her life with.

"I'm happy for the two of you. May I be the first to congratulate you both on your engagement?" Pa reached inside his suit's breast pocket and handed Delia the engagement ring she'd placed in his desk drawer for safekeeping alongside the one from Thaddeus since she'd found either difficult to wear while undecided about her suitors. "I didn't know at the time why I thought to bring this, but I had a feeling you might be needing it."

"Oh, Pa! Thank you!" Delia slid the ring on her finger and held it out for Aunt Mae to admire.

"It's a beautiful ring. Well done, Jake. Welcome to the family," her aunt said, shaking her fiancé's hand.

"Congratulations." Apparently, Harvey had trailed them into the grandstand. He shook Jake's hand too.

"Thank you, everyone. I can hardly believe I have the most beautiful bride-to-be." Jake kept gazing at Delia with a wide smile.

His smile was contagious, telling her she would be safe in

his care forever, cherished, and loved. She couldn't help but return the smile, contentment and relief filling her finally untangled heart.

"I see we have a lot more celebrating to do when the race is over." Aunt Mae grinned at them. "And a great deal of shopping for someone's wedding trousseau when we get back to New York."

"Oh, Aunt Mae..." Delia couldn't find words to express her affection for her father's sister who'd done so much to help them already. She wouldn't turn down shopping.

Harvey inched toward the steps. "I should probably be going now."

"Don't leave, Harvey. Stay and watch the race with us." Delia held her hand out to him. "I want you to see what a champion Horizon is, as well as celebrate the love on our own new horizon."

A flag waved, simultaneous to a gunshot. The race began, and they turned their attention to the horses as they dashed toward the clubhouse turn, their speed kicking up a cloud of dust behind them. The familiar thunder of their hooves rumbled as the pack grew closer. Observers held their breath, watching the riders navigate around the first turn of the oval. They moved along the far side of the track, and then finally into the final turn.

Coming out of the turn, everyone began cheering as Gold Dancer and Horizon took the lead. Bluegrass Blaze stretched his neck out but fell behind in a pocket of other horses, all of them vying for a chance at third. Neck and neck, Gold Dancer and Horizon sped alongside each other for the victory, approaching the finish line, both way out in front with a five-length lead.

"Look at them go!" Delia couldn't help but squeal, jumping up and down. Even Aunt Mae clapped. Jake hollered for joy, as did Pa.

The horses crossed the line at the same time for a stunning finish. Several horses Delia didn't recognize came in behind them, but they had to wait for the announcer to know if their horses and jockeys had tied. A few moments passed, and finally, the announcer's voice proclaimed a tie between Gold Dancer and Horizon.

They cheered so loudly on their balcony corner, Delia hadn't heard who took second or third, but she didn't care. Both horses were champions. She would be going home to Kentucky soon, engaged to a man who would love her fully, having waited patiently for her. God had chosen him to be her husband, erasing all of her doubts and fears.

CHAPTER TWENTY-THREE

Now when they saw the boldness of Peter and John, and
perceived that they were unlearned and ignorant men, they
marveled; and they took knowledge of them, that they had
been with Jesus.

—Acts 4:13

June 3, 1903

Delia's train arrived in Lexington from New York on a
sunny Wednesday afternoon. Jake picked her up at the
station. When he finished loading her trunk and they settled
into his carriage, he handed her a copy of the *Lexington Gazette*,
folded open to the page featuring one of her short stories.

"My pirate story!" she exclaimed. "They accepted it."

He smiled at her. "I loved every word, and especially the
fact you used your own name."

Setting the paper aside, she threw her arms around his neck

and gave him a kiss on the cheek. "I couldn't have done it without your encouragement."

"Ruby will enjoy reading it too. She's already seen it, but we were running late this morning. I told her she could read it after school." He drew back and took up the leads. "We're picking them up next."

"I can't wait to see them. Have you told them about our engagement?" She arched her brow.

"I have. They are overjoyed. They want to be in the wedding." He snapped the reins, and the carriage pulled away from the train station.

"They can be our bridesmaids."

"I'll let you tell them," he said, a tone of approval in his voice as he leaned toward her with a smile. He focused on driving for a while before he stole a glance in her direction. "We need to set a wedding date."

"How does Saturday, June twenty-seventh sound?" She tucked her arm in his elbow, looking up at him with hope in her heart.

"Can we be ready by then? I'll need a new suit."

She nodded. "My aunt helped me find a seamstress who will be shipping my wedding gown here next week. I'm sure Mama's local seamstress can make little bridesmaid dresses for the girls. And since it will be a parlor wedding at Velvet Brooks as we agreed upon, everything will be simple and elegant. I'll order a cake, we'll have daisies for flowers, and we can ask our preacher to perform the ceremony. We'll need a light meal, and we'll only have a few invitations to pen. If we send those out soon, your parents and my Aunt Mae will have time to make arrangements to attend."

"I like everything you've said. It sounds perfect. We can't forget to invite Red, Carter, Gabriel, Charlie, Thimble, and Brady."

"Yes, everyone from Velvet Brooks and Leonora too."

Delia breathed a sigh of relief. The details of their wedding paled in comparison to her anticipation of belonging to him.

∼

JUNE 8, 1903
VELVET BROOKS

Gladdie peered out from one of the dining room windows. "Thaddeus is on the veranda, pacing, looking around for you."

"Thaddeus is here?" Delia, seated at Mama's secretary, finished signing her letter to Aunt Mae sharing a few details about her impending nuptials. Should she speak to him?

Mama had gone to town with Pa to pick up the bridesmaid dresses from the seamstress. Ruby, Ella, and Mary had enjoyed several trips to town for their fittings and could hardly contain their excitement.

She hadn't seen Thaddeus since Pimlico. In truth, he was the very last person she wished to see. Jake's investigation had come up empty, but it remained open, though Pa and everyone else had doubts about it being resolved. What could Thaddeus possibly have to say now? Had he come to apologize? Wish her well? She'd returned his ring.

Twisting in her seat to see her sister's face, she bit her lower lip. "I don't suppose I could prevail upon you to tell him I am incapacitated?"

Knocking on the door gave them further pause. Martin's polite greeting drifted from out in the hall.

Gladdie crossed her arms over her elegant white blouse with its high-neck lace collar. "You can't delay speaking to him forever."

"I suppose you are right." Reluctantly, she rose from the desk as the butler stepped inside the room.

"Thaddeus, requesting to speak with you, Miss Delia. I left him on the veranda and told him I would see if you were receiving callers." Martin's brows lifted as he waited for her instruction.

"Against my better judgment, I'll see what he wants." Delia breezed past Martin and stepped outside, closing the door softly behind her.

The sight of him standing near his horse, the dapple-gray named Sir Rodger, tethered to a hitching post alongside the veranda, filled her with sorrow. Sorrow for his choices, and perhaps a twinge of remorse over her inability to help him become the kind of man he could be.

"Hello, Thaddeus. What brings you to Velvet Brooks?"

He turned away from the horse and stepped closer to her. "Delia, sweetheart. I have come to insist you reconsider my proposal. I know how happy we can be together. Haven't we proven that over all these years? Don't we deserve this chance?"

She shook her head, staring at him, surprised at his audacity. But then, why should that surprise her? Didn't he see the very opposite was true? They could never be truly happy together. "No, Thaddeus. I can't marry you. I'm sorry, but I just can't."

She'd spent years living in fear and trepidation at his side, worried about acceptance, worried about his reaction to everything she said or did. Always trying to soothe his temper. Never fully free to reach her full potential. Seldom encouraged by him.

Their relationship aside, he had done everything possible to undermine Jake's chances at happiness, regardless of whom he might hurt along the way, selfish about his own ambitions in nearly everything he did. It had taken her so long to see the truth.

Thaddeus stepped closer, his hands wrapping around her

forearms. "You must marry me, Delia. I insist that you marry me. We make the perfect couple." His grip tightened.

Wincing, she shook her head and took a step back, but he didn't let go. "No, Thaddeus. Please, release me. You're hurting me."

He ignored her plea. "Delia, if you don't marry me, I will tell everyone how your grandfather acquired his riches. Everyone will know Colonel Lyndon is nothing but a common thief, a fraud. It will destroy you and your family. No one will come to the Velvet Brooks Vintage once they know the truth about his involvement in raiding the good families of the South during the war."

"You wouldn't dare!" Her mouth dropped open that he would threaten to stoop so low, thinking he could succeed in forcing her to marry him. Had he lost his mind? She squirmed in his grip, trying to free herself, but he only tightened his hold.

"I will. And when no one brings their horses to your pa for training, then what? Where will you be then?" He dropped his hands from her arms and took a step back. "I expect your answer before the week is out."

She put her hands on her hips and tilted her chin up. "You will never hear from me!"

He laughed in her face and crossed to his horse. He untied his horse and swung up into the saddle. Gathering the reins, he grinned down at her. "I know better. Your family will be ruined, and you know it too."

Delia spun around and went inside, slamming the door. Shaking, and glad to be rid of him for now, she returned to the desk. She would have a cup of tea, say a prayer, and regain her composure. Would he really spread this tale, this horrid rumor, all over Lexington? What would Pa say? What would Jake tell her?

~

A few hours later, Delia had recovered the best she could from the earlier confrontation. She sat at Mama's little desk penning her reply to the second note she'd received from Jake that day. Martin had delivered both notes on the little silver tray he carried with the household mail and calling cards.

Jake's first note had simply read, *I just wanted to tell you how much I love you.* She had replied, *We are living a beautiful dream I never want to wake up from. I love you too.* The note had arrived prior to Thaddeus's horrid visit.

Jake's second note read,

I've placed an ad in the paper for a cook and a housekeeper, but I thought you might like to conduct the interviews as replies arrive.

She skimmed what she had thus far written in response.

Yes, I would very much like to conduct the interviews. Are Ruby's little legs getting tired delivering these notes back and forth between our homes?

In fact, Ruby waited in the hall while Martin made small talk with her, so Delia bent her head and began a new paragraph with reluctance.

I have some disturbing news. Thaddeus appeared on the veranda only an hour ago, insisting I marry him. He is threatening to tell a family secret about my grandfather, Colonel Lyndon. I do not know how, but he has knowledge of my grandfather obtaining a vast sum after raiding plantations owned by wealthy Confederates during the Civil War. Pa told me it is how my sisters and I have such a generous dowry. I haven't told anyone of his visit, yet I spent part of this morning in tears. Clearly, he has never truly cared for my happiness if

She melted some candle wax and sealed the page with the stamp bearing her initials. How she looked forward to the one she'd ordered with her new initials for use after her wedding.

Delia rose from the writing desk and stepped out into the hall. She gave the note to Jake's niece. "See that you always look both ways before crossing Cornflower Road, Ruby."

"Yes ma'am." Ruby grinned and dashed out the front doors, leaving Delia with a smile on her face. Frown lines returned to her forehead when she returned to the writing desk.

Buggy wheels crunched over the gravel in the drive. Carter greeted her parents, back from town. They entered the house, and her mother fussed at the mirror, removing her hat while Pa brought in the package with the bridesmaid dresses and placed it on the dining room table.

Mama poked her head around the corner. "Was that little Ruby delivering another love note from Jake?"

"Yes. She enjoys it so, and it's summertime. No school. And she's doing so well with her riding. We've practiced with her through the Velvet Brooks Vintage showmanship jumping course at least a dozen times now. She is clearing all of the obstacles on Gallant Maiden."

Mama entered the room, her wedding planning notebook under her arm. Pa patted Delia's shoulder and headed toward his desk in the library.

Mama smiled as she flipped her notebook open to one of her lists. "I've seen her practicing. She's a natural, just as you were, Delia. You are going to enjoy having those three girls to mother once you are wed." She placed her index finger on the page before her. "I've ordered the flowers and the cake. I know you and Jake completed his fitting yesterday."

"Yes. Gladdie and I enjoyed the outing. We saw Jake's suit.

He looks so handsome, and the girls will look adorable in their white dresses and peach sashes."

"Excellent. Once you select the dishes, Martin and Frances will see to the china and the crystal and polish the silver. Have we forgotten any last-minute invitations for any out-of-town folks?"

"All mailed last week," Delia confirmed, biting her lower lip. What would Mama say when she heard about the latest provocation from Thaddeus?

"All that remains is trying on your wedding dress, then finalizing a menu and renting some chairs for the parlor. We'll tackle those things over the next few days. I think we deserve a break today, though."

"Thank you, Mama. I appreciate your help."

"I can't tell you how happy I am about the fact you are marrying Jake." Mama closed her wedding planning ledger. "If we can get through the competition for the Velvet Brooks Vintage, we'll be fine."

"I'm glad too. Jake loves me with all of his heart. He will look after me properly and be an honorable husband. None of us could have known about Thaddeus. It was such a shock." Sighing, she told her mother about his recent threat.

"Don't panic." Mama touched her shoulder. "I'll tell your pa. He'll know what to do."

A knock on the front door gave them no time to continue the discussion.

"I have a feeling it's Jake. I'll let him in. I told him about Thaddeus." Delia rose from the writing desk.

"I'll get your pa. The four of us can put our heads together. Bring Jake to the library."

Her mother crossed the hall to the library while Delia welcomed her fiancé. A few minutes later, they gathered around Pa's desk.

"I think Delia and I should stand up to Thaddeus," Jake

announced, sitting up tall and straight in the chair beside Delia. A commanding presence in the room, he rested the palms of his hands on his knees. "Unless you think we need to drive into Lexington to ask the colonel about the validity of this threat, which seems a waste of time. Lots of soldiers on the Northern side conducted those kinds of raids during the war. Sherman raided all the way to the Atlantic. I can't imagine why Thaddeus thinks it would upset us now, fifty years later."

Delia looked to her father. "He has a good point. What do you think, Pa?"

Pa shifted in his seat. "Jake, you know history better than our opponent, and Thaddeus was a history major. I know all about the raids. My father told us stories about them many a time. I agree with you. Thaddeus won't back down or give us a moment's peace until someone calls his bluff. What kind of confrontation do you have in mind?"

Delia held back a moan. Would their attempt to confront Thaddeus backfire and ruin their wedding?

～

June 20, 1903

The day of the annual showmanship competition arrived. Locals and guests from across the state arrived to participate as observers and competitors. The lawn of Velvet Brooks filled with neighbors, friends, and family. Ruby waited astride Gallant Maiden, next in line to compete on the course. Stiff in her saddle, she gave Delia and Jake a quavering smile.

Delia held Mary while Jake held Ella's hand as they took their places at the railing to cheer Ruby on. With her wedding to Jake only a week away, Delia hoped his plan to confront Thaddeus would bring an end to his relentless attacks.

However, at the moment, all of her attention centered on Ruby. They'd worked hard to simultaneously plan the wedding and practice jumps with Ruby.

Her big moment finally arrived, and the announcer introduced her as Ruby Williams, age nine, from Lottie Belle Farm. The crowd clapped as she waved and sat up straight in the saddle. She wore the new fashionable riding breeches called jodhpurs which Delia had made for her from a sewing pattern, a tweed jacket, and a white blouse with a fancy high-neck collar. Her cap hid most of her hair, pulled into a sleek bun at the nape of her neck.

"Atta girl, Ruby. You can do it!" Jake called out.

A smile appeared on her face. She'd heard her uncle's words.

Delia exchanged a smile with Jake.

When the flag lowered, the clock started with an official clicking a stopwatch. Ruby urged her horse forward. Gallant Maiden sailed over the first jump. The crowd clapped. She made the second and third jumps, too, gliding through the air like a professional champion.

Delia bit her lower lip, praying for Ruby. If she could make the next two jumps without any trouble, she would have a chance at one of the best times in the event. Ruby leaned in for the final jumps without any hesitation, completing the course in record time to thundering applause. Now they only had to wait and see how the last two competitors would do.

Delia had to restrain herself from biting her nails while waiting for the others to finish the course, but finally, the announcer stepped up on the platform to read the top three names. "Third place goes to Amelia Bloom from Jefferson County, second place to Elizabeth Gardener from Lincoln County, and first place goes to..." The announcer paused. Then he raised his voice. "Ruby Williams from Fayette County! Please come forward and accept your trophies, ladies."

Jake and Delia clapped vigorously, and when Ruby stepped onto the platform to receive her award, a huge smile on her nine-year-old face, Delia released a contented sigh. The sweet girl deserved it. She had worked hard to earn it, sometimes riding for several hours each day to master her jumps.

Later that night, Velvet Brooks came alive for the grand ball held under the tent erected on the front lawn. Lanterns lit up the dancing platform, and candles glowed from hurricane globe lamps. Waiters circulated with trays offering finger foods, punch, cider, and hors d'oeuvres to their guests. Ladies dressed in ball gowns waited for gentlemen in their finest suits to ask them to dance. Children danced, too, and outside the tent, visitors could look up at the stars dotting the sky. A sinfonia of musicians took up several rows of chairs beside the platform where couples swirled in each other's arms.

Jake approached where Delia sat in her cream-colored ball gown trimmed in lavender lace. "Care to join me in a dance?" He extended his hand, looking ever so handsome in his dinner jacket. When had he purchased the new suit?

"I'd love to." Delia accepted his hand, allowing him to pull her to her feet.

How wonderful it felt as Jake held her close and they swirled about in a waltz amid other couples. She could finally —unequivocally, without shame, reservation, or fear—hold her head up before Aunt Eliza. For the first time in years, the pressure to prove her worth by becoming a Sullivan had melted away. She had the joy of being accepted and deeply loved simply by being exactly who the Lord had made her.

After the dance, Jake escorted her to their seats and offered to return shortly with punch. Veronica bounced little Edward on her knee while her husband looked on with a smile. Gladdie had given in to a dance with Percy. Pa and Mama circulated among guests. Both sets of her grandparents sat together around a large table with her Louisville relations, including

Aunt Eliza and Aunt Ida. They would return next weekend for her parlor wedding, one she wouldn't need to run away from. Aunt Celia Jane had agreed to play the piano again too.

What was taking Jake so long? When a tall form appeared before her, Delia glanced up expectantly. But it wasn't Jake. Thaddeus didn't ask her to dance. No, he merely pulled her onto her feet and dragged her to the dancing platform, too shocked to protest. Squeezing her arm, he forced her to follow him up its three steps.

"Enjoying the ball, Delia?" he asked as he swirled her around in time to the music, his face unreadable.

Judging from his mood, it wouldn't do to further displease him. "Y-yes, I am. A-and you?" Her head spun from the way he whirled her around too many times and too fast.

"You're making a mistake by marrying Jake. You know he isn't good enough for you. It was always meant that our families and our two farms should merge." Thaddeus gazed into her eyes, his expression strangely hard. "There's still time for you to change your mind. You could run away from him as you once ran from me...only this time, you could run *to* me. We could marry at a justice of the peace and go away on a luxurious honeymoon, anywhere you like."

"As I've said, I can't marry you, Thaddeus. We'd never be happy." How could she convince him? "I'm sure there are a dozen girls here you'd be happier with."

"No. There is no one for me but you." He grimaced. "But perhaps you have decided you want me to tell everyone about your stealing, cheating grandfather, Colonel Lyndon."

Delia prayed silently, imploring the Lord to rescue her from Thaddeus. They hadn't planned for Thaddeus to find a way to be alone with her when they had talked about the confrontation.

Abruptly, the music ended. Everyone looked toward the musicians.

Jake stood before them, waving for them to stop. In one smooth leap, he jumped onto the platform and then strode in their direction. Reaching her side, Jake pulled her away from Thaddeus. "Thaddeus Sullivan, you are no longer welcome to dance with Miss Lyndon, my fiancée."

All eyes focused on them. Would Thaddeus take the bait and protest?

"Your fiancée? She is *my* fiancée!" Thaddeus's eyes glazed as he fairly shouted his reply.

"No, she is not your fiancée. She is mine. Why is she mine? I think all of Lexington deserves to know, and the rest of those here from throughout Kentucky. We know you are the one responsible for burning my barn to the ground. We have a witness."

"A w-witness isn't proof," Thaddeus sputtered. "Witnesses can be mistaken. Or bought."

"*And* we know you are responsible for hiring two men to beat up my jockey. They left him for dead in an alley with broken ribs, a broken nose, and a broken wrist." Jake glared at him. "He's lucky to be alive." Jake pointed toward Brady Danford.

Brady stood up, his wrist still in a cast, his arm in a sling. Gasps and murmurs ran through the crowd.

"I did no such thing. You're making all this up."

"Oh, just like you hired Harvey to make Horizon disappear before the Preakness Stakes at Pimlico." Jake shook his head. Delia clung to his side, thankful her fiancé spoke with such courage. "But the man you hired came forward and led us to find Horizon and bring him back in time to ride to victory. But to think what you put that horse through and the fact you tried to cheat me out of a fair race. It's unsportsmanlike conduct on the highest of levels. You deserve a prison sentence, but I'm choosing to offer you mercy instead."

Thaddeus crossed his arms over his chest, apparently unable to think of any reply.

"If all that wasn't enough, you spread false rumors all over Lexington about me. I should sue you for defamation of character. If I brought in a prosecutor from a different state, I'd have a chance to win. But since you keep running to daddy to pay off the sheriff and the district attorney, and maybe judges, too, I suppose you think you can continue your sinful deeds. And finally, you threatened to bribe Delia into marrying you by messing with Colonel Lyndon, Delia's grandfather, a pillar and a hero in this community."

Harold Sullivan rose from his seat, but he didn't interrupt Jake. More gasps and murmurs.

"I d-did n-no such thing." Thaddeus dropped his arms to his sides, inflating his chest.

"Yes, you did, Thaddeus." Delia stomped her foot on the dance floor. "You threatened me. You can't force me to marry you."

"But the truth is, your own Grandfather Sullivan led those raids. Didn't he?" Jake waited for his reply. When Thaddeus didn't respond, Jake grabbed his shirt by the collar as he had done on the veranda before Delia's trip to New York. "Didn't he?"

"Okay, okay. Yes, he did. My grandfather led the raids. You can let go now." Thaddeus raised both hands.

More gasps shuddered through the crowd.

"If you so much as lay a hand on Delia again, I'll whip your backside all the way from here to Tennessee. Do I make myself clear?" Jake held him by the collar until Thaddeus nodded.

"Now say you're sorry."

"I'm sorry, Jake."

"Tell Delia you're sorry."

Thaddeus gulped. "I'm sorry, Delia."

"Now get out of here." Jake let him go with a slight push. "I don't want to see your face for a long time."

Thaddeus scurried down the platform steps, heading toward the tent exit. His face was beet red, and he could only look at his feet. Jake had finally defeated him, as evidenced in the applause coming from all those present.

"Hit it, boys," Jake said, waving to the sinfonia.

The director nodded with a smile, and the musicians resumed with a robust rendition of "Dixie."

Jake turned to Delia, holding his hand out as he bowed. "Would you care to dance, my lady?"

Delia smiled, offering her best curtsy. "I would love to, kind sir."

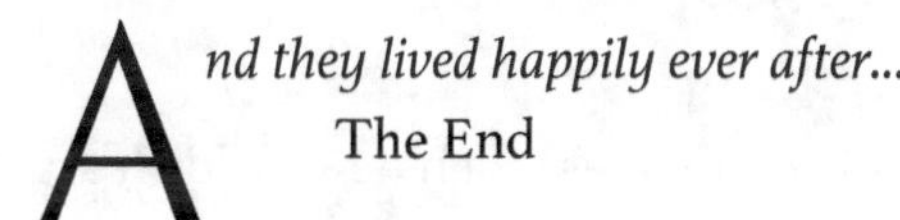

*A*nd they lived happily ever after...
The End

Did you enjoy this book? We hope so!
**Would you take a quick minute to leave a review where you
purchased the book?**
It doesn't have to be long. Just a sentence or two telling what
you liked about the story!

Receive a FREE ebook and get updates when new Wild Heart
books release: https://wildheartbooks.org/newsletter

Don't miss the next book in the Kentucky Debutantes of the Gilded Age!

The Debutante's Second Chance
Releasing January 2025!

February 14, 1908
Velvet Brooks Farm, Lexington, Kentucky

"Is that you, Gladdie? It's Henry Billings...from the Lexington Stockyard." The clerk's voice crackled through the recently installed telephone line. "I've got a horse here for you, just arrived this morning with your name as the recipient."

"A horse? Are you certain, Henry? We weren't expecting any deliveries today, and certainly not a horse." Seated at Pa's desk in the library at their horse farm, Velvet Brooks, holding the receiver to her ear, Gladys Lyndon leaned forward. Surely, Henry was mistaken. Pa hadn't mentioned anything about a horse being shipped by train.

261

"Yes, I'm sure. She just arrived on the nine o'clock from New York. She's a real beauty too. Three years old, according to the paperwork."

"A filly? From New York?" Her brows rose. Pa wouldn't have forgotten to mention such an important detail, would he? He had been somewhat forgetful prior to his departure for South Carolina, a symptom of the strain he'd been under lately that had led to his recent stroke. But to forget a new horse purchase seemed unlikely even then. Or had he planned it as a Valentine's Day surprise?

"Probably another champion for your stables. When can you pick her up?" Henry sounded anxious, talking a bit fast. A variety of indistinguishable noise and voices in the background added confusion to the crackling on the line.

"*When* can we pick her up?" Gladdie repeated into the mouthpiece. Taking the base of the telephone with her, she swirled around in Pa's desk chair until facing the front of the house, the old floorboards creaking as she rose and stepped before one of the two windows. She parted the lace hanging between the drapes with one finger while holding the receiver to her ear, peering toward the big horse barn. It looked quiet outside, but the men employed by her father would be working hard inside the barn or doing something useful somewhere on the property. And it was beginning to rain. She bit her lower lip. Maybe Hank Parker, the farm's manager, knew something about this horse. "It's so unexpected, Henry. I'll do my best to send someone over before the end of today, or I'll come myself."

"Very good. The sooner, the better." He cleared his throat. "Word of caution. She's on the feisty side. You may want to send a couple of farmhands or bring someone to help you."

Feisty? No wonder Henry sounded nervous. He'd probably had a tangle with the filly while unloading her from the train.

"Thanks for the warning. Someone will be there as soon as

we can manage it. Does your paperwork indicate who the sender of this horse is?" Gladdie arched her brow and held her breath.

"Uh, let me check."

Rustling papers and more crackling on the line filled her ears.

"Ah. Here's what I'm looking for. There's some history about this horse amongst the papers the sender included." He paused and more papers shuffled. "No, it just says a gift for Miss Gladys Lyndon. Unfortunately, the filly was sent anonymously, so I can't help any with who the sender is, but if I knew, I'd tell you."

"A gift for me? Hmm." She had a couple of ideas who might be behind such a grand gesture, but both possibilities seemed unlikely.

"Yes, Gladdie. I'm curious to know who sent her too. On another note, how's your pa doing?"

"Mama says he improves a little each day. Thank you for asking, Henry." Gladdie untwined the long cord wrapped around her hand and turned around to face the desk again. She set the slim base of the telephone back onto Pa's desk, delighted with the convenience. Her father had dragged his feet for years about installing a telephone, just as he did about automobiles, but it was long past time Velvet Brooks entered the world of progress. What a surprise it had been the day the telephone installers had arrived.

Speaking of surprise...Pa and Mama would be shocked to see the jodhpurs she currently wore with her riding boots.

"Yes, of course. He's in our prayers. I guess we'll see you soon, then. Remember now, we close at five o'clock. Happy Valentine's Day to y'all."

"Thank you." She leaned forward to speak into the funnel-shaped mouthpiece. "Happy Valentine's Day to y'all at the stockyards as well. Goodbye for now." Because of her preoccupation with fitting in with her elite friends of New York society,

Mama would cringe to hear Gladdie using words in her Southern drawl with no regard for proper grammar, but even her mother displayed her Kentucky heritage now and then.

Gladdie disconnected the call by hanging the receiver on the device, frowning. Would Pa have shipped her a horse on his way through New York before heading south to Chesapeake Manor? He had traveled with Mama, Gladdie's sister Veronica, her sister's husband, Edward, and their two sons—her nephews, Edward Junior and Creighton—to Edward's boyhood vacation home situated on the coast of South Carolina. They'd arrived ten days ago, hoping to improve Creighton's constantly delicate health with the salty ocean air and give Pa the rest he needed so much to recover.

It seemed highly unlikely that her father would have had time to purchase a horse while traveling through New York by train—if indeed they had even stopped in the state. Perhaps Pa had ordered the horse *before* his departure, or maybe this had something to do with her sister's husband's family who lived in New York. And yet...Mama had failed to mention any new horse in her first letter, nor had she mentioned the filly in any of their few telephone conversations.

The ticking of the clock above the fireplace mantel caused her to glance up. Almost noon-thirty. Pa would be finishing his luncheon, maybe even taking a leisurely afternoon lie-down by now. Rather than disturb his rest or a meal, she'd telephone later and ask if he knew anything about this turn of events.

If not Pa, had Harvey sent the filly? Harvey Higginbottom, a writer for the *Lexington Gazette*, was the gentleman her parents and Grandfather Lyndon considered a suitable candidate to become her future husband, but someone she didn't find herself attracted to romantically. What did they admire in Harvey that she failed to see?

Sure, he owned a comfortable two-story house with a big front porch in town. He had an interesting career as a newspaper journalist. He attended her church, too, but he was a quirky sort of fellow with an overly meticulous nature.

Shaking her head, she crossed her arms over her chest. No, not even the gift of a champion filly could entice her into becoming Mrs. Harvey Higginbottom. If he had sent such an extravagant present, she should return it at once—except for the fact she didn't know if he had sent the horse. Nor could she bring herself to call him to ask. It would be considered forward of her to telephone him—except perhaps to thank him for sending the gift.

She drummed her fingers on Pa's desk. Harvey might be the most likely sender, since he *had* recently returned from New York on some sort of journalism assignment. He'd resided next door to her grandfather, Colonel Lyndon, who'd served in the war between the North and the South on Lincoln's side. Her grandfather had established the legacy of Velvet Brooks before retiring to live in the city where things were easier for him and her grandmother. Harvey loved chatting about old war stories and politics with Grandfather Lyndon. They relished long discussions about horses and farms since Harvey had grown up at Fern Ridge, a small horse farm in the vicinity of Velvet Brooks.

Hadn't he mentioned something about a surprise the last time he'd called on her? She rose from Pa's leather chair. Circling around to the front of the desk, she paced, hands clasped behind her back as she tried to recall. Yes. She'd offered him tea in the sitting room to be polite. But a *horse?* It seemed rather presumptuous, even for Harvey.

Nonetheless, despite the fact he sometimes worked from his city home when he wasn't at his *Gazette* office, she simply refused to telephone him to inquire about the matter. Why get his hopes up for a match between the two of them with a call? While she considered him a friend, Harvey Higginbottom was merely another nice gentleman she would never marry.

She had no intention of marrying anyone.

Just as her oldest sister, Veronica, had nursed a hidden broken heart before meeting Edward, Gladdie's heart ached, and she remained firmly convinced it would never fully mend. After Clay Grinstead had jilted her, failing to show up to catch the train to Richmond, Kentucky, for their elopement, she'd telephoned her grandfather, a man who had a little faith in modern inventions, the next morning. "Grandpa, I'm in trouble. Big trouble. Will you come and get me?"

She'd rushed into Pa's and Mama's embrace the moment her grandfather brought her inside the front door. She could still remember, after telling the whole story, what her mother had said. "Well, honey, we don't know why things happen the way they do. Sometimes they don't make sense until years later. We must do the best we can to go on in the meantime. Find purpose and meaning in life in other ways, through whatever God gives your hands to do."

Gladdie had eventually heard the rumors that her beau had betrayed her, marrying Alice Parker within a few days or perhaps hours of when he should have shown up on the train to elope with Gladdie. The only saving grace had been the fact it was a secret elopement. If he'd jilted her in front of all of Lexington, she'd never have survived.

Sure, folks had gossiped plenty about the fact Clay had married Alice when he'd been courting Gladdie unofficially. An ache still pulsed with every beat of her heart, but no one seemed to think it would still be so. Nothing could be further from the truth, even after all these years. She had turned twenty-three a few months ago, and by now, he would be about twenty-six. Seven years had gone by.

Her parents and most other family members now urged her to consider marrying Harvey...or Percy Sullivan...or some other gentleman caller. She preferred to make a game of hiding from the callers with a bevy of excuses, despite Mama's protests.

After all, they had more important matters to contend with than marrying her off—chiefly, Pa's failing health due to his stroke and the survival of Velvet Brooks. The stroke had left Pa with problems not only with his memory, but also in his speech and mobility. According to the doctor, he needed rest and tranquility to recover. Hence, his journey to Chesapeake Manor on the South Carolina coast to enjoy Edward's family vacation home.

Things had changed at the estate where Gladdie had spent her whole life. While the Sullivans still owned the horse farm on most of their western border below Rose Glen Cottage, the owners of Blue Acres on their eastern perimeter had sold their farm and moved away to live in another state. Someone had torn down their old farmhouse and currently, what looked to be a mansion was under construction. Everyone stared at the limestone mansion as they passed Blue Acres, curious about who the owner might be.

For another thing, her sisters weren't as involved with Velvet Brooks as they might have preferred before they married —and at a time Gladdie needed them most. Her older sister, Delia Williams, had her hands full caring for her toddler, Isadora, and her husband Jake's three nieces. Not to mention the country inn and boardinghouse they operated in their home across the street and a second baby on the way. Jake had a few horses they occasionally entered into races too.

Her oldest sister, Veronica, and her husband, Edward Beckett, still resided for most of each year on ten acres of neighboring land at Rose Glen Cottage, a wedding gift from Pa. But as proud owners of their own business in Lexington, they focused on making Edward's artwork a success. Beckett's Art Gallery kept them quite busy—when they weren't galivanting off to New York or South Carolina. Unfortunately, their second son, Creighton, did not enjoy the same good health as his older brother, Eddie Junior. Veronica spent most of her time providing extra care for Creighton, who'd been susceptible to colds and fevers ever since his birth.

And now any issues at the farm fell to Gladdie. She carried a heavy load, and only the Lord could see them through. Big changes in the horseracing industry weighed heavily on everyone's minds. Worry was evident in the eyes of their staff. With so many racecourses closing around the country because of new laws enacted due to bookmakers skimming the purse—not to mention a growing sentiment against betting and horseracing in general—fewer folks contacted them to train their horses. And with fewer races, chances of winning a purse had become even more elusive, making the sport less lucrative for breeders and trainers.

The ledger book lay open on her father's desk where she entered income in one column and expenses in the accounts payable column. Some funds remained in their account at the bank, but the figure decreased with each passing day. If the Phoenix Stakes Race at the Lexington Association Track and the Derby at Churchill Downs went on as usual, and if they could take any of the top winning places, she could use the funds to make payroll and keep Velvet Brooks afloat without dipping into Pa's savings.

Her hands flew to her hips. She really should stop pacing and also stop her thoughts from becoming a jambalaya soup. She'd best head to the barn and ask if Hank could designate two strong men to wrangle Miss Feisty Filly into the horse wagon. And sooner rather than later so Henry wouldn't have a conniption at the stockyards.

A tingle of anticipation shot through Gladdie. It had been a long while since they'd won any races. What if this filly turned out to be a champion just as Henry had said? Could the new horse help her save Velvet Brooks in Pa's absence?

AUTHOR NOTE

Dear Reader,

I hope you enjoyed shy and demure Delia's story with its theme of perceptions. Thank you for following along with her journey to find truth about her heart, the Lord's will for her life, and the men who loved her. It was as if she could see dimly through a glass or a veil...but slowly, after much prayer, soul searching, Bible study, and revelation, gained an understanding of the truth until the blinders finally fell away. Isn't that the way life can be sometimes for so many of us?

The book features more of the competitive horseracing world in Kentucky during the early 1900s. I based the saddle dispute at the auction on an actual advertisement I found in the newspapers from the earliest days of horseracing in Kentucky.

Racetracks had entered a steep and sharp decline in America by the early 1900s as they diminished from over 300 tracks to less than 75 throughout our nation. Some of this had to do with the Great Depression in the 1930s, and some of it had to do with bookmakers accused of taking unfair cuts from the gambling purse, but most if it had to do with a popular opinion regarding the ills of gambling.

It wasn't until France's pari-mutuel betting system (or pool betting as opposed to fixed odds) came to America that some states decided to continue horseracing. The pari-mutuel system led to the installation of machines to calculate the complex bets, and it also gave the operator a profit while allowing any number of bettors to win. We may see a mention of this in Book 3.

At the dinner party where Jake is seated beside Delia by her matchmaking mama, a fun trope in this series, I included a number of actual tidbits from my research for changes made at Churchill Downs which indeed became a turning point leading to the popularity of the Kentucky Derby. I took a little liberty for the timeframe of these changes as most of them rolled out a few years beyond the setting of my story.

Two of the songs I mentioned at the dinner party were very popular in this era according to some music charts from the Gilded Age. "In the Good Old Summertime" by the Haydn Quartet was a popular recording played on the Victrola in 1902. "Melody of Love" by Hans Engelmann, popular music for the piano in 1903, had lyrics by Tom Glazer. You can find both songs and some of the others mentioned on YouTube if you'd like to hear actual music from the era. The few recordings we do have from the Gilded Age are rare, so I wanted to share this research.

The real-life winner of the Kentucky Derby in 1903 was a horse named Judge Himes, a descendant of Longfellow, a real-life champion horse with an astonishing legacy. And the foal from Runnymede that Colonel Clay mentioned to Colonel Lyndon, Agile, was a real-life horse that went on to win the Derby in 1905. Runnymede is one of the oldest horse farms in Kentucky, and I thought it might be delightful to mention it in my story, purely in a fictionalized sense.

You may also be interested to know that some say the tradition of singing "My Old Kentucky Home" at the Derby began around 1922, and others say it began in the 1930s. The song has been "cleansed" because the original lyrics contained controversial words, though Stephen Foster wrote it from an abolitionist perspective to show that slaves had feelings at a time in history when ignorance was still prevalent in the minds of some people.

The Preakness Stakes race was added to the featured races at Pimlico after an amazing horse won the Dinner Party Stakes by an astonishing ten lengths. Inspired by the colt with the name of Preakness when he crossed the finish line in first place on that day in 1870—though he wasn't a favorite and many considered him a longshot—the Baltimore racecourse, fondly called Old Hilltop, then added the Preakness race named in his honor that we now herald as part of the Triple Crown.

I enjoyed drawing a connection between my book *A Summer at Sagamore* and the characters in this story since they share the same era. I hope you enjoyed the connection too. If you love mysteries, romance, and the Gilded Age, I highly recommend reading *A Summer at Sagamore* and the other books in the *Romance at the Gilded Age Resorts* series.

As mentioned in Book 1 of this series, my horse names, other animals, racing winners, jockeys, trainers, and characters are purely fictional figments of my imagination. Any resemblance to any horses, other racing winners, or any other characters from real life are coincidental.

Thank you so much in advance for your kind reviews.

Warmest Blessings,

Lisa

ABOUT THE AUTHOR

Lisa M. Prysock is a *USA Today* Bestselling, Award-Winning Christian and Inspirational Author. She and her husband of more than twenty-five years reside in beautiful, rural Kentucky. They have five children, grown. Empty nesters, they are slowly reclaiming the house.

She writes in the genres of both Historical Christian Romance and Contemporary Christian Romance, including a multi-author Western Christian Romance series, "Whispers in Wyoming." She is also the author of a devotional. Lisa enjoys sharing her faith in Jesus through her writing and has authored more than 50 published books in both Contemporary and Historical Christian Romance. She loves to make readers laugh and enjoys writing humor in many of her stories.

Lisa has many interests, but a few of these include gardening, cooking, drawing, sewing, crochet, cross stitch, reading, swimming, biking, and walking. She loves dollhouses, cats, horses, butterflies, hats, boots, flip-flops, espadrilles, chocolate, coffee, tea, chocolate, the colors peach and purple, and everything old-fashioned.

She adopted the slogan of "The Old-Fashioned Everything Girl" because of her love for classic, traditional, and old-fashioned everything. When she isn't writing, she can sometimes be found teaching herself piano and violin but finds the process "a bit slow and painful." Lisa enjoys working with the children and youth in her local church creating human videos, plays, or programs incorporating her love for inspirational dance. A few of her favorite authors include Jane Austen, Lucy Maude Montgomery, Louisa May Alcott, Charlotte Brontë, and Laura Ingalls Wilder. You'll find "Food, Fashion, Faith, and Fun" in her novels. Occasionally, she includes her own illustrations.

She continues the joy and adventure of her writing journey as a member of ACFW (American Christian Fiction Writers) and LCW (Louisville Christian Writers). Lisa's books are clean and wholesome, inspirational, romantic, and family oriented. She gives a generous portion of the proceeds to missions.

Discover more about this author at **www.LisaPrysock.com** where you'll find the links to purchase more of her books, free recipes, devotionals, author video interviews, book trailers, giveaways, blog posts, and much more, including an invitation to sign up for her free newsletter.

Connect with Lisa:

*Lisa's Author Website:

https://www.LisaPrysock.com

*Lisa's Facebook Reader & Friends Group:

https://www.facebook.com/groups/500592113747995/

*Follow Lisa on Goodreads:

https://www.goodreads.com/author/show/7324280.Lisa_M_Prysock

*Get a Free Book When You Sign Up for Lisa's FREE Newsletter:

https://www.LisaPrysock.com/sign_up_for_my_newsletter

If you love historical romance, check out the other Wild Heart books!

A Not So Peaceful Journey by Sandra Merville Hart

Dreams of adventure send him across the country. She prefers to keep her feet firmly planted in Ohio.

Rennie Hill has no illusions about the hardships in life, which is why it's so important her beau, John Welch, keeps his secure job with the newspaper. Though he hopes to write fiction, the unsteady pay would mean an end to their plans, wouldn't it?

John Welch dreams of adventure worthy of storybooks, like Mark Twain, and when two of his short stories are published, he sees it as a sign of future success. But while he's dreaming big with his head in the clouds, his girl has her feet firmly planted, and he can't help wondering if she really believes in him.

When Rennie must escort a little girl to her parents' home in San Francisco, John is forced to alter his plans to travel across the country with them. But the journey proves far more adventurous than either of them expect.

~

Ranger to the Rescue by Renae Brumbaugh Green

Amelia Cooper has sworn off lawmen for good.

Now any man who wants to claim the hand of the intrepid reporter had better have a safe job. Like attorney Evan Covington. Amelia is thrilled when the handsome lawyer comes courting. But when the town enlists him as a Texas Ranger, Amelia isn't sure she can handle losing another man to the perils of keeping the peace.

Evan never expected his temporary appointment to sink his relationship with Amelia. Or to instantly plunge them headlong into danger. But when Amelia and his sister are both kidnapped, the newly minted lawman must rescue them—if he's to have any chance at love

~

A Heart's Forever Home by Lena Nelson Dooley

A single lawyer whose clients think he needs a wife.
A woman who needs a forever home...or a forever family...or a forever love.

Although Traesa Killdare is a grown woman now, the discovery that her adoption wasn't finalized sends her reeling. Especially when her beloved grandmother dies and the only siblings she's ever known exile her from the family property without a penny to her name.

Wilson Pollard works hard for the best interest of his law clients, even those who think a marriage would make him more "suitable" in his career. And when the beloved granddaughter of a recently deceased client comes to him for help, he knows he must do whatever necessary to make her situation better.

As each of their circumstances worsen, a marriage of convenience seems the only answer for both. Traesa can't help but fall for her new husband—the man who's given her both his home and his name. But what will it take for Wilson to realize he loves her? Will a not-so-natural disaster open his eyes and heart?